INTOXICATED
by YOU

An Exposed Hearts Novel

KRISTIN MAYER

Intoxicated by You
An Exposed Hearts Novel
Copyright © 2018 by K. Mayer Enterprises, Inc.
Published by K. Mayer Enterprises, INC.
Cover Design: Sommer Stein with Perfect Pear Creations
Interior Designer: JT Formatting
Editor: Jen Matera at Write Divas

Intoxicated by You (An Exposed Hearts Novel) / Kristin Mayer – 1st ed.
Library of Congress Cataloging-in-Publication Data
ISBN-13: 978-1-942910-29-9

:
VISIT MY WEBSITE AT
http://www.authorkristinmayer.com

This book is dedicated to everyone who has been part of this journey. Thank you from the bottom of my heart.

Prologue

Alexa

The last few days had been a blur. One moment, my father was alive, and the next, Drake called to tell me he'd died. I'd spoken to him only three hours before he passed. And now he would never pick up the phone again when I called.

Something had seemed off the last few times we'd spoken. Like there was something he'd wanted to tell me but hadn't. *What's wrong?* When I'd asked, he'd deflected, which only made the anxiety of what it might have been worse.

Will I ever find out?

My dad was my rock—the person I could go to with anything. And now I would never be able to ask for his advice or make furniture with him when something was on my mind.

At least I still had Drake. Together, we would find our way.

Through it all, the love of my life had been by my side.

i

Drake had been there for me in every way imaginable. He was my soul mate.

But inside, I was numb, and my mind was a mess as I tried to process the loss of my father. It felt like I was a stranger in my own skin. And I hated that feeling. Normally, I was self-assured and ready to tackle the world. But since my dad died, I was simply lost and not sure what my next step would be.

If only my dad could guide me.

My hands trembled as I opened the letter—the last piece of communication I would receive from my dad. After the reading of his will, his lawyer had given me the letter and said Dad had brought it by a couple of weeks ago.

Alexa.

As I traced the familiar handwriting, my throat tightened. That afternoon, I had slipped away to the pond behind my parents' house to read the letter by myself. The ground was thick with snow and it was bitter cold, but I didn't care.

A slow tremor started in my hands as I prepared myself. Maybe this was the guidance I needed to keep moving forward. Maybe fate had impressed upon Dad to bring this letter to the lawyer, knowing his time here on Earth was limited. I was a firm believer that everything happened for a reason.

I slipped my finger under the flap of the envelope and opened it.

The first line drew a sob I wasn't aware I'd been holding back.

My darling Alexa...

Dad would never say those words to me again. We'd never make any new memories ever again. I closed my eyes and tried to calm down. *I can do this. I can read this letter.*

Taking a deep breath, I focused on my dad's words.

My darling Alexa,

You have always meant the world to me. I've been struggling with something that I need to tell you. I couldn't find the words while we talked on the phone. I hope to take you to the cabin and tell you during your next visit. But if that time doesn't come, I've written this letter. I have to protect my little girl.

I know you love Drake, but you need to listen to me.

Drake is not the right man for you. I know this comes as a shock, but I need you to trust me on this. As your dad, I implore you. End things with him. It will be for the best. I know this doesn't make much sense, but I need you to do as I ask. Do this one thing for me. In time you'll understand why. This may be the last piece of fatherly advice I can give you.

I love you, Alexa, with my whole heart.

Dad

When I reached his signature, my world imploded. My heart shattered into a million pieces, and nothing made sense.

How can I give up Drake?

How can I not listen to my dad?

CHAPTER
One

Alexa

"Answer your phone," I whispered, peering into the window. The entire town of Skagway was in the Red Onion Saloon, celebrating Mayor Richmond's reelection. I'd arrived in Skagway two days earlier and so far had managed to go unnoticed, which was quite a feat for such a small town. But I wasn't going to go unnoticed today. Oh no, Teagan had insisted I meet her there to get the keys for the property I'd bought. Why she took them in the first place still perplexed me.

The real estate agent, Nancy, had driven to Ketchikan for a convention. I'd gotten a text saying she'd given the keys to Teagan. I'd never asked Teagan to get them and couldn't get a straight answer why she had. The previous night, I texted her to say I was just going to have a locksmith come open it up for me. Magically, I got a response to meet her at the Red Onion Saloon to get my keys.

I'd gotten the place for a song, which worried me. Something felt off about the whole situation. But things with Teagan normally did. And I needed to start cleaning up the soon-to-be clinic as soon as possible.

Inside the bar, people cheered while the mayor stood on a chair in the middle of the room. Drake was inside—I could feel it. Whenever he was near, my body came alive and excitement danced along my skin.

But I wasn't ready to see him. I'd hoped these feelings would have disappeared over the last two years. But if my current state of awareness was any indication, they hadn't in the slightest. Which sucked. Drake Foster was the one person I couldn't be with. Ending things with Drake had been my father's last request before he died.

Teagan knew this. She *knew* it.

Drake had probably moved on, but I'd refused to ask. If he'd found someone else, I didn't know if I could face it. The thought caused my chest to ache. I knew at some point it would be necessary to see him. Face what I had done. But not today. *Not today.* I needed to get myself grounded and face other demons from my past.

Facing Drake would happen, of course. I'd returned to my small hometown to open a clinic with my friend Hollis. *Well, technically, he's Dr. Hollis Fritz.* Skagway didn't have its own doctor. For major medical crises, the injured had to be airlifted to another town with a doctor. It cost thousands of dollars after insurance; that alone could put severe financial stress on a family here. Waiting for transport delayed treatment for critical cases. And if the weather was bad enough, even airlifting wasn't possible.

That was the reason my father had died two years ago after a logging incident. There was too much ice, and the chopper couldn't get to my dad in time. With a focus I'd never had before, I'd gone back to college my sophomore year and buried myself in my studies to finish my nursing degree in record time.

My phone vibrated, and I crouched down lower to answer Hollis.

Hollis: *Decided to come up a day early. I'll be there later today.*

Me: *Want me to pick you up?*

Hollis: *Nah, my car is being delivered to the airport. I'll get settled at the hotel. We can meet up tomorrow. You still going to the clinic?*

Hollis had always been a bit of a loner. That was why we'd clicked two years ago. He was a trust-fund baby who wanted a break from the leisurely life of the rich and famous. Our little town of Skagway, Alaska, would provide that escape.

I hunkered down a little lower to ensure my head wasn't visible above the windowsill.

Me: *Yeah, that's the plan. I'm currently standing on a crate outside the Red Onion trying to get Teagan to give me the keys. She's holding them hostage.*

Hollis: *Umm... is that normal for Skagwayians?*

That made me laugh. Hollis and Alaska were going to be an interesting combination. His mother was livid he even considered wasting his talents up here. He'd graduated first in his class. We'd met during clinical while he was working on his residency. Even though he was four years older, we'd hit it off as friends instantly.

Me: *No... not really.*

Hollis: *Oh... well good luck with that.*

Me: *I need to go. My calves are starting to hurt.*

Hollis: *Just talk to him.*

I put my phone away, not answering his text. Hollis thought I should tell Drake everything. For two months after I left, Drake had tried to contact me. Finally, I'd changed my number and moved to a different location in New York so I would be unreachable. Otherwise, I knew I'd have gone back to him.

I am such a bitch.

Drake hadn't deserved that. He was a good guy—the best. Before the logging incident, I'd planned to spend the rest of my life with him. I'd loved him. I still loved him. But Dad had known something. He would never have led me astray.

I rang Teagan again and held the phone up to my ear. "Come on, Teagan. Pick up. I'm not in the mood to play your games today."

Voice mail again. *Damn it.* I wasn't sure why I had a soft spot for her. Her selfishness and games drove Drake nuts. But I knew it was Teagan's way of protecting herself. Her parents had been as shitty as they came. If I had been in her spot, I hoped someone would try to help me—a true friend.

When I asked if I could stay with her, she'd been hesitant at first but then agreed. Since I arrived, though, I'd only seen her the one time when I arrived. Then she'd taken off with Donnie.

That meeting had been awkward, almost strained. I needed to find another place to stay. Maybe I'd go to the hotel.

Inside the bar, the crowd cheered. I felt like a serious creeper, standing on a shaky wooden crate with my head just above the windowsill, watching. Teagan was in the back with her boyfriend, Donnie, who had rubbed me the wrong way since day one—nearly three years ago—and rang a ten on my creep-o-meter. I'd have to walk through the whole bar just to get to her. *She's doing this on purpose. Or maybe she's just being Teagan.* The thing was, with Teagan, I never knew. With a frustrated sigh, I blew out a breath.

"Hey, Lex. Who are you spying on?"

The deep voice took me by surprise, and I jumped with a scream and fell off my perch. Pain shot through my ankle. "Ouch!"

Why me? Why?

The circumstances looked much worse than they were— an innocent situation gone terribly wrong. All I'd wanted was to avoid the man who still affected me in more ways than he should. And now that man was standing less than two feet away. My skin danced with the familiar electric current that left my head buzzing.

Be strong.

The crate had given me a nasty scrape on my calf. *Damn it.* It was superficial but bleeding nevertheless. I knew I shouldn't have worn shorts that day, but the weather was unseasonably warm. I looked around to make sure no one else had heard my shriek, buying some time to pull myself together. Judging by the racket inside, I had most likely escaped additional embarrassment.

I gave another quick scan around us to make sure no one else was there. Skagway had a local gossip newsletter that went out on a weekly basis via email. The Twiner sisters ran it like world-class paparazzi. Sometimes, for *red hot* news, there were even special editions. They had a knack for being in the "worst" place at the "best" time.

Every. Single. Townsperson. Was. On. The. Subscription. List.

The people of Skagway enjoyed the gossip. Hell, even *I* read it. When my email pinged with the newsletter each week, it called like a beacon.

Jean-clad legs I was all too familiar with stepped closer. "Need a hand?"

The deep timbre of his voice still made me weak in the knees. It was deep and husky and took *manly* to a whole new level. Already my resolve was weakening. I would have to read my father's letter again to reinforce my walls. I carried the note around with me in case I ever felt the need to call Drake, which was often.

The men in New York City were nothing like Drake. They were too refined, lacking the edge—the wildness— Alaska infused in the men who lived here. Drake was savagely protective, romantic, strong, and loving all wrapped up in one ridiculously hot package.

I glanced up, meeting those warm chestnut eyes I remembered all too well. His dark hair was still short like I remembered. I swallowed and said, "Drake." My voice cracked.

Yeah, I sound nervous. Stay calm. Drake knows you. He knows you better than anyone.

I cleared my throat. "I wasn't creeping. I was waiting for Teagan."

"Why not come in? She's inside with Donnie."

That was the million-dollar question. "Umm... I... You know..." I gave up and stood. Immediately, I felt the blood trickle down my leg.

Ugh. I need to get this cleaned up.

Drake leaned against the post and crossed his right leg over his left. He was all muscle. "Let's get you fixed up. I've got a first aid kit upstairs at my place. We can take the back stairs."

I took a step back. "I'll be fine. I can walk."

Drake looked at my leg. "Ol' Man Rooster is talking with the Twiner sisters out front. If you go that way, you'll pass right by them." He shook his head. "I'm sure that'll give them something to talk about for a while. You'll be the star of the weekly Twiner Tellings newsletter."

His smirk caused me to take a deep breath. He knew I hated being in the newsletter. Hated it. And in the two years I'd been gone, Drake had only been in it once—for something inconsequential. I'd secretly scoured it for any news about him. Was he seeing someone? *Don't think about that. It doesn't matter.*

Lurking outside the Red Onion was not how I wanted the Twiner sisters to find out I was back in town. The rumors would be rampant. And if truth be told, now that I had him near, I wasn't ready to be without him again.

Just a few minutes. I want to be near him for just a few more minutes. Then I'll leave. I'll go read the letter and re-

mind myself why I stayed away for so long.

"Lead the way."

Drake handed me a towel from his back pocket. When working at the bar, he always had one tucked there. "It's clean. Hold it to your cut, and I'll carry you. We don't want you leaving a trail of blood up the stairs."

Without an argument, I took the towel. Drake's strong arms wrapped around me, and he easily picked me up.

I yelped. "It's—"

"I don't remember you being this jumpy."

I clamped my mouth shut. I was a nervous wreck around him. *What do I say?* Any kind of explanation would only make the situation look worse than it was. "I promise I wasn't lurking."

"Then why not come inside to see Teagan? You nervous to see me?"

Of course, Drake was straightforward. He always had been. We'd known each other since we were babies. When I was a senior in high school, he'd stopped to help me change a flat tire on the side of the road. From there, we started hanging out. With my father's blessing, Drake took me out on our first date. He was two years older and had wanted my father's approval since I was still in school.

Why did Dad change his mind?

Drake shifted his hold on me as he climbed the stairs, which brought my thoughts back to the oh-so-familiar feeling of being in his arms. Goose bumps formed along my skin where he touched me. Two years apart from him had done nothing but amp up my desire for him.

He paused at the door. "Why are you nervous, Lex?"

Lex. He was the only one who ever called me Lex, and it

still did things to me—made me feel like I was still his.

Outside his door, we stared into each other's eyes. "You know why I'm nervous. It's been two years since we saw each other, spoke to each other."

"Don't be. I'm still just me. The same man I was two years ago."

Not according to Dad.

Regret surged through me, and I blinked a few times. "Yes, of course. I figured facing a large crowd would be awkward after what I did. I deserve it if you hate me."

It was too much; I had to break eye contact. If he hated me, I wouldn't be able to stand it. *Why does it feel so right to be near him?* In just mere minutes, my world felt fuller than it had for the last two years. This was why I had to cut off all communication. Drake Foster consumed me.

Shifting his hold on me, he was able to open the door without putting me down. I'd forgotten how strong he was. "I could never hate you." The softness in his voice brought me up short, and I blinked several times to clear my thoughts. Gently, he set me down. "Let me get the first aid kit. It's in my room."

"Thanks."

My body instantly missed his touch. *If only I could be back in his arms.* He deserved to know what happened two years ago. But the knowledge that my dad hadn't approved of him might hurt him more. Drake had loved my dad. They'd been close. Which was why my father's last letter telling me to end things with Drake had gutted me. How could I even consider spending the rest of my life with a man my father didn't approve of? When I'd first read the letter, I hadn't been myself. I'd felt like a stranger in my own skin. And now that I was in Drake's presence again, I felt doubt at my father's words for the first time.

Did I make the wrong choice?

I shook my head and tried to get my thoughts straight. Drake's place was just as I remembered—masculine. The furniture was solid wood—handmade by Drake's father, Ike. Things were tidy-ish, as usual. The shirt he wore yesterday was on the back of the couch where he probably removed it to watch TV. A lone beer bottle sat on the table. I had so many memories of us here together—cuddled on the couch as we watched a scary movie, making love by the fireplace, celebrating when I'd been accepted into college with a nearly full scholarship.

It had taken me three years to save up enough money to go to college to study nursing at twenty-one. The scholarship supplemented my savings so I hadn't needed a loan. It had been a blessing. Being a nurse had been my dream since I was a little girl.

Drake reappeared in the doorway and paused while our eyes met. Time had been good to him, and he looked fit as ever. His T-shirt hugged his muscles and showed off how broad he was.

With a quick shake of his head, he snapped out of it and brought the first aid kit to me. Quickly, I set to work cleaning the cut and putting a Band-Aid over it. "Good as new. Thanks, Drake."

"Anytime."

A few moments passed as we stared at each other. I knew I should leave, but I couldn't bring myself to do it. I wanted more time.

Finally, Drake said, "Mom told me about the clinic."

The mention of his parents caused pain to shoot through

me. I missed them so much. Weakly, I smiled. "Yes, Skagway is going to finally have a doctor. Hollis is amazing."

Something shifted within Drake, and he expelled a breath, taking a few steps back while raking his fingers through his hair. "It's a good thing you're doing."

My throat grew thick. "Thanks. Maybe Dad... well, you know."

He grabbed my hand, and the fierce protectiveness I always associated with Drake came rushing back. "I know. He'd be proud."

I had made a terrible mistake leaving Drake Foster.

CHAPTER

Two

Drake

I dragged a hand down my face as the door closed. Lex was back. And I still fucking loved her. Hell, I never stopped. When she came home to bury her father, I thought we were okay. I had been there for her in every way I could be. At least I thought I had. Replaying our time together, I still had no idea what I'd done wrong.

Then the morning she left, everything changed. She ended things between us. Something had happened, and she'd shut down… completely.

Hollis fucking Fritz.

The name itself made me see red. I hated the fucker, and I'd never met him. After Lex had left, I'd kept trying to reach out to her. She wouldn't return my calls, emails, letters. Nothing. I'd hoped she would work through whatever was bothering her and then reach out. But that never happened. Finally, I went after her. She was mine. The problem was when I got there two months later, she was running into that bastard's arms.

So, I left and buried myself in the Red Onion and the town. I joined the city council, started playing cards with my buddies every other week, got nominated for an Alaskan business board, and helped my dad build furniture on the side. Anything to keep my mind off what had happened. And I thought it had worked. I thought I'd managed to pick up the pieces and move on... until today.

I felt sick to my stomach as I opened the fridge and cracked a beer. For a mere moment with her in my arms, I'd forgotten she had a boyfriend. So, I would keep my distance from now on. Cheating wasn't something I condoned. Never had. Never would.

In the two years she'd been gone, she'd only gotten more beautiful. Her blonde hair was a little longer, but other than that, nothing else had changed. Lex's petite body fit perfectly in my arms. With that thought came the realization that trying to forget Lex was a waste of energy. There was no forgetting her.

I am so screwed.

That night I was going to Moochie's house to play cards with some of the guys. We'd all been friends since school and got together when we could. They were all married with kids—or kids on the way. I'd be bringing an extra case of beer for sure. The distraction would definitely help.

Lex being back was going to fuck with my head, especially since her boyfriend was coming back with her.

But if she needed something, I would be there for her. I'd made a promise to her father that I had to keep. It was what he whispered to me as he was dying.

Take care of my Alexa. She's going to need you.

Besides losing Lex, the day Lloyd passed away was the worst day of my life.

From the time we started dating, when Lex was in high school, I knew she wanted to be a nurse. I'd supported her going away to pursue those dreams. I thought our love would last. All that shit they say about distance making the heart grow fonder was utter bullshit. If that was the case, we'd still be together.

There was a soft knock on the door. *Damn it.* I needed to be alone and gather my thoughts and control before I went back to the bar. Snapping at customers wasn't good for business. Lex being back in town and bringing that jackass city boy changed everything.

How do I not punch the fucker?

I opened the door, and Lex stood there, still beautiful as ever. She twirled a piece of her blonde hair where it spilled over her shoulder, and she chewed on her lip.

Is she as messed up as I am about this situation?

"Sorry, I forgot my phone."

Remain calm. Neutral. Unaffected.

"Come on in. Want a beer?" I opened the door wider to let her in.

Her sweet smile nearly did me in. "No, thanks. Maybe another time. I got the keys from Teagan. Finally. And I need to go check out Doogle's place. I'm hoping to open the clinic within a week. I know it needs some TLC, but with a little elbow grease, it should be fine. At least that's what Nancy said."

Without a team of people, there was no way she'd make that date. Nancy drove me fucking nuts, too. She would say anything to make a sale. But she was the only realtor in Skagway. And she only did it part time. She also helped coordinate tours for tourists during the season.

Lex picked up her phone and put it in her back pocket. The way she tapped her fingers against her leg told me she was nervous. And I imagined that was from the thought of going out to the Doogle place by herself. My grip tightened on the bottle at the mere thought of Hollis being in Skagway, but I couldn't let her go by herself. *Where is the bastard?* I already hated him. "Do you want some company?"

She paused for a second, her hand relaxing. And there was another gorgeous smile on her face. "That would be nice. Empty old houses creep me out. Teagan can't come. She's headed somewhere with Donnie. They're always heading somewhere, it seems. I haven't seen her but for a couple of minutes since I've been home."

Sometimes Teagan didn't think things through. More than once, I'd had to pick Lex up because Teagan had abandoned her for some random hookup. Pissed me the fuck off.

"Let me get my keys."

"Oh, I'll drive. I have a bunch of stuff in my car. Or you can follow me. It's up to you. But you don't have to. I don't want to wreck your afternoon." Her eyebrows crinkled as she rambled.

Yeah, this is hella confusing to me, too, sweetheart.

What I wanted was to understand what happened. Closure. For me. Maybe then I might be able to move on. Because, honestly, it made zero fucking sense. Lex was it for me. I knew this, but I'd have to figure out something.

We made our way down the stairs, her peach scent taunting me. "You sure you don't need to go back to the bar?"

"Yeah, I'm sure. Crete has it under control."

15

I pulled out my phone to let him know.

Me: *Won't be back until later.*

Crete: *No problem.*

Crete was a good kid. He helped support his mom and two sisters. His dad had been involved in the same accident as Lex's. It had rocked the town when the three loggers lost their lives by some freak malfunction in the logging equipment.

I followed Lex to the car and saw the Twiner sisters leaning around a pole, watching us. There was no escaping them. We'd be in this week's newsletter for sure. During the tourist season, they dressed up in gear people wore to do gold mining. They thought it added to the impression of the town.

They. Were. Crazy.

Lex blew her hair out of the way. "The Twiners've made us."

"They have?" I glanced again at the dark-haired twins.

"I wonder if we'll make a special edition?"

She isn't worried about Hollis? Do I ask about him? I decided to keep it surface level for now. If I started asking about her boyfriend, things would get awkward. I commented back, "Probably. I think Elvira had her camera out."

"Oh, we're for sure making a special edition. Shit, I hate being in that stupid thing."

It was hard to suppress my laugh, but somehow, I managed. Lex's leg bounced from nerves as she drove. I stretched my legs out in her dad's old red Chevy truck. "Your dad's truck still runs good. I've been going over to the storage unit and cranking it from time to time."

When she glanced my way, Lex had that look I remembered getting anytime I did anything for her. Her adoration made me feel like a fucking king.

"Thank you. I appreciate it. Makes me feel like I still have a piece of him."

"I know."

We turned into a driveway on the outskirts of town and got out of the truck. From there, it was obvious the place was run down. A lot of the deck needed to be replaced, and the yard was overgrown and filled with branches. I imagined inside would be the same.

We walked up to the door. It was hot as hell today, and I wiped the bit of sweat that had formed on my brow. "Did you hire anyone to fix up the place?"

"No." She stepped on one of the broken boards. "Before I bought the place, I asked Mom to take a look. She didn't have time but said it was in decent shape the last time she saw it. And... umm... you know how she can be."

Yeah, I knew how she could be. And supportive of her daughter's ambitions wasn't an example. Irene and I had a rocky relationship, to put it mildly.

Touching one of the broken railings, Lex blew out a breath. "I think I'm going to have to push back the opening. It's a little different in person. I guess it's true... the saying. You get what you pay for."

I kept my mouth shut. Things between Irene and me were strained at times. For the most part, she tended to favor Raquel, Lex's sister. A parent should never show favoritism to one of their children over another. My parents never did between my two brothers and me.

Lex unlocked the door. Everything was covered in dust and smelled musty. I rubbed the back of my neck. Yeah, it needed a lot of work. "Maybe Fred can squeeze you into his schedule."

Around this part of Alaska, Fred was about the only option for repairs, which meant he stayed busy.

"Yeah, I'll call him." Lex kept walking through the room. Pausing, she took a deep breath and pointed to the front area. Something changed, and her face brightened. "Can't you see it? Patients come in here. There's exam rooms over here. Offices. Upstairs can be a residence. It's going to be wonderful."

Her excitement was contagious. It had always been that way with her. "Yeah, I can see it. It'll be great."

She got that sweet look in her eyes. "Thanks, Drake. I know you get how important this is to me."

"I do."

Things shifted between us, and I took a step back. *She has a boyfriend.* "What did you need help with? I need to get back to the bar."

Was that hurt that flashed across her face? After this was over, I was going to need a stiff drink. Maybe two. Or three. A case of beer wasn't going to do at Moochie's. I was going to need whiskey and a lot of it.

"Oh yeah. I'm sorry. I forgot. Can you help me take some measurements of the rooms? I need them to create a layout for when all the equipment comes. I'm going to take pictures, too. This way I can make a budget of what needs to be done."

I picked up one of the tape measures from her bag. "I'll start upstairs."

"Thanks."

Again, things felt awkward, or maybe it was what was left unsaid between us. *Just ask her what happened.* But the words died in my throat. Instead, I walked upstairs and took all the measurements and noted them in my phone. The second floor was just as bad as the first. Maybe worse. Some of the drywall needed to be repaired, and the plumbing looked shot.

I could hear Lex cursing as the measuring tape retracted, making a racket. *So damn cute.* She was impatient and had a temper to match. Another snap of the measuring tape made me smile and drew me to her.

I trotted down the stairs. "How's it going?"

"Stupid thing is trying to kill me." She threw it down on the floor and stomped on it.

"I think you've effectively killed the tape measure."

We smiled at each other and then laughed. I had to fight the urge to sweep her up in my arms and kiss her until we couldn't breathe. Her lips were addictive. I could happily drown in her touch. Instead, I cleared my throat. "Upstairs is done. I'll finish downstairs if you want to take pictures of the upstairs."

In no time, we were done and headed back to the Red Onion. Lex pulled up to the front and said, "I'll let you out and go park."

I chuckled. "This time, try not to lurk outside the window."

"I will try. I can see how it might become a habit. Lex the Lurker."

"Definitely has a ring to it." Laughing, I got out of the truck and walked inside, unable to wipe the pussy-ass grin off my face.

The bar had slowed down some. Most of the party had left, leaving a few locals. I waved and chatted for a minute before going behind the bar.

A new guy was here; had to be a tourist. From the looks

of his loafers, he was a city boy. Lots of those came here thinking they'd tame the wild. If I were a pussy and rolled my eyes, this would be the time to do it as I watched him, imagining his thoughts. People like him drove me crazy.

Two of the local girls—Samone and Jane—had saddled up close to him. Those women would sleep with anyone. The city slicker smelled of money, which meant those two girls would be after him.

"Oh, Hollis, it's going to be so nice to have a doctor in town," Jane said.

My head snapped up and I stared at the guy. There was no fucking way this was a coincidence. This was Skagway, for shit's sake. The guy gave Samone a smile, and I felt rage shoot through me. Lex didn't deserve this. No rich asshole was going to cheat on the woman I'd give my right arm to still be with.

Jane slid him a piece of paper. "Call me."

He took the piece of paper, and I lost it.

CHAPTER
Three

Alexa

I blew out a breath as I listened to a message from the loan officer who wanted to meet with me. The papers had been signed for the Doogle place. I'd used a piece of land Dad had given me as collateral since I was technically jobless. The entire process was a little confusing since I had to get a collateral mortgage. In the end, they needed my land to ensure the loan would be covered if I should default. There was probably some additional paperwork they needed signed.

Putting my phone in my pocket, I decided I'd call Morgan, the loan officer, tomorrow. I knew I was being a glutton for punishment; I wanted to spend more time with Drake. And I needed to talk to him about what happened, see if maybe there had been a misunderstanding with my dad. My heart was alive for the first time in what felt like forever.

After being in his presence for just a few hours, I missed him. I wanted to sit in my truck and take deep breaths, savor his spicy smell that was a mixture of him and the outdoors. Pure ruggedness.

From across the street, the wind blew some dust around, and the Twiner sisters waved from their bench. "Hello, Alexa."

"Hey, Elvira and Sylvia. Taking the day off?"

Elvira patted her gray hair and straightened her old-timey gold-digging uniform. "A news reporter never sleeps."

Of course. "Good to know. Found anything worth writing about?"

They giggled. "Want to give us an interview?"

"Maybe next time," I called and hurried onto the wooden porch of the Red Onion. There was some sort of commotion going on inside. I walked in, and it was like a scene happening in slow motion. Drake had murder in his eyes as he moved toward a man like an unstoppable force.

"Lex deserves better than a piece of shit cheating bastard."

In the blink of an eye, Drake punched the blond man. When he spun around, I gasped. *Hollis.* My eyes widened as Hollis fell off the stool. "Oh my! No!" I yelled.

Drake turned to me and dropped his fist. I ran to Hollis's side as he held his face and moaned. He sat up, looking at the Alaskan madman. "What the hell, man? Is it a crime in Skagway to take a number?"

"Hollis, what happened?" I asked, looking at Drake with narrowed eyes. He was not a bit sorry for punching the town's newest member and future doctor.

Hollis pointed to Drake. "That Neanderthal just punched me. For no reason."

I winced as the bruise started to form. Hollis needed ice.

"Drake?" I prodded. There had to be some sort of explanation.

Drake folded his arms over his chest, which only made his muscles look larger. Definitely intimidating. "He was taking a woman's number."

Okay... I looked around to see if there was something I was missing. Samone and Jane were holding onto each other for dear life. *Overdramatic.*

I looked at Drake. "Why can't Hollis get a woman's number?"

Drake's eyes narrowed. "A man doesn't cheat on his woman."

I paused, waiting for him to continue. When he remained silent, his lips pressed into a thin line, it all started to click.

Oh no. He thinks Hollis and I are together.

Hollis stood. "No, he doesn't. I agree. Good thing I don't have a girlfriend."

Drake's eyes widened, and I realized people were staring at us. The Twiner sisters were "lurking" at the door and writing down everything that was going on. We had probably given them enough fodder for three special editions. No, more. "Can we go to your office, Drake? Get some ice for Hollis?"

Drake nodded, grabbing an ice pack from Crete on our way back to the office at the end of the hallway. The tidy, wood-paneled office was just as I remembered. I whispered to Hollis, "You okay?"

He moved his jaw and winced. "No wonder you wanted a doctor here if this is how they greet newcomers."

"I think Drake thinks we're together."

Hollis nodded, probably already piecing together the situation. In the office, Drake handed Hollis the ice pack, which he put on his jaw.

Drake began to speak, but I cut him off, more than a little agitated. "You owe him an apology, Drake. Hollis and I aren't together. We have never been together. Why would you think that?"

For a moment, Drake simply stared at me. Then he took a step toward Hollis. "Sorry, man. I had some bad information."

"I can respect you looking out for Alexa. But next time, ask before you punch." They shook hands. Hollis handed Drake back the ice pack and then turned to me. "I'm going to head to the hotel. What time are you going to the clinic tomorrow?"

"Probably eight or nine. It needs more work than I expected. I'll call you when I leave here."

Hollis grinned. "Sounds good. This is already starting off as an adventure."

I let out a breath and rolled my eyes. Only Hollis would think getting punched was part of the Alaskan adventure he was looking for.

At the door, Hollis said, "I'll meet you in the morning. We'll be carpenters together."

In some ways, Hollis was sheltered. He'd traveled the world but had never camped. He'd dined at the top of the Eiffel Tower but had never tried a s'more. Our worlds were miles apart, yet we'd connected due to our losses.

I waved. "I'll bring the hammers."

"Can't wait."

It was going to be a disaster. I doubted Hollis had ever held a hammer in his life.

The door closed, leaving Drake and me alone. Before I had a chance to speak, Drake said, "You're not together?"

"No."

He took another step toward me. "You've never been together?"

"No."

My body hummed with excitement as he came closer. Light danced in his eyes.

"Are you seeing someone?"

"No."

"You're single?"

"Yes."

I knew he had a lot of questions, judging from the way his caramel eyes searched mine. I had them, too. The connection between us was undeniable. There would never be anyone like Drake Foster in my life. Never. I knew this. *But what do I tell him?* He deserved more than I ever gave him. I wanted him to understand there had been no one. I tucked my hair behind my ear. "I haven't seen anyone since I left two years ago. Not even a date."

"Then why, Lex? Why?" The anguish in his voice twisted a knife in my heart. I had done this to him... to us.

"I... it's just... Dad..."

Knock. Knock. Knock.

Drake swore when the door opened. Crete poked his head around the corner, his dark hair a mess. "Drake, inspector is here. Wants to speak with you about some new codes to make sure you're aware."

"Okay, give me a few."

"Will do."

The door closed, and Drake turned back to me. "I have a lot of questions. Lex, I need some answers."

"I know. I did it all wrong. I was messed up when Dad died. Really messed up. I'll explain everything. Answer any question you have."

His eyes softened. "I know it was tough. Where are you going to be later? I want to see you so we can talk."

With all that had happened, I needed to stop by Mom's house before her feelings were hurt. Not that it mattered much. When I'd tried to tell Mom when I would be in town, she'd blown off my comments and only wanted to talk about Hollis. And honestly, I was nervous about going home. I hadn't been back since Dad died. I knew it would feel emptier now with him gone. And that scared me. When I'd been home the last time, his shirt had still hung on the back of the chair, and things had been as he'd left them. If I closed my eyes, I could still sense him. But I doubted Mom had left anything of his out.

I wasn't sure what I would find when I went home. But I needed to face it and face my mother. "I'm going to head to see Mom after this. I haven't seen her yet."

"Okay. Text me your new number. Later, I'll text you so we can meet up."

I pulled out my phone and sent Drake my number. He went to the door. "This isn't over between us, Lex."

The door closed, and my heart thudded double-time in my chest. Drake Foster still wanted me. And I wanted him.

What am I going to do?

I drove up the long drive, anticipating the owens b&b sign. Some years ago, I helped carve our last name on the sign and then painted it with Dad. As I made the turn, I stopped abruptly. The sign was gone. The place had fresh paint, new landscaping, and new furniture in the yard. It looked like a completely different place. More sophisticated. Not the rustic B&B I'd called home for so many years.

Blinking a few times, I sat, frozen. This wasn't home. This was something... new and not part of my dad. All I could see was the loss of what had been. The bench Dad and I made was gone. His rustic rocking chairs, too. My heart ached. I hoped Mom still had them.

I closed my eyes, remembering what it had looked like before, needing to have that connection to my dad. Our home. The place where he taught me to ride a bike. The pond behind the house was where I learned to ice skate. Dad had pushed me on the tire swing for hours on end.

Maybe this is a dream.

When I opened my eyes again, I realized it wasn't. This was a foreign place to me. My eyes stung. *Why didn't Mom tell me she was doing this? Why?* I would have come home sooner to see it one last time.

At least the tree where Dad and I used to read together was still there. Drake and I had memories under that tree, too. When we'd first started dating, we had to stay in public places because I was seventeen and Drake was nineteen. Every day, Drake came over to help me study under that tree.

Drake.

He'd thought I was dating someone. I wanted him more than I wanted anything else in the world. My head was still torn, but my heart felt alive for the first time in two years. Dad's words bounced around in my head like a ping-pong ball.

Don't settle. Drake is not the one for you.

The lawyer had given me the letter two days after Dad died, at the reading of his will, and it had turned my world upside down. I had loved Drake... I still loved him. But I never knew Dad felt that way about him. They hunted, fished, and did so much together. They were close. And yet it all felt like a lie. *Did something happen while I was at school?* The letter had been dated two weeks before he died, and I just couldn't imagine Drake doing anything to break my trust.

A lump caught in my throat. Drake was a good guy, but at some point, for some reason, Dad had no longer approved. His last piece of parental advice had warned me against the man I loved. And now I was more confused than ever. If it had been the right decision, I didn't think I should feel this conflicted.

Later, Drake and I would talk, and I'd work on sorting it out.

Mom stood on the front porch, stiffly waving. The grimace on her face probably meant I hadn't come at the most opportune time. I got out of the car anyway and waved back. "Hey, Mom."

She paused with a look of surprise. "Alexa, I thought you weren't arriving until tomorrow. When did you get here?"

Well, that wasn't the greeting I'd hoped for. Normally, I would correct her, but I felt out of sorts at the moment. Like I was a stranger in the one place that was supposed to bring me comfort. From the looks of it, the inside of the house had been changed as well. And it seemed I was a glutton for punishment; my feet brought me closer to the door. At least the flowery scent of forget-me-nots still filled the air. That was the smell of home.

I cleared my throat. "Yesterday. I came back to open the clinic."

"Where are you going to open it?"

That was when I wanted to scream out in frustration. I'd

asked her to look at the Doogle place for me—explained all my plans. Trying to keep the irritation out of my voice, I said, "The Doogle place, remember."

She sighed, "Oh, Alexa. I had hoped you'd decide not to go through with that. Stay with Hollis in New York. That's where the two of you belong."

Deep breaths. Deep breaths.

I walked up the steps, holding out my arms. Mom greeted me with a stiff hug. Not the one I'd have expected from her after not seeing me for two years. Mom and I had never been super close. I mean, yes, I loved her, and she loved me... I thought. But she was closer to my sister, Raquel. My sister was married to the richest man in town, who was an asswipe, from what I could tell. *Chazz thinks... Chazz says... Chazz agrees. Chazz, Chazz, Chazz.* From the emails Raquel sent me, it was like my sister had lost all independent thought when she married him. But I'd never met him.

Opening the door, Mom said, "Come on in. I took a pie out of the oven."

The smell of freshly baked apple wafted through the air, which helped ease my tattered soul. Pie was just what I needed. This was another familiar smell, helping to ground me. Dad and I ate apple pie so many times while working together.

"A lot has changed," I commented. In the will, Mom had been given the B&B and the land around it. Raquel and I had received separate parcels of land that weren't connected to the B&B.

Behind me, Mom let out a deep, disappointed sigh. She probably wanted me to tell her how wonderful all the renovations were. The lie died on my tongue. I couldn't. It felt like the memory of Dad was purposefully being erased. I pressed again, trying to get answers. "What happened to the B&B sign?"

"I stopped doing that. Your sister wanted me to relax and not work so hard. Chazz agreed. With his stature in town, they thought it would be best if I stopped."

Not her, too, with the Chazz stuff. I kept my thoughts to myself, though it was getting harder to stay quiet about Chazz.

"But you loved it. It was something you and Dad enjoyed."

She shrugged. "Raquel understands the sacrifices I've made. I deserve to have a chance to take it easy."

Move on. Nothing will come of saying anything else.

I touched one of the new chairs in the entryway. It was covered in fancy silk. It seemed out of place—or maybe I was the one out of place now. I felt like a stranger in my childhood home. The thought turned my stomach a little queasy. With her face set, Mom watched me. To keep the peace, I said, "I'm happy for you, Mom. Where did all the furniture Dad built go?"

"It was sold at auction. How about some pie? Tell me about Hollis."

The words stung, and my heart seized in my chest. *She auctioned off his stuff and didn't ask me if I wanted it? Dad's furniture is gone?* The thought alone was a heavy weight on my chest. All those hours spent building the furniture together—all the precious memories. It was a pastime he'd learned from Drake's dad, Ike.

Mom turned her back to me and began to cut the pie. Suddenly, the acid churned in my stomach. The earlier inviting aroma now had the opposite effect. The walls began to close in on me, and there was no way I could stay there. I'd rather sleep in my truck.

"Alexa? Tell me about Hollis."

I blinked a few times, trying to not cry. Mom hated tears. "He arrived today. But, Mom, we're just friends."

After I broke up with Drake and met Hollis... Mom had been convinced he was the one for me. The room grew a little smaller, and I had to fight to stay calm as I searched for something concrete to remind me of *home*.

"I can't wait to meet him. He sounds like such a nice man. Maybe he'll be able to convince you to move back to New York."

I felt like I was talking to myself. Always had been that way. It was why Mom and I had a "harder" relationship. Man, I missed Dad. He would've wanted to know everything about my plans. Dad would have insisted on helping me get the Doogle place ready. I kept glancing around the room. All the family photos... gone. Anything familiar... gone. Bile rose in my stomach. I needed to leave.

Before she cut another piece, I took a step toward the door. "I just remembered I need to do something. Rain check?"

"Sure. I had planned to meet Raquel for dinner, anyway."

Mom looked almost relieved she no longer had to entertain me. *Of course.* Nothing had changed since I left.

There were only so many times my heart could break.

CHAPTER
Four

Drake

L ex was single.

Had been single.

I drummed my fingers on the steering wheel as I drove out to my favorite thinking spot. It was still early evening, but I wasn't ready to see her yet. I needed to get my head on straight and calm down before I jumped the gun with Lex. This new information changed *everything*. I just needed a few minutes. Then I'd text her.

She'd seemed ready to talk. I hoped we could get to the bottom of what happened.

Moochie had been understanding when I texted him to let him know Lex was back in town. He'd said I had a seat and could come later if I wanted to. If things went south, I'd probably take him up on it.

I thought back to everything that had been said over the last two years. Irene had insinuated that Lex had a big-city boyfriend. But, as I thought back, she never actually confirmed it. Her mother always alluded. *Why?* I'd made an assumption when I saw her running into his arms. I slammed my fist against the steering wheel. *Why the fuck didn't I talk to her that day? Why?*

I parked my truck and caught sight of her small frame on the end of the dock my parents owned. It was a small parcel of land not too far from their house. *What are the chances?* I shook my head and threaded my hands behind my head. This had been our place when we were together—to talk, to sit, to just be alone. Her head lifted from her knees and she glanced my way, a sad smile on her face.

I hated that look. And even though what she had to say might scare the shit out of me, I got out of the truck and headed her way. The pull to her was instinctive; the need to protect her was primal.

"You came here to think, too?"

She tilted her head back to look at me. "I did. Want me to leave?"

I tried to read what were behind those sad blue eyes. Shaking my head, I said, "No, I don't. Not at all."

I sat next to her and dangled my legs off the dock. There were so many conflicted emotions on her face. The breeze picked up, alleviating some of the stifling heat we'd had that day. Lex rested her chin back on her bare knees and looked out at the lake. "It's so peaceful here. I should have called your parents and asked if I could come. But I—"

"You never have to ask to come out here."

We grew silent again. I was impatient to get the answers I needed, but Lex couldn't be pushed. From the distant look on her face, I imagined a war raging within her.

Finally, she responded, "I was a coward. And I was confused."

"About?"

She looked me in the eye, and I could see the hurt she'd been hiding. It was raw, anguished, and I wanted to hold her until I could convince her everything would be okay.

Sighing, she shook her head. "Everything I thought was right in my life was suddenly wrong."

That makes no fucking sense. I watched her closely, waiting.

"Remember after the reading of Dad's will, Montgomery handed me a letter?"

"Yeah." I swallowed, anxious to hear what had happened.

"It was from Dad."

Again, I felt like she was spoon-feeding me information. I prodded her to continue, "What did the letter say?"

Her eyes brimmed with tears, and I couldn't stand it. I reached out, and Lex came into my arms willingly. I held her to me, searing the moment into my mind. She began to sob.

"Lex, what happened? Did someone hurt you?"

If someone had, I would kill them.

She shook her head. "No. No one hurt me."

I rubbed her back as she cried, and slowly she calmed down. When she pulled back, I saw the heartbreak on her face. "I'm so confused. It was easier when I was far away. I could keep you out of my mind. But you're here and..."

No. No. No. She needed to finish that sentence. A hell of a lot hung on that sentence. "I'm here and what?"

"Dad told me to leave you. That, in time, I would understand why. He said it was his last piece of fatherly advice." Her voice caught, and she closed her eyes. "I was so confused,

Drake. So confused. And I simply reacted. I wasn't thinking. I wasn't myself. I just did as he asked."

The air left me in a rush, and I couldn't quite catch my breath as I tried to process the words. *Ike wanted Lex to leave me?* I stared speechless at Lex. I was barely able to ask, "What?"

"I know Dad loved you. I had just lost him. And the letter. It was too much. I reacted. I was emotional. And I regret everything."

Stay calm. Lloyd told Lex to break up with me? That made no sense. "Do you have the letter?"

She sniffed and pulled it from her back pocket. It was soft and worn. Really worn. It looked like it had been refolded thousands of times. Through a couple of sniffles, she said, "Every time I felt weak and wanted to call you, I read the letter."

It had been read a lot. "Can I?"

"Yeah."

I unfolded the letter; it was short.

My darling Alexa,

You have always meant the world to me. I've been struggling with something that I need to tell you. I couldn't find the words while we talked on the phone. I hope to take you to the cabin and tell you during your next visit. But if that time doesn't come, I've written this letter. I have to protect my little girl.

I know you love Drake, but you need to listen to me.

Drake is not the right man for you. I know this comes as a shock, but I need you to trust me on this. As your dad, I implore you. End things with him. It will be for the best. I know this doesn't make much sense, but I need you to do as I ask. Do this one thing for me. In time you'll understand why. This may be the last piece of fatherly advice I can give you.

I love you, Alexa, with my whole heart.

Dad

The air left my lungs for the second time, and I felt nauseated. I checked the date of the letter. Lex's actions all made sense now. "This makes no fucking sense."

"Why?"

I swallowed, unsure how to tell her. But if we were going to have a chance, there was no holding back. "This was dated two weeks before he died."

"I know."

Do I tell her? I ran my thumb along her jaw, debating. Her blue eyes searched mine, pleading, and I knew I had to. "A month before that, while you were at school, we'd gone to his cabin for a few days to hunt."

A faint smile emerged. "I remember. It had been in September. He had a good time. You guys got a moose."

I took a deep breath. "Lex, that weekend I asked your Dad for permission to marry you. He gave me his blessing."

A million emotions flew across her face—shock, joy, sadness. Hopefully this knowledge would change our future. I still wanted her to wear my ring, have my last name, be mine in every way. We just needed to find our way back to each other.

Lex grabbed onto me, desperate. "What? You did? He did?"

"Yeah. I've never lied to you before. And I never will. That letter wasn't written by your Dad—I don't care what anyone says. You know he would've said no if he didn't agree. And if I'd done something wrong, he would have told me about it. I've been nothing but faithful and loyal to you. I swear it."

I would have done anything to wipe away all Lex's pain, absolutely anything. Continuing, I said, "He wouldn't have asked me to take care of you with his last breath. You know I was there. He said, 'Take care of my Alexa. She's going to need you.'"

"He did?" Her voice was soft, and she closed her eyes. We had both suffered needlessly for the last two years. If only we'd talked.

"Yes, he did. I swear it. I didn't tell you because when you came home for the service I just wanted to support you. And then you were gone."

She clutched my shirt. "What have I done? Oh, Drake, what did I do?"

"Nothing that can't be undone." *I hope.* If only she'd give us a chance.

Lex held me tighter.

I had her back in my life now, and I would never let her go.

CHAPTER
Five

Drake

The sun dipped below the horizon while we sat, holding each other. We didn't say much, just sat and soaked up the moment. *I have Lex in my arms again. She's here.* So many fucking times I'd wondered if it was truly over between us. Hoped to hell it wasn't. She shivered and burrowed into my chest a little deeper. This felt right. She was mine to protect and watch over again. Truly mine.

"Let's get out of here," I said.

"It is getting cold. I just don't want to leave. I'm scared you're going to want things to be over." This vulnerability wasn't like Lex. She was usually strong and self-assured.

I waited for her to look up at me. The last rays of the sun were nearly gone, and Lex's face was illuminated like an angel's. Fuck, she was gorgeous. When her eyes met mine, I leaned closer until we were a breath apart. "That isn't going to happen. From the moment I helped you change your tire on the side of the road, you held my heart."

"Drake…"

Just a small taste. Only a small one. What we had was still fragile. If I rushed it, it could shatter us forever. I pressed my lips to hers, savoring the feel of her warm lips against mine. Her lips tasted of vanilla. Pure fucking heaven. Before the kiss could deepen, I pulled back. "Do you feel it?"

"Yes."

"When things get tough, we hold on to this feeling. We fight like hell to never lose it."

She pulled me closer. "I'm all in."

Thank fuck. I let out a breath and held her tight. The letter from Lloyd confused me. He'd approved of me asking Lex to marry me. And he hadn't been a man to go back on his word without giving you a valid reason. Secret letters and shit weren't his thing. The handwriting was a man's, but the words weren't his. I was sure of it.

Someone had fucked with our lives.

But why?

Somehow, I would get to the bottom of it. But first, I needed to get Lex somewhere safe. She shivered in my arms. Against her forehead, I whispered, "Let's get out of here."

"Sounds good."

Hand in hand, we walked to her truck. "Where are you staying?"

"I've been camped out on Teagan's couch—I came into town, and they left. It feels like I'm cramping their style. They locked the bedroom door. I told Teagan today at the bar I would find somewhere else to stay, and she said that was great. I thought about asking Mom if I could stay there, but with all the changes she made, I don't think I can do it. I might check into the hotel or go stay at Dad's cabin. I just don't know if I'm ready to go out there."

When I heard about the B&B closing down, I knew Lex would be upset. Irene had nearly gutted the place. It was like she wanted to erase all the memories. Lloyd's belongings had been auctioned off. It hadn't been about the money. It had been about Raquel dealing one final blow to Lex. *Bitch.* And the cabin had been special to Lloyd and Lex. As a kid, she used to go up there with him and help him work on it. Together, they'd restored it to how it had looked when his grandparents built the place. I got why it would be hard to stay there.

The breeze blew, and Lex shivered again, tucking her hair behind her ear. I wasn't ready to be without her. I could offer my place, but that was likely something Lex wasn't ready for. She needed somewhere safe to process everything. The letter was still going to be an issue to overcome, mentally. But at least we were going to do it together.

It hit me, and I stopped, pulling Lex up short. "Why don't you stay at Mom and Dad's? They have the extra space, and you love it out there."

For a second, her smile grew, but just as quickly, it dimmed again. "I couldn't do that. They must hate me after what I did."

I brought her hand to my lips. *I have Lex. She is mine.* I took a deep breath and focused back on the situation. "No, they don't. You're like a daughter to them. They never stopped loving you. I think they knew we'd find our way back to each other somehow. Mom already called when she got the newsletter."

Within an hour of Lex leaving the Red Onion, the *Red*

Hot Twiner Tellings newsletter landed in everyone's email box. According to the Twiner sister, Lex and I were back together. Hollis had tried to break us up. The story was complete with pictures of me carrying Lex up the stairs to my place and us getting in her truck together to head to the Doogle house. And of course, Hollis leaving the Red Onion sporting a bruised jaw. I'd managed to avoid being in the newsletter for two years. Within a day of Lex being back in my life, I was in it again. Life was fucking great.

Hell, in this town, you couldn't take a piss without someone knowing.

Lex groaned. "I've been avoiding checking my email. Is it bad?"

I chuckled. "They've got pictures, according to Mom. I haven't looked."

"I bet Raquel is going to be mad." She leaned against her truck door and laughed.

Her sister was a piece of work, acting as if she was better than everyone else. "Has she reached out?"

"No. She'll track me down tomorrow, I'm sure. Once she finds out Hollis comes from money, she'll swoop in and try to control that, too. Just wait." Her fists were clenched at her side. Lex was a firecracker when she got pissed off. With a huff, she released some of the building energy. At some point, she would explode.

Finally, she nodded. "It'll be fine."

"It will be. And if she pisses you off too much, we can put food coloring in her mouthwash again."

Lex laughed out loud, and I smiled at the memory. When Lex was a senior, Raquel had borrowed a pair of Lexi's shoes and ruined them. In retribution, Lex put green food coloring in her mouthwash. That shit stained her teeth for a while. She looked like she had mold in her mouth. *Disgusting.*

Lex giggled. "Oh, man, could you picture her at a function with moldy-looking teeth?"

"Classy."

Things were getting easier between us. She touched my chest and I loved it. Soon I'd get to feel her fall apart in my arms. I grew hard just thinking about being insider her again. *Down boy. Just a little more time.* "I missed this."

"Me, too." The breeze picked up. In her tiny little shorts, Lex had to be cold. "I'll follow you to Mom and Dad's house."

"Okay." She opened the door but stopped before getting in. For a second, she looked down and kicked at a rock on the dirt road. "I'm scared, Drake."

I pressed in closer and kissed her jaw. "Me, too. But... I would risk it all for you."

She wrapped her arms around my waist; it felt so fucking right to have her in my arms. I wanted to lay her down and make love to her underneath the Alaskan sky the way I had so many times before. But we needed to take things slow.

And we needed to figure out who the hell did this.

Sweetly she murmured, "You're worth it all, too, Drake."

I closed my eyes as I held Lex, relishing her words.

CHAPTER
Six

Drake

We were almost to my parents' place when my phone vibrated.

Moochie: *Glad things are working out. I'll let you know when we're having the next card night.*

Me: *Great. I'll be there.*

We pulled up to my parents' place out in the country, about fifteen minutes from town. They had a large spread. My two brothers and I each had a hundred acres my parents had given us. The only stipulation was that if we ever wanted to sell it, family got to make the first reasonable offer.

It was heaven on earth.

In Alaska, you could go from a populated area to dense forest in the space of a quarter mile. Summers were beautiful, but winters were brutal. It took a strong person to survive this place.

As I got out of the truck, I checked for my brothers' vehicles, but it looked like they were gone. They'd been there earlier to help Dad load some furniture. Mom had probably shooed them away when I texted her that I was bringing Lex out to stay with them.

Mom came out on the front porch as I hurried around the truck to open Lex's door for her. She smiled at me. "Thanks."

When I got to her door, I saw the warmth in her eyes that had always been there. There was no doubt that Lex owned me, body and soul.

Before I took her hand to help her out, I checked the back seat and the bed of her truck. There was nothing. "Do you have any bags?"

"Oh, no! Everything is at Teagan's. I need to run over there and get some clothes."

Lex started to climb back into her truck, but I put my hand on her elbow. I could tell her mind was going in a million different directions. "I've got something you can wear, or Mom will. We'll get your stuff sorted tomorrow."

"Alexa, oh, I have missed you so."

I should have known Mom wouldn't wait for us to get to the door. She pushed me to the side and had Lex in her arms in a bear hug in a nanosecond. It was the best fucking feeling in the world to see them together. Lex's hug was just as fierce as they held on and whispered to each other. They'd been close. Really close. Lex had been the daughter Mom never had. And in some ways, Mom had been a mother figure for Lex.

To be honest, I liked Irene just fine as long as she didn't meddle in my and Lex's business. But Lex and her mom were different. They didn't see eye to eye on much of anything. There had been many times I'd shown up to catch Irene criticizing Lex for not wearing enough makeup or dressing up enough. It pissed me the fuck off. Lex was perfect as she was. No changes were necessary.

Did Irene write the letter?

I hoped it wasn't her. But I couldn't rule her out. Too many times, she'd made insinuations about Hollis and Lex in front of me.

Mom ushered Lex toward the front door. "Come on in. I hope you'll stay with us until you find a place. This place needs more women."

"I'd like that. But I don't want to impose."

Mom reached the top of the stairs first and turned around with her hands on her hips. Oh man, I knew that look by the cock of her head. I'd received it many times growing up here.

"Alexa Marie, get that thought out of your head right this instant. You are family and will always be family."

"I like the sound of that." Lex glanced my way and gave me a breathtaking smile.

Mom ushered her inside. "Have you eaten yet?"

"No, but that's not necessary."

Mom clapped and tucked a piece of blonde hair behind her ear. "Perfect. I'll get something prepared while Drake gets you settled. Drake, take Alexa upstairs. She can sleep in whichever room she wants." We started up the steps when Mom called, "Drake, are you going to stay the night?"

"Yeah, I am." There was no way I was leaving here until Lex left with me.

"Perfect. I'll call up when dinner is done."

We made it to my bedroom door. Lex's cheeks were a lit-

46

tle red as she touched the doorknob. Many nights we'd spent in here, making love when my parents were away. When I moved out, after Lex graduated high school, she stayed with me at my place.

"This feels like old times."

I rubbed the back of my neck as images of Lex spread beneath me flashed through my mind. Fuck, I was going to have to take a cold shower tonight. "I could never forget a moment we spent together. Not one."

She gasped and pressed her lips together. Without responding, she opened the door to my bedroom. I watched as she walked in the room and looked around. If something had changed, I wouldn't notice. Mom had been insistent on keeping our rooms as they had been when we lived here. She wanted to make sure we felt welcome to come home whenever we wanted. I only stayed out here when Dad needed help during the winter. I helped chop wood, clear the snow so Mom could drive, make deliveries, and help some of their elderly neighbors who weren't quite as mobile as they used to be.

Lex walked over to a framed picture of my brothers and me. "How're Hayden and Kane?

It was probably smart to change the subject. "They're good. Hayden's still flying planes and helps Dad. His business has grown a lot over the last couple of years. Hayden has three planes and has hired a second pilot. Kane's still doing the executive hunts and hates people in general."

It was amazing how different my brothers and I were from each other. I had never been afraid of relationships and wanted the commitment I'd seen in my parents my whole life. Hayden wanted the freedom to be with whom he wanted when he wanted. And Kane... who the hell knew? He kept his shit close to the vest.

She set the picture down with a laugh. "Kane is probably counting down the days until he can go hide in his cabin in the woods."

Kane loved the harsh winters. If it were up to him, he'd live off the land and only visit us sporadically. "Yep. He came back from a hunt today. I'm surprised he hasn't stranded some poor bastard in the woods."

Being a guide up here paid well. And it allowed Kane to hide away from the world more often than not.

Lex laughed. "Me, too. And I bet Hayden is sad that the tourist season is coming to an end. Have you met his flavor of the summer?"

"Come to think of it, I haven't. He hasn't said anything about a girl this year." That was odd. Normally, Kane and I couldn't get him to shut up about his bachelor life.

There were footsteps on the stairs, and I leaned against my desk. From the sound of it, Dad was coming to say hi. A few second later, he appeared in the doorway, wearing a huge smile. Kane and I favored our dad in coloring. Hayden was blond like my mom. "Aren't you a sight for sore eyes. Amie mentioned you were coming."

Lex smiled at Dad and hugged him. "Hey, good lookin'. How are you?"

Dad chuckled and hugged her back fiercely. Lex's and my separation had been hard on all of us. Mom and Dad's relationship reminded me of Lex and me. We never fought much. Yeah, we disagreed, but we worked it out.

Dad patted Lex on the back as he released her. "I'm good. Glad you're back in town, kid. Drake told us what you were doing. Mighty proud of you. Your dad would be proud of you, too. He was always telling me how you were going to make a difference with your fancy degree."

Lex blinked a few times to keep the tears away; it was clear my dad's words had touched her deeply. "Thanks. That means a lot. Hopefully, you can stop by the clinic sometime to meet Hollis. Skagway is lucky to have him as a doctor."

"I'll be sure to stop by soon." He gave a wink. "And I've heard the Twiner sisters think mighty highly of him, too… so it must be true." There was a pause, and Dad smiled as Lex shook her head. "They had a juicy excerpt on you two, as well."

Lex blew out a breath and threw her head back with a groan. "I swear they are part bloodhound."

Dad and I chuckled. Everyone loved those stupid newsletters. But it was a pain in the ass when you were the subject matter.

Dad gave Lex another hug and walked to the door. "I'm going to see if your mom needs any help. Dinner should be ready in about ten minutes."

When Dad left, the room grew silent again. I opened the dresser drawer Lex had claimed once upon a time, and just as I'd expected, her stuff was still there. Mom probably hadn't been able to bring herself to throw it out. It had been so long since I lived there I couldn't say what was in most of the drawers. I found a pair of her pajamas and placed them on the bed. "Looks like you're in luck. Mom never throws anything out."

Lex played with a stray thread on my bedspread, and it was clear there was something on her mind. *Let her work it out.* My nerves were frayed after the day I'd had, waiting and wondering where her mind was. It took everything in me not to demand she tell me what she was thinking.

After a few more seconds, which felt like a lifetime, she softly asked, "Did you date anyone while I was gone?"

I tilted my head and watched her closely. When I closed the bedroom door, she looked up, her expression stiff and filled with dread. My parents weren't nosy, but some things needed to remain private between a man and his woman. I needed Lex to see my face. Really see me when I answered her. Words alone might get misconstrued. "I tried—once. But I stopped it before it went anywhere. She was a random tourist who came to the Red Onion. But I knew it would be a mistake. So I dropped her off at the ship and went home."

Relief flashed across her face followed by hope. "Really? You didn't sleep with her?"

I took a step forward. "No, I didn't. It's been only you since the flat tire."

After I changed Lex's tire on the side of the road, I canceled the date I'd had planned for that night. It had taken me a while to convince her my sleeping-around days were over and to give me a chance. To be fair, I had earned the reputation. But after I saw Lex, I knew I would only ever want her.

She released a breath with a shake of her head. That wasn't a good sign. I thought she'd be glad I hadn't fucked another girl. "What are you thinking?"

"I'm so sorry for what I did. I nearly ruined us. If you had... I just... I..."

I knelt in front of Lex, resting my hands on her knees. "No more sorrys. Let's just move forward and see where it takes us. I wish I'd talked to you when I came to New York. There's a lot I wish I'd done. But we've found our way back to each other. That's what counts."

"You came? To New York?"

I nodded. "Two months after it ended. When I realized you weren't going to reach out, I got on the first plane. When I got there, I saw you run into Hollis's arms. I hated the son of a bitch. I turned around, got on a plane, and left. Never told anyone but Mom and Dad what I saw."

Adamantly, Lex shook her head. "Oh no. We're just friends. Always been just friends. I promise. Nothing has ever even gotten weird between us."

It was good to have the reassurance. As long as he kept his interest away from my girl, we'd get along great. "We good?"

"We are. More than good. But, Drake, I still don't understand why someone would want to do that to us. Write a letter from my dad. That seems so cruel. And I don't understand why. It makes no sense."

"No, it doesn't." *But, baby, I'm going to find out who. Stay calm. Don't get worked up right now.* I took a deep breath. "We'll figure it out. Together."

"I like the sound of that."

Whoever it was would pay for nearly ruining our lives.

CHAPTER

Seven

Alexa

I wiped my brow before I began to scrub another window. At least the weather was mild today. Since most Alaskan homes didn't have air conditioners because of the permafrost, hot days were hell. For the tenth time, I checked my phone to see if Teagan had texted back about me getting my clothes. But there was nothing. *What's wrong with her?* When she gave me the key to the place, it had been as if she couldn't leave fast enough. And she hadn't asked about my encounter with Drake. It made me wonder if she'd been holding the keys hostage to force me to see him. *Or is it something else?*

I sprayed more cleaner on the glass and started scrubbing again. Hollis was upstairs, attempting to sweep. I didn't think he'd ever held a broom before in his life. After I showed him, he walked upstairs with pep in his step, twirling it about. He was such a goof. But he was a brilliant doctor. New York-Presbyterian Hospital had all but begged Hollis to come work for them. The hospital ranked number eight in the nation.

I stepped back and surveyed the window. The windowsill was slightly askew. *Oh man, this place needs a lot of work.* I was handy, but this would take me months by myself. We were going to have to postpone the opening, which was disappointing.

There was some sort of cry of pain. I called upstairs, "Hollis?"

There was cursing before he yelled, "Coming!" He came trudging down the stairs. "I swear that broom is out to kill me."

On the opposite side of his face from his bruised jaw was a red welt.

"What happened to your face?"

He pointed to his jaw. "Crazy Alaskan." Then pointed his cheek. "Crazy Alaskan broom. Apparently, Alaskan things and I are not getting along."

I put my hand to my mouth, trying not to laugh. Hollis pointed to me with a glare. "Don't you dare." He tipped his head to the left and then the right, cracking his neck. "Surgery is easier than this wilderness."

Shaking my head, I tried to control my giggles. Sweeping was hardly *wilderness.* "I think we're going to need to hire this project out. I don't know how we can open on time if the contractor can't fit us in."

Throwing his head back, he dramatically whispered, "There is a God. Finally, my friend has come to her senses. No more manual labor."

I punched his shoulder. "It wasn't that bad. And you wanted to be Mr. Fix-It."

With a raised eyebrow, he looked me square in the face.

"Not that bad? Have you seen my face? I might have misjudged the situation."

That made me giggle at the angry red mark all over again. *How in the world did he manage that?* Hollis tossed the broom like it was on fire. "I won't be needing that anymore."

I blew out a breath. There was so much to do, and we were in over our heads. "I should have asked someone else to come look at the place. I'm sorry, Hollis."

We leaned against the wall and took in the room. The place smelled a little better today, at least. A mixture of Pine-Sol and Dusty Old Room. I noticed some of the spindles were missing from the second-floor railing. *Ugh. Just great.* I nudged Hollis's shoulder. *How is he so easygoing about this?* Medical equipment would be here before we knew it, and we were far from ready.

"Listen, Alexa, I saw the pictures, too. I agreed on the place. Yes, it's rougher than either of us thought. But once we get it fixed, it'll be great. The location is key, the layout is great, and the property is large enough for expansion. Plus, I can have a residence here, which will be helpful. I'm not worried."

Of course he wasn't. Hollis never worried. But I had a mortgage to pay and needed the income from the clinic. Though Hollis had offered to buy the property, I'd insisted. It was important for him to know I was all in.

More for myself, I said, "We'll figure this out. I can start calling around to see if anyone can fit us in their schedule. It might be a bit before they can."

I wanted the clinic to be spruced up and perfect before we had our first patient. Having a doctor here was more important than all the rest. It would come. But I wanted Hollis to be happy with his decision. In New York, he wouldn't have to look at broken spindles on a railing.

"Are you listening?"

I focused back on Hollis. "Sorry. What did you say?"

"I think you should let me buy this place. I do want to live here. It'll be easier, and I like it." I was quiet for a second, unsure what to say, and Hollis continued. "Just think about it. I know you want to show you're invested in this. I already know you are. And I know you can afford this place. But it makes more sense. Otherwise, I'm going to pay you an obscene amount of rent."

Oh, Hollis knew how to push my buttons. "You wouldn't."

He winked. "Just think about it. It honestly makes more sense. And I want to make this place a home. My home."

I hadn't thought about it like that. As a kid, Hollis had grown up in mansions, not regular homes. And I knew he desperately wanted a place filled with love. This was something he needed.

"Okay."

"Okay... I can buy it? Or okay, you'll think about it?"

"You can buy it."

A genuine smile spread across his face. "Thanks, Alexa."

"Thank *you*, Hollis. For coming here."

He put his arm around me. "I'm the one who should be thanking you. You saved me in more ways than you'll ever know."

"I feel the same way."

We stared around the room. I chewed on my lip as I thought about everything that needed to be done. We'd be lucky to get it completed within a few months. The problem was the equipment Hollis ordered would be arriving here in six days.

Hollis snapped his fingers in front of my face. "Stop worrying. We'll make this work." He cocked his head to one side, and I knew he was about to ask a question. "So… Drake? You two are back together?"

"We are. We're taking it slow."

"I think that's smart. I'm glad you two finally talked. That man can throw a punch. But I feel like an official Alaskan now. I've been in a brawl."

I shook my head, laughing. "You're crazy."

Hollis puffed out his chest, and I had to laugh. He'd gone to the local store and bought what he thought was official Alaskan gear yesterday after his run-in with Drake's fist: some tough, rugged fabric pants with midleg utility pockets. He paired them with a button-down cargo shirt that had all different size pockets. Definitely over the top. "What's so funny?"

"You, in your Alaskan gear."

"What? I look like an official Skagwayian."

"Yes, you do. Completely official." Or not. But I wasn't going to say that out loud.

CHAPTER
Eight

Alexa

The rumble of vehicles pulling in brought us both to the window. Four large trucks were parked in the yard. I recognized them as belonging to the Fosters. In near unison, Drake, Ike, Hayden, and Kane got out of their trucks. Instantly, Drake's head lifted, his eyes searching for me, and I gave a wave. A smile spread across his face. *I love him so much.* Never again would I leave him. Never. He'd asked Dad if he could marry me. If I hadn't been rash, Drake and I would be together. I wanted that with him desperately.

The letter still bothered me. Who would do that? And why?

With a bump to my shoulder, Hollis brought my attention back to the men outside. The Foster men got out and headed to the beds of their trucks, grabbing tool belts and toolboxes. Ike's truck had a bed full of lumber. Hayden and Kane's had machinery. My heart soared. Drake had done this for me.

"Looks like the cavalry just arrived."

"Looks like it."

Drake caught my eye and gave me a wink. His strong muscles flexed as he buckled his tool belt, and desire pooled within me. I swallowed hard when he grabbed a toolbox from his truck bed. *Heaven have mercy, the man is hot.*

"Why didn't I think to get one of those tool things while I was at the store?" Hollis asked.

I waited for him to laugh, but when I looked at him, he was serious. "I bet they have an extra one you can borrow."

Hollis's eyes lit up. "Now we're talking. Let's go get me Alaskan ready."

It was hard not to giggle, but somehow I managed. Outside on the front porch, the Foster men walked up the cement pathway. Amie and Ike followed them. I hadn't noticed Amie at first. Drake had captured my attention.

I didn't even try to contain my smile. "What are you guys doing here?"

Drake skipped two of the steps and met me on the porch. I nearly melted into him when he greeted me with a kiss on my cheek. His breath tickled my ear when he said, "Here to help my girl get her clinic opened on time."

That warm, soft feeling filled my heart. "Thank you."

With a nudge, Hollis raised his eyebrow and nodded toward Drake's tool belt. *Oh, right.* I turned to Drake. "Would you, by chance, have an extra tool belt for Hollis? He's trying to become a native Alaskan."

Approval was evident in Drake's eyes. He called over his shoulder. "Dad, do you have an extra tool belt for Hollis?"

From halfway up the walk, Ike called. "I'm sure I do. I'll get it." Beside me, Hollis vibrated with excitement.

In a flash, I was picked up and twirled around. "Well, if it isn't trouble."

I laughed. "Hey, Hayden. It's good to see you, too."

"You missed your chance to go after the right Foster brother." Hayden had that happy-go-lucky personality. It was hard not to remain unaffected by his charisma. He'd always been playful and innocently flirted with me to irritate Drake.

It still worked. Drake smacked him in the back of the head. "Don't make me beat your ass."

Hayden hugged me tighter. "What? I'm saying hey to Lex. I need an extra-long hug to make up for lost time."

Drake narrowed his eyes; I knew he hated when Hayden used *his* nickname for me. Only Drake called me Lex. And he was fiercely protective of it. "Stop being an ass."

Laughing, he set me down with a wink. "Man, it's good to have you back. I haven't been able to get under his skin in a while."

Under his breath, Drake muttered, "Fucker."

I giggled. Next to Drake, Kane stood with his normal, somewhat grumpy, expression. His husky, Mariah, sat at his feet. On a hunt about four years ago, Kane had found her abandoned in the woods. Since then, they'd been inseparable. "Hey, Kane. Hello, sweet Mariah."

The husky wagged her tail but stayed glued to Kane's side. She was the most well-behaved dog I'd ever met.

Kane gave me a quiet smile. "Make the dickhead work for it."

This time, Amie hit Kane in the back of the head. "Language."

Kane rolled his eyes, and I whispered, "You counting down the days until the snow?"

"Hell, yes. But then, for about a month, I'll have to deal with the rich asswipes who think they know how to hunt, but don't. Fu—foolish idiots."

Amie nodded in approval. The Foster brothers respected their parents.

Ike handed the tool belt to Hollis, who looked like a kid in a candy store. I made the introduction. "This is Hollis Fritz. Skagway's new doctor."

Hayden whistled when he looked at Hollis. "So the rumors are true."

"If they include Drake punching me for cheating on Alexa—who is *not* my girlfriend—yeah, they'd be true."

Amie tsk-tsked and gave Drake a scornful look. "Oh dear. I'm so sorry. I'm Amie Foster, mother of these three. I swear we taught them manners."

With a polished move, he took Amie's hand and gave it a light kiss. "My condolences, ma'am. You must have received a lot of calls when they were younger."

"Oh, trust me. These three gave me every gray hair I have."

The boys chuckled and nodded. The Foster brothers had been hell on wheels back in the day. Hayden was two years older than Drake, and Kane, the baby, was my age.

Drake and Ike put together a game plan. And in the next minute, lumber was brought in and the men got to work.

Hollis grabbed a hammer.

"What are you doing?"

With the hammer held the wrong way, Hollis looked at me like I was stupid, tucking some nails into one of his many shirt pockets. "Going to hammer some things. Be all Alaskan manly. I'm going to need the survival skills. These guys seem like the right ones to learn these manly things from."

Oh, they are. I handed Hollis a tape measure. "You'll probably need this, too. Watch out, though. If you thought the broom was bad, this is much worse. It's my nemesis."

"Good thinking."

The Foster men all stared at Hollis as if he'd lost his mind. Ike clapped Hollis on his shoulder. "Come with me. We'll get you hammering right away."

"Perfect." The excitement coming from Hollis was contagious. He wanted to fit in and figure things out. You'd never guess he was a brilliant doctor. My heart hurt at all the things he'd missed out on as a child.

As they walked up the stairs, I heard Ike ask, "Have you ever held a hammer before?"

"Nope. No time like the present to learn."

Drake touched my hand. "Mom's going to take you to the paint store. Her quilting circle and members of the local church are coming tomorrow to help paint. We'll have this place ready in no time, and you'll meet your deadline."

This was incredible. My heart swelled. Since the day Drake changed my tire, he'd always been there for me. He made me his first priority. Leaning toward him, I put my hand on his face. "You are amazing. Thank you."

"Anything for you. Anything."

Drake leaned toward me, and our lips almost touched.

Kane called from upstairs, "I'm not here to do this by myself, Drake. Stop playing kissyface with Alexa, or I'm going to beat your ass."

Amie groaned, and Drake gave me a quick kiss. "Better go before Kane gets his panties in a twist."

"I heard that, dickhead."

Amie sighed, "Lord, give me strength."

It was wonderful to be back with the Fosters again.

CHAPTER
Nine

Alexa

Almost twelve hours later, I stood in the middle of what would be the reception area. The broken spindles on the top railing had been replaced, the walls were primed to be painted, and the musty smell had been replaced with fresh cut wood and cleaning supplies. All the major repairs were done except for the upstairs kitchen and the restrooms. The latter would have to wait a day or so, when the new plumbing would arrive. Kane was going to help Drake finish up tomorrow since Hayden had a flight. Old wallpaper had been stripped, and the walls were ready to paint tomorrow. Everyone but Drake and Hollis had left about twenty minutes ago.

This was happening. And we would open on time. All thanks to Drake. Without him, everything would have taken much longer.

Hollis came down the stairs looking exhausted. Throughout the day, I'd heard Ike teaching Hollis what he needed to know. But now his hammer was stowed in his tool belt correctly.

"I don't think residency was this exhausting. I'm going to bed. Ike is a force to be reckoned with, and he's twice my age."

I gave him a hug. "Night, Hollis. You're halfway there to being a full Alaskan."

"I hope so. Stitches, setting bones, diagnosing illness... piece of cake. Sawing, hammering, screwing, leveling and every other *ing* word... I'm too tired to even be clever. Drake's gathering his tools and will be down in a second."

"Sounds good. Get some sleep. I'm meeting the church members and the quilting circle here at ten tomorrow for painting. You don't have to come."

"No, I want to. It feels good to accomplish this. I'm going to go soak, crawl into bed, and pass out—unless you need anything."

"Nope, I'll lock up with Drake."

He threw up a hand and walked to his car. "Night."

Although he was completely out of his element, Hollis had hung in there to the very end. When Ike had left, he'd given Hollis the tool belt to keep. My friend had more money than he could spend in a lifetime and could have bought as many tool belts as he wanted. But judging by the way he touched the belt, I knew he would treasure it for the rest of his life. Most things in Hollis's life had come with strings. With the Fosters, friendship and kindness weren't a bargaining chip.

The taillights of his SUV faded as he drove away, and I thought about my friend. He was desperate for a new start after his father's suicide two and a half years ago. Hollis's father had owned a medical equipment company, and about three years ago, his parents separated. One night, after his shift at the hospital, Hollis had stopped by for dinner only to find his father dead. In his office, a one-word note was left on the desk. *Sorry.* I think Hollis and I ultimately bonded quickly because we both lost our fathers in a tragic way.

I walked into the room on the right. This would be one of the exam rooms. *If only we had this place when Dad got hurt. Things might have been different.* The day of the accident, three men had died. The pistons from the log splitter had exploded, and Dad had bled out internally before the helicopter could get to him. If Skagway had had a surgeon, the bleeding might have been stopped.

The air charged when Drake walked into the room, and I felt his heat behind me. "Mom said everything is set to paint tomorrow."

It was because of Drake and his family that this had happened. I turned, and we were so close our noses touched. "Thank you... for everything. You helped make one of my dreams come true."

Dragging his nose along mine, he said, "And I will spend the rest of my life helping you achieve your dreams. Every one of them."

"I want to do that for you, too."

"You already have."

Goose bumps erupted along my skin. It had been so long since I felt this alive. I ran my hands over his chest and felt him shudder from my touch. He was all sweaty. I missed the feel of him. Butterflies danced in my stomach in anticipation of his lips touching mine.

"Lex, I—"

"Yoo-hoo. Alexa?"

No. No. No.

I wanted to grab that moment between Drake and me back. It felt important, and I could have sworn he'd been about to tell me he loved me. I closed my eyes and let out a sigh as Raquel's familiar voice—a sound not unlike a cat being strangled—drifted into the room. Drake stood up straight and muttered a curse. "Impeccable timing."

That was an understatement.

CHAPTER
Ten

Alexa

I turned to face the door, preparing myself to see my sister. We hadn't spoke in the two years since I left, other than a few random emails to finalize Dad's estate and her gushing about her fabulous life. She'd cashed out the plot of land Dad had left her almost immediately. I was a little sore she'd let it go without giving me a chance to purchase it, but Dad had left me the land with the cabin on it—the one with all the memories. Mom had gotten the B&B with the surrounding land. I took a deep, fortifying breath.

"Alexa? Where are you?" If it was possible, her voice got higher, and I cringed. She peeked in the doorway. "Oh, there you are. Why didn't you answer me? I had to yell. You know how that stresses my vocal cords. Chazz doesn't like when my vocal cords are stressed."

Oh yes, the vocal cords. Raquel had a beautiful singing voice. It was odd, considering her speaking voice nearly drove me up the wall. But she sang like an angel. Mom, of course, loved the attention Raquel garnered and generally sided with her. They had hoped one day Raquel would make it big. Mom always said that someday, word of Raquel's voice would travel and bring an agent to Skagway to sign her. They were delusional. *"Mom, Alexa is stressing me out. It'll affect my vocal cords."* That was the most commonly heard phrase in our house when we were growing up. Dad, on the other hand, would ignore the complaints and take me fishing. Anything so we could escape the house.

Raquel wore her dark hair in a tight chignon and some over-the-top designer suit. In Skagway, she stuck out like a sore thumb. As she walked in, her strong perfume filled the room. I wanted to gag from the overly flowery taste in my mouth.

Maybe things will be different now. Hopefully.

"Hey, Raquel. It's good to see you."

I stepped forward, my arms outstretched. Raquel's reaction was almost comical. She patted my shoulders like I was diseased. If we'd been in public, she would have greeted me with excessive affection.

Nope, she hasn't changed.

Without a word, Drake stepped beside me and rested his hand on my hip. Raquel's eyes focused in on the motion, her mouth flat. She'd never approved of Drake. The thought of being connected to someone who owned a *bar* was unimaginable to her. Time and time again, she'd begged Dad to make me break up with him. Needless to say, Drake barely tolerated her.

What am I supposed to say?

The situation grew awkward as I waited and Raquel

peered around the room. Disapproval rolled off her in waves. There was no question that the clinic was definitely beneath her.

Well, truth be told, anyone who didn't believe money and status were everything was beneath her.

My parents had been financially comfortable from Dad's logging and Mom running the B&B during the tourist months. But there wasn't much excess. Which was why I'd had to scrimp and save for college.

After Dad died, Raquel and Chazz started dating—they got married two months later. The moment he came to town Raquel had schemed to get Chazz's attention. I had overheard a conversation between her and Mom after the funeral in a back room. The poor guy never stood a chance.

I hadn't been invited to the wedding, which hurt. But it had always been that way—Raquel intentionally did things to spite and hurt me. She'd known that I would have wanted to be there. Family was important to me.

I'd found out about Raquel's engagement through the Twiner sisters' newsletter. Yeah, it had stung. Sooner or later, I'd grow completely numb to anything my sister did.

Once she'd completed her survey of the room, Raquel twisted her expression and waved her perfectly manicured hand in front of her nose. "The dust is beginning to upset my allergies. I'll need to make this quick. Chazz hates when I'm stuffy and sound nasal. We need to talk about welcoming Dr. Fritz to Skagway. Chazz agrees."

Chazz Hennington. I'd never met the guy, but hearing his name was like fingernails on a chalkboard. No one knew much about his family other than the fact that his parents were dead and he had a brother in California. From what I understood from the Twiners, they'd made their millions from a grocery store chain in California.

I wanted to wipe the smug look right off Raquel's face. "I think we're going to do the meet and greet at the Red Onion. Hopefully, Chazz will understand." I kept my face neutral, but my voice dripped sarcasm. There was only so much I could take from my sister before my temper flared. And I hated when my temper got the best of me. It normally resulted in me doing something I regretted.

One time in high school, I dumped an entire tray of food on my sister in front of the whole school. Yeah, I'd gotten in trouble for that one. She'd dropped her backpack on my school project, ruining it. It had pissed me off and I reacted. Poorly.

"Pardon me?"

"You heard me, Raquel. We'll do a welcome party at the Red Onion." Well, I hadn't really cleared it with Drake, but he wouldn't care.

She gasped, her hand to her chest, and I felt Drake's frame shake as he tried to contain his laughter. "I don't know if a *bar* is the right place to welcome the town's doctor."

Cocking his head, Drake stared at Raquel. "I promise to make sure the floors are mopped and the tables have been wiped down. *Chazz* can stop by to check it out if he'd like."

I mashed my lips together at Drake's overemphasis of *Chazz*. At one point when we were dating, Raquel had gone off on how she doubted the floors and tables in Drake's bar were ever cleaned. Apparently, Drake remembered.

Raquel's green eyes narrowed, and her lips thinned to nonexistent. If looks could kill, Drake would have vaporized. She walked around the room a few times, circling her prey... probably me. Maybe Drake. The clicking of her heals echoed through the room. Raquel pinned her eyes on me trying to intimidate me into submission. It wouldn't work. I refused to turn around and follow her movement. Drake remained relaxed beside me. It always amazed me how composed he could remain.

Finally, she asked, "Is the fodder in Twiner Tellings true?" before sighing dramatically.

Fodder? Who talked like that?

Before either of us had a chance to respond, she continued. "Alexa, things have changed since you left. I do not need a member of our family gossiped about in that horrid newsletter. It's upsetting to me. And Chazz hates when I'm upset. He plans to run for mayor in the next election. You understand, right?"

Mayor Richards would not like that news. He'd been elected seven years ago and served the people of Skagway well. If Chazz were to win, I imagined my sister would want Skagway to be renamed *Raquelville*.

Yeah, I'd have to move.

Again, there was no time to respond before she said, "So, I'll let you know the details of the welcoming party. I imagine we'll do it at our home. It's a lovely place, more than fitting to welcome the new doctor. And Chazz agrees."

Chazz. Chazz. Chazz. My temper soared, and I felt the burning heat on my neck that often accompanied this level of fury.

"I'm glad we're on the same page, Alexa. I'll let Chazz know and get the details to you."

I stepped out of Drake's embrace and addressed my sister. "No, *Raquel*, we are not on the same page at all." She was not going to dictate my life. I fisted my hands to remain calm, but when Raquel tilted her head and raised her eyebrow condescendingly, I lost it. "Does Chazz wipe your ass, too, Raquel? Because it seems like you've lost any independent thought since marrying him."

She gasped and put her hand to her chest again with a staggered, dramatic step backward. I rolled my eyes. If there had been anyone else there besides Drake, she'd have fainted for the attention. "I have never heard such crudeness."

"Well, it's a legitimate question, Raquel. Are you able to take a shit in private?" I held up my index finger. "Wait, don't answer that."

She narrowed her eyes at me. "Dad would be so disappointed in you for acting like this. I'm trying to help."

On the inside, I was shaking with rage. *How dare she bring Dad into this! How dare she!* There was a bucket of dirty water two feet away. *Stay calm. Don't let her bait you.* I took a deep breath. "Raquel, I think it's time you left."

From the flash of victory in her eyes, Raquel knew she'd hit a nerve. And now she was going to go in for the kill. With a sinister smile, she added, "Does the truth bother you, Alexa? I know if my father didn't approve of my choices, it would haunt me."

Lies. It was all lies. And manipulation.

Anger surged through me. Nothing had changed. Raquel would say anything to get her way. Anything. In the blink of an eye, I was a teenager again, hurting from all the terrible things she used to say.

No more.

I picked up the bucket and tossed the dirty water at Raquel. "You have always been a bitch."

She screamed while I fumed. If I'd had ten buckets, I

72

would have dumped every single one of them on her. "Never, ever, bring up Dad to me again. Do you understand? In fact, just avoid me altogether."

I stood, gripping the empty bucket while Raquel shook with hate. *Oh, I'll be getting a phone call from Mom tomorrow, no doubt.* But tonight, I had set a boundary with my sister. I waggled my fingers the way she had done to me so many times. "Run along now, Raquel. Go tell Mom. But I won't warn you again. Never mention Dad to me again or I will make it my mission to create more *fodder* than you could ever dream of. *Chazz* wouldn't like, considering his plans to run for mayor. Do you understand me?"

Raquel's nostrils flared while she opened and closed her mouth, unable to speak. Without another word, she turned and huffed out of the place, dripping nasty, dirty water. I threw my head back and sighed. *I shouldn't have done that. I should have walked away.* Tomorrow, there would be hell to pay with my mom. Raquel had deserved it, without a doubt, but now I'd have more stress.

And the mood had effectively been ruined. *Bitch.*

I turned to Drake and he said, "None of it's true. You know that, right?"

A lump formed in my throat, and I nodded stiffly. Drake gently put his hand on my cheek. "Don't let her poison you. Your dad was proud of the person you were. Never doubt it, Lex. Don't let her win."

Weary, I closed my eyes for a second. *Dad loved me. I know this.* I grabbed a towel and began to clean up the water. Silently, Drake helped me.

"I'm ready to head to your parents' place."

Drake nodded and escorted me to the door. "She's not

worth it."

I flicked off the lights. "No, she's not. I bet Chazz would agree."

Drake's deep chuckle helped ease some of the stress. "Maybe we should invite her to sing at Hollis's welcome-to-town party? Unless her vocal cords are too stressed. Who knows, maybe there'll be an agent there to sign her."

Since the moment I'd met Drake, he'd been able to bring light to the darkest of situations. He kept me grounded. I laughed, and he smiled down at me.

After locking the door, I headed to my truck. Drake opened the door, but we remained there, staring at each other. *How did I stay away from him for so long?* He traced his finger down my jawline, and something raw flickered in his eyes. Maybe we'd be able to recapture what had been about to happen earlier. I still wanted to know what he'd been about to say.

"Lex, I—"

Blingbring. Blingbring. Blingbring.

"Damn it all to hell," he cursed.

The world was against us.

He looked at his phone with a frown and sighed. "I need to take this." I nodded, and he accepted the call. "This better be good, Crete. Fuck. Yeah, let me get Lex home and I'll be right in."

Oh, this isn't good.

With another curse, he ended the call.

"Bad news?"

"Yeah. Bernie came in, pissed off at the world. Mack said something. Bernie swung. Roy came. I've got to go." Roy was the sheriff in Skagway.

In the past, our dates had been ruined on more than one

occasion because of a similar situation. About once every other month it had seemed to happen. "You don't have to follow me to your parents'. I'll be okay."

"Roy can wait. I want to make sure you get home."

That warm, squishy feeling made its way back. Drake winked at me and headed to his truck. As I drove to his parents' house, it was impossible to wipe the grin off my face with Drake's headlights in my rearview mirror the entire way. With Drake Foster, I always felt like his number one priority.

CHAPTER
Eleven

Drake

It was past midnight, and I sat on the back porch of my parents' place drinking a beer and unwinding. Lex was already asleep—she hadn't stirred when I opened the bedroom door to check on her. She'd wanted me to wake her when I got there, but after seeing how peacefully she was sleeping, I couldn't do it.

Once I'd gotten to the bar, it didn't take long to get things sorted. But I ended up staying to make sure things remained that way. Bernie and Mac had gotten into a fight about who'd caught the bigger fish. *Fuckin' stupid.* They'd probably both been so drunk they'd only caught some tiny perch.

I was still pissed they'd interrupted things with Lex. I'd wanted to tell her how much I still loved her, but twice that night, something had gotten in the way. *Is fate stopping me from moving too quickly?* Fuck if I knew.

I took another swig of my beer, thinking about Lex's letter from Lloyd, which was still in my back pocket. Since the moment she handed it to me on the dock, I hadn't let it out of my sight. *What are we going to do about it? How do I prove Lloyd didn't write it?* Lex believed me, but this still had to weigh on her. Shit, it weighed on me and I *knew* it was a damn lie.

Maybe I'd talk to Dad and see if he had any idea how to sort this out that wouldn't take forever.

As if he'd known I was thinking about him, Dad walked out the back door. "Thought I heard you come in." He sat and scrubbed a hand down his face with a yawn.

The blackness of the night calmed me. "Sorry, Dad. I thought I was quiet. I needed to decompress."

"Something on your mind, son?"

"Lex." There wasn't a moment she didn't consume my mind.

"Are you regretting getting back together?" Dad asked hesitantly.

I looked him straight in the eye. "No. Never. She's it for me. Always has been."

The tension in Dad's shoulders relaxed. "Then what's going on?"

It had been awhile since I talked—truly talked—with my father. For the last two years, I'd bottled everything up and pretended I was okay. But I hadn't been. I'd forgotten how much talking helped. I pulled out the note from my back pocket. "You know I asked Lloyd to marry Lex. And he gave his blessing."

"I remember. You had the ring and were going to ask her that Christmas."

Before I'd asked Lloyd, I'd talked to my Dad, wanting to

make sure I did things right. I handed over the note. "Well, I found out why Lex broke up with me. She got a note at the reading of his will. I remember the lawyer handing her the envelope, but she didn't open it. The letter was supposedly from Lloyd and told Lex to break up with me."

Dad swore as he read it. "I never understood what happened. But that would make sense. Her dad's last piece of fatherly advice. They were close. How could she stay with a man her dad didn't approve of?"

The thought made my blood boil. Lex had been all sorts of messed up and feeling guilty for not being home when he died. And then she gets the letter from her Dad... Yeah, it would fuck with anyone's head.

"Exactly." I took a deep breath. "I told her I asked Lloyd for his blessing to marry her and what he'd said when he was dying. I do not believe Lloyd wrote that letter."

Dad kept starring at the note. "I don't, either. Lloyd wasn't one to be underhanded. His word was his bond. And he wouldn't have asked you to watch over Alexa. He would have told you to leave her even with his last breath."

It was true.

"Who would do this, Drake? Why?"

I scrubbed a hand down my face and sat back in the rocking chair. "Raquel is the first name that comes to mind. She paid a visit to us at the clinic tonight. Still filled with hate and piss. Or Chazz. Maybe Irene. She's always thought the sun shined out of Raquel's ass and was harder on Lex. And neither liked me. All I know is someone needed access to the will. Maybe it was the lawyer. Hell, it could have been Teagan, considering how weird she's been acting. But she's always been that way. As for why, I have no fucking clue."

Dad refolded the note and handed it back to me with a shake of his head. "You're going to have to be careful if you start accusing people."

"I know. But whoever it is nearly fucked up my life." I sighed and took another pull of my beer. "Something just isn't sitting right with this. I don't know if Lex has put much thought into it, but someone went to a lot of trouble to break us up. Now that we're working things out, I wonder what they'll do."

"You sound worried."

"I am. This person has remained in the shadows for two years. Now Lex is home, and we're back together in less than forty-eight hours."

"Has Lex mentioned anything out of the ordinary happening?"

"Not that I can think of."

Before Dad could respond, the door swung open. Lex walked out in a T-shirt—no bra—and tiny-ass shorts. My dick was not going to survive this going-slow stage, which we really hadn't defined.

"Ike, do you still chop wood in the same place?"

Oh shit.

Dad pointed across the yard. "Same spot. There's wood there now."

"Thank you."

Lex took off across the yard, her ass shaking as she threw her arms in the air, obviously talking to herself. By the way her volume rose and then lowered, it was clear she was pissed off. She looked like she was asking the world a question and then answering it. I wasn't sure what had happened, but I knew it was best to not suffocate her. Something had added to her fury with Raquel earlier. Her body grew more animated the more she got worked up, and then she disappeared behind Dad's shop.

"Boy, something got her agitated." Dad chuckled. "I forgot what a firecracker she could be."

The fucking grin on my face wouldn't disappear. I had Lex back, and she was still the same. Crazy antics and all.

"I'm going to see what happened. Say a prayer she doesn't take a swing at me."

Standing, Dad patted me on the back. "Good luck, son."

When I was halfway down the stairs, Dad stopped me. "You know… We could ask Butch if he knows anyone who could look at the letter. Maybe compare the handwriting."

Butch was ex-military intelligence who'd moved here a year ago to start over. He was a good guy and came to eat at the Red Onion from time to time. He preferred to stay under the radar. I'd totally forgotten about him. "You're a genius."

Then, it occurred to me… if Lloyd had written the letter, I might lose Lex forever. This was uncharted territory. I heard the wood splinter off in the distance and glanced that way. I couldn't lose her. And I'd fight like hell to keep her.

Dad touched my shoulder. "From experience, it's always best to know rather than wonder."

Yeah, except if it ruins your life. "Probably."

But it wasn't my call to make. This was something Lex and I needed to discuss together. As I made my way across the yard behind the shop, my phone vibrated.

Hollis: *The rumors aren't true. Don't hunt me down and punch me again. We city folk don't fight with our fists.*

I chuckled. Hollis was growing on me. He was a fish out of water up here, but he wanted to make a difference. The man couldn't swing a hammer, cut wood, or use a tape measure for shit, though. Alaska would be an interesting match for him. I typed back a response.

Me: *What happened?*

Hollis: *Something to do with the Twiner sisters and their newsletter. You Alaskans are nuts. Seriously, code red release? It's nearly one in the morning. They called me looking for a comment.*

Me: *Welcome to Skagway, Doc.*

Hollis: *I'm going to have to raise my rates.*

Me: *Probably smart. Going to check on Lex.*

Hollis: *Good luck. She's quite irritated.*

I put my phone away and walked to the side of the shop. As long as I had Lex in my life, I'd weather any storm with her.

CHAPTER
Twelve

Drake

The floodlight outside the shop had been turned on. Lex had a log up on the block and was mid-swing. As I watched, a piece of wood splintered off.

My Alaskan firecracker.

With each swing of the ax, Lex growled, "I hate her. I hate her. I hate her."

This wasn't good. We'd gone straight to hating whomever. I kept my distance and leaned against the wall. "Who do you hate?"

Lex swung again and broke off another piece of wood. "Raquel."

Raquel most likely deserved it. "What'd she do?"

"Apparently, she called the Twiner sisters, probably to vindicate her name and take revenge on me for the dirty water. Then she proceeded to tell Elvira that it was her and Chazz's idea to bring Hollis here. Stupid, stupid Chazz. I've never even met him, and I can't stand the sound of his name."

Whack!

Another piece of the log split off. Sylvia and Elvira must have struck gold with this newsletter. Lex loaded another piece of wood and swung, but this time she missed. "It was *not* her idea. At all. She told me I was an idiot when I left for New York with this idea. Ugh!" She gave the log another whack. "Then Sylvia chimed in and asked what it felt like to be Raquel's sister. I tried to remain calm. I really did. But then, on top of that stupid-ass, ridiculous question, they asked me for a quote for their newsletter regarding my opinion of how wonderful Raquel and Chazz were for the community. How wonderful they were for finding Hollis Fritz."

I was afraid to ask, but I did anyway. "And you said?"

She gave four more angry swings before she placed the ax down and turned to me. She put her hands on her hips, fury radiating from every pore of her body. "That Raquel had nothing to do with Hollis Fritz coming to town. Nothing. He doesn't even know her. He's my friend, and I asked him to come here. And then the sisters called Raquel, who said I was cheating on Hollis with you. My mother confirmed that I was dating Hollis. My *mother*! She knows I'm not."

Now I was getting fucking pissed, too. These two were trying to make waves where there weren't any. Which definitely made them letter-writer suspects.

"Drake, I have never, ever dated Hollis. I swear it."

"I believe you." I wanted to take the ax to a few logs myself. *Motherfuckers.* "What happened next?"

Lex began to pace. "They called me back and asked about us. What Hollis thought about me and you rekindling our romance. Would I break up with Hollis. I tried to calmly explain the situation. Then they said they needed to finish gathering the information and would let me know. This is my *fucking* life. I know who I'm seeing. I seriously want to—"

My phone rang, cutting off Lex. It was Sylvia, one of the Twiner sisters. I held up my finger. "You're going to want me to take this. It's Sylvia."

Lex marched over and grabbed for the phone. "I'd like to finish where I left off."

I tried to reason with Lex while barely keeping the phone out of reach. Going back and forth could take all night. I was fucking exhausted and just wanted to focus on us. "Let me talk to her."

For a second, Lex looked like she wanted to argue, but she stepped back with her hands up. "Be my guest. So stupid. Stupid. *Stupid*." She grabbed the ax and took another swing, muttering, "It's been two freaking days, and I've been in three newsletters. Three. *Three*. That's got to be a record."

I pressed Accept on my phone, trying to hide my smile. "Sylvia, how are you?"

Lex stopped and watched me, her eyes narrowed, and I swore steam was coming out of her ears. She set another log on the stump and began to swing again.

"Hey, Drake. We've got a code red newsletter we want to get out to the people of Skagway, stat. Seems we may have uncovered a scandal. We'd like your side before we send it out."

A scandal would put Lex in a *fourth* newsletter. A record, for sure. I chuckled. "What scandal would that be?"

"Does the name Hollis Fritz mean anything?"

Oh good. I was going to be able to nip this shit before it started. "Sylvia, get your pencil or turn on your recorder. This is going to be good. You're not going to want to miss any of it."

Lex stopped swinging, put down the ax, and walked my way. On the other end of the phone, I heard a flurry of activity. The Twiner sisters lived together and had never married. I swore they took shifts sleeping so they wouldn't miss anything. I heard Sylvia say, "Oh, dear. Elvira, this is going to be good." There was more noise, and then she came back on the line. "Go ahead, Drake."

I stepped closer to Lex, watching her face to make sure she understood how serious I was. "Lex has never been involved with Hollis. And *she's* the reason Hollis is here. So the people of Skagway can have a doctor. Raquel and Chazz had nothing to do with it. And I hate to say this, but Irene knows that Hollis and Lex never dated." And because the Twiner sisters needed something else to focus on, I said, "Rumor has it from a very reliable source that Chazz wants to run for mayor next year. I think that's probably a better addition to your newsletter than Lex and me dating again, don't you think?"

I could hear gasps on the other end of the line.

"Oh, this is good stuff. What, Elvira?"

They began to whisper. "Okay. Okay. Give me a second and I'll ask. Shh... this isn't my first time, Elvira." Sylvia cleared her throat. "So, Drake?"

"Yes."

It was hard not to smile. Lex's mouth was still a thin line.

There was more commotion on the other end. "Yes, I know. I'm asking. Stop it." She cleared her throat again. "Tell me, Drake, for the record. Are you and Alexa back together? Like *together*, together? The people will want closure."

I got the impression the sisters were going to move onto

Raquel if they were talking closure. *A-fucking-men.* I put my arm around Lex's waist and brought her to me. Slowly, we walked back toward the wall. So many emotions passed over her face: love, fear, desire, irritation. Once her expression softened a little, I said, "Lex is mine. Always has been. And I plan for her to always be."

Lex sucked in a breath, and her eyes flared with desire, while the sisters giggled like little schoolgirls. "Oh dear, this is going to be good." I was pretty sure that was Elvira.

The sisters had enough for another red-hot newsletter. Chat time was over. "Okay, ladies, I need to go kiss my girl now."

They continued to giggle. "Bye, Drake. Thank you for the tip on Chazz. Do you want to stay anonymous?" they asked in unison.

"Sure."

With that, I ended the phone call. Lex was leaning against the wall. I braced my hands on the wall on either side of her face, caging her in. Hell, I wanted her bad. But I needed to remember not to rush things until we had some answers. I leaned in closer.

Quietly, she asked, "Always has been?"

I searched her eyes as she licked her lips.

"Yes. And I hope always will be."

"Me, too."

That was all it took for me to press my lips against hers. She moaned into my mouth, and instantly my dick hardened. I knew I'd be jacking off to this memory later, wishing things could have gone further. All too soon, Lex pulled back, and I pressed my forehead against hers. Everything just felt *right*. "I've missed you."

She leaned her head against my chest with a gentle sigh. "Missed you, too."

CHAPTER
Thirteen

Drake

I lay in my bed, staring up at the ceiling. In the room next to me, Lex was asleep. Outside her room earlier, I hadn't wanted to stop kissing her, but when she finally opened the door to her room, she hadn't asked me to follow. With the restraint of a fucking saint, I'd stayed outside. But hell, I wanted to hold her, just have in her my arms. I sounded like a sap, sure, but I missed her lying next to me at night. Kane and Hayden would give me hell if they knew how far gone I was—had always been—for Lex. On more than one occasion, they'd called me pussy, whipped, whatever they could think of. But it had never fazed me. And if they ever met the right person, I was going to give them hell.

The memory of her lips brushing against mine made me hard again. Shit. A cold shower and jacking off twice hadn't helped. Maybe a third time would do the trick—that or five stiff drinks.

Creak.

I froze.

"Drake?"

I shot up, my dick stiffening further at the sound of her voice. "Yeah, I'm awake. What's going on?"

"Can I come in?"

If she turned on the light, she'd see the tent I was pitching with my blankets. Thank God she didn't. I adjusted myself with a wince. "Of course. Come here."

The door opened wider before closing again, cloaking us in darkness. I heard Lex's feet on the carpet as she padded over to me.

"I can't sleep."

"Me either." I swallowed hard before I asked, "Do you want to join me?"

"Yes," she breathed on a whisper.

I pulled back the covers. "Come here."

I was hit with all-too-familiar sensations as she joined me. The peach smell was nearly my undoing. If we hadn't been in this awkward limbo, she would have snuggled into my side and placed her hand across my abdomen. Instead she kept some space between us and lay facing me. Our breaths mingled. I wanted her. All of her.

A few minutes passed in silence.

"Drake?" I could hear the worry in her voice.

"Yeah, baby. I'm still awake."

She took a deep breath. "What if my dad really did write that letter?"

Her sadness tore through me. I knew this wasn't over yet. There was no way it could be. The situation had my heart and mind warring with each other, which meant it had to be a full-scale war for Lex. I'd hoped to have more time to make us stronger as we dealt with this. But time hadn't been my friend for a while.

I reached out and rubbed my thumb over her hip. "Then you'll need to decide what to do."

Lex ducked her head to muffle a sob. "I don't want to live without you, Drake. These last two years have been miserable. I just can't do it."

"Then don't."

She didn't say anything else as we lay in silence. *Is she having second thoughts?* I wanted to ask but wasn't sure if I wanted to hear the answer. Lex had left me once before. *Will she be able to do it again?*

At some point, a worried sleep claimed me.

CHAPTER
Fourteen

Drake

"**D**rake."

I jolted in bed and reached for Lex. She was already sitting up. "Lex, are you okay?"

It was still dark, and I was nearly blinded when she turned on the light. There were dark circles underneath her eyes, and she looked exhausted. "Can we talk?"

Oh shit. The three words no man wanted to hear. They rarely began a good conversation. I sat up straighter and looked at the clock. It was almost five in the morning. "What's on your mind?"

"I've been thinking…"

And those were three more words I didn't want to hear.

I knew I had to proceed carefully. "And…"

She lay her hand on my cheek. "I can't walk away from you again. Even if Dad wrote the letter, I can't. Dad wanted me happy. I'm happy with you."

In one swift motion, I pulled Lex into my lap. "I don't think I could either. Even if you wanted to leave, I would spend every day of the rest of my life convincing you to choose me."

She placed her hands on my chest. The intensity between us hadn't changed. "Can you feel it, Drake?"

"Yes, I feel it. It never stopped."

She shifted on my lap, and her eyes widened. *Yeah, baby, I'm hard for you.* From the change in her breathing, I knew she wanted more. If I slipped my fingers into her panties, I was sure I'd find her wet. The tips of her nipples hardened against the fabric of her shirt. My thumbs drifted over their peaks and slowly moved back and forth. I watched her eyes to see if this was okay. They were cloudy with lust; there was no hesitation there. She wanted... no, she needed this as much as I did. With each slow stroke, her nipples grew stiffer. Lex squirmed.

"You sure about this?" I asked.

"Yes," she said on a breathy sigh.

I'd make her feel good for now. Later, when I could make it special, I'd make love to her like she deserved—multiple times. I slid my hand up the inside of her thigh, where her skin was smooth as silk.

"Drake." The sound of my name on her lips made my dick excruciatingly hard.

She moved against it, and fucking hell if I didn't almost come in my boxers like a teenager.

Pound. Pound. Pound.

"Let's go."

Motherfucker. It was Kane. We weren't supposed to meet until seven.

Lex and I froze on the bed like two kids caught doing

something we weren't supposed to be doing. I had no idea if the door was locked. I called out, "Just a sec."

Lex jumped off me and dove under the covers in a flash right before the door opened.

"I don't have all day. Let's get going."

"I said just a sec, asshole."

"Your door was unlocked. If you're going to wank off, lock the door."

Sometimes, I swore Kane had to be adopted. Beside me, Lex stiffened. He paused and looked at the lump of covers next to me. *Yeah, bastard, I have Lex in here.* He smirked, which made me want to punch him.

"What happened to seven?" I snapped, not bothering to hide the irritation in my voice.

"I have to meet the city fuckers at eleven now. They're paying top dollar to go earlier for a two-day hunt. I texted you on my way over, but I see you were otherwise occupied."

Mom called from below, "Language, Kane. And don't wake Alexa."

He called back, "Too late, Drake already did."

"Asshole."

"Wanker."

Lex popped her head out from under the covers. "Morning, Kane. You're chipper this morning."

"Fucking with my brother has that effect on me."

Mom called again from downstairs, "Kane Foster! Stop aggravating your brother. And watch your language! Drake, you, too!"

"Sorry, Mom," we answered in unison.

Kane motioned to me as he walked backward. "Come on, dickhead. I'll pour you a cup of coffee and drive so we can get the lumber from the shed."

Leaving the door open, Kane backed out of the room and plodded down the stairs. I couldn't understand how, in the woods, he moved without making a sound. Here, he was as delicate as a bull in a china shop.

Lex threw a hand over her face, mumbling, "Is it too much to ask for one orgasm? Just one that isn't machine generated. The world is against us. Seriously, every time we're on the cusp of something—*bam*—we're interrupted."

She was honestly irritated, and I chuckled. At least until the thought of Lex using a vibrator had me returning to full mast.

"Don't laugh! It's not funny."

I grabbed her hand and put it on my massive erection. "No, it's not."

"Oh my."

"Yeah. And he's fucking pissed he's going to have to wait. I jacked off two times already before you even came in here."

Sitting up, she bit her lower lip. "Really?"

"Really."

Those must have been magic words because she leaned over and kissed me. Maybe I could buy us five minutes.

Kane called from below, "I'm leaving! You better hurry unless you want to do it yourself."

That ass would leave me, too. Hauling lumber was definitely easier with two people. I threw off the covers and grabbed my clothes. In less than two seconds I was halfway dressed. Leaning down, I kissed Lex goodbye. "Will you drive my truck to the clinic? In case I need to get anything else after Kane leaves?"

"Yes, I'll be there shortly. I think I need a cold shower first, if you get my drift."

I groaned. "Not helping."

With one more kiss, I was out the door and heading for my brother's truck. For shits and giggles, Kane put the truck in reverse and backed up about ten feet before stopping and letting me in. Mariah sat in the backseat, watching us with interest.

When I was halfway in, Kane put his truck into gear. I righted myself and slipped my shirt on. "You're an ass."

"Yeah, I am. But at least I'm not a whipped fucker."

Giving him a Cheshire Cat grin, I nodded. "When that girl walks into your life, I'm going to give you *so* much shit."

Mariah barked from the backseat. "She's warning you. I'm my own man, and I'm not going to let some girl lead me around by my dick."

I said nothing, and Kane raised his eyebrow. "Fuck you."

"What?"

"I see your smug smirk. Not happening."

"Okay." I held my hands up, knowing it would aggravate him more. "Not happening."

We approached one of Dad's lumber sheds. As the family's main source of income, Dad and Mom ran a lumber mill business. He'd donated all the supplies to fix the clinic, even though Hollis had offered multiple times to pay for it as we worked yesterday. From what I could tell, Hollis had little experience with people just doing something for you with no strings—simply because it was nice. In Alaska, there were times when we needed each other to survive. Off to one side of the shed, one of Dad's nightstands sat, unfinished. Seeing it brought back a lot of memories. I never would have imagined the little blond-haired, pigtailed girl who used to come with her dad to buy lumber would one day intoxicate me. At that age, she'd followed me around, asking a million questions. When she left, she'd give me a hug and skip off to her dad's truck. She'd stopped coming about a year before I really saw her for the first time. Man, it was like she had blossomed overnight.

Dad and Lloyd had bonded over making furniture. I believed it was one of my only saving graces that convinced Lloyd to let me date Lex.

"Looks like you and Alexa are figuring things out." Kane's voice brought me out of my memories.

"We are." Rolling my neck, I tried to get my thoughts together. I needed someone other than Dad to talk to. Though Kane was insensitive, he was always there for his family any time we needed him. "Lex broke up with me because she got a letter her dad left with his will telling her he didn't approve of me. I know someone else wrote it. I'd just asked Lloyd if I could marry Lex, and he gave his blessing."

Kane put the truck in Park and looked at me. "Come again?"

One summer in high school, Kane had come back from doing some work in Ketchikan a changed man. He'd never told anyone why, as far as I knew. Mom worried about him, but he swore to her nothing horrific had happened. Somehow, I knew he'd talk to me when he was ready. And through all the fighting and arguing, we were always there for each other.

I explained the situation. When I finished, there was anger burning in his eyes. "One thing you don't do is fuck with a Foster. You going to figure out who it was?"

"That's the plan. The most reasonable place to start is

with the lawyer. Raquel or Irene are likely suspects."

He shook his head in disgust. "Why would they do that to Alexa?"

"Jealousy. Irene clearly plays favorites. Lex wasn't told her mom closed the B&B. She wasn't even invited to Raquel's wedding."

Kane's eyes widened as his lips thinned. "I had no idea. Alexa is like a sister. They better watch their fucking step around her. Watch her back, okay? Yours, too."

The words left me uneasy, but I understood what he meant. Someone had sabotaged our relationship two years ago. It was highly unlikely we were going to be left to go our merry way now that we were back together. No one, not even me, thought we'd manage to work things out.

I clapped him on the shoulder. "Thanks, man."

One of the workers waved to us as he left the shed. Kane asked, "What does she think about it all?"

"I think she's still trying to wrap her head around it all. For the last two years, she conditioned her mind to reject the thought of us. Then she comes back, and... I don't know... we couldn't stay away from each other if we tried. But it's some heavy shit to process. It felt like we had a breakthrough last night, though. Lex told me that even if her dad did write the letter, she was choosing me."

He blew out a breath. "That's some fucked-up shit."

"Yeah, it is."

With an intensity only Kane could have, he looked me in the eye and vowed, "If you need anything, call me. I don't care if I'm in West Buttfuck, Alaska. Call me, and I'll be there."

"Thanks, Kane. I appreciate it. Dad mentioned that I should contact Butch Cowart, see if he'd look at the letter.

Then at least we'd know if it was forged. I'm going to get his number from the Red Onion. I think I have it in my office." The finality of knowing whether Lloyd had written the letter made me uneasy.

Kane thought for a second. "I can't imagine what you're going through. But I'd want to know. I wouldn't want that shit hanging over me. Something like that would gnaw away at a man. You want me to call Butch? I think he's planning on heading up to the woods to meet me this evening. He's helping me with the hunt. Not sure if there's cell reception out there." He chuckled. "Butch may kill these bastards, so you might want to get his thoughts before he's in jail."

"Why is he going with you?"

"Demand for private hunts is high—even when I raise my prices. I'm charging nearly quadruple what I was last year. I'm going to raise them again for any new ones I book. Butch mentioned looking for some extra income, so he's going with me on a few hunts over the next two weeks. We'll see how it works out."

Kane and Butch were good friends. They'd hunted together from time to time. "If you don't mind. It would be great if he could look at it before he leaves town. I just need to run it by Lex first."

"Sounds good. Let's get loaded up, and I'll make the call."

CHAPTER
Fifteen

Drake

I t was early evening, and there was a chill in the air. Since the day Lex arrived home, Skagway had returned to normal temperatures. But a cold front had come through today, putting us in the forties, which was colder than normal for late August.

After we finished the repairs at the clinic, I had a meeting with the city council. Then Moochie and I had a quick bite to eat. It had been a hell of a busy day. Now Lex and I were in my office while Crete manned the bar for me. I was going to give him a bonus. Over the last few days, he'd been available at a moment's notice.

Butch sat at my desk, studying the letter against samples of Lloyd's handwriting.

When I arrived at the clinic, Lex and I decided we needed to know the truth. Either way. Dad was right—it was better to know the truth and deal with it than let uncertainty linger.

But hell, I was nervous. Lex paced, and then sat, and then paced some more. I was on my second beer but probably needed something stronger. The tension seemed to bounce off Butch. He was laid back, like we were sitting at dinner, talking about the weather. I'd have bet he'd had one hell of a life.

The sound of shuffling paper filled the otherwise silent room. Thankfully, Mom had found some lumber orders with Lloyd's writing. Mom kept everything. For the last twenty minutes, Butch had methodically studied the letter and the lumber orders. Each time he shifted his focus, the anticipation in the room grew. It felt like a fucking elephant on my chest.

Tick.

Tick.

Tick.

I swore I could hear the second hand on the wall clock ticking the time away. Lex chewed on her nails, paced some more, and then sat next to me and fidgeted.

Tick.

Tick.

Tick.

It felt like my life was hanging in the balance. Yeah, we'd find our way. But if Lloyd had truly wanted me away from his daughter, it was going to hurt like a son of a bitch.

Tick.

Tick.

Tick.

I was about to explode when Butch finally looked up and leaned back in the chair, his face an unreadable mask. The chair made some awful squeak. I sat straight up, my mouth suddenly going dry. The pressure increased as Lex stepped beside me and grabbed my hand. I wanted to stand, but I knew it would only add to the stress.

Deep breath in, slow exhale.

Butch scratched his graying beard and nodded to himself. "The handwriting on the letter does not match Lloyd's handwriting on the orders. It's damn close, but it's not a match. I would guess someone paid a lot of money to have this done."

The air left me as I contemplated his words. Lloyd had not written the letter. His blessing stood. He'd wanted me to take care of Lex. He'd wanted her to be mine.

Without thinking, I stood and picked up Lex. The black cloud lingering over us disappeared. The weight lifted. We were free to love without any emotional consequences.

Lex let out a sob and clung to me as if her life depended on it. "It wasn't my dad."

"No, baby. It wasn't."

I held her tightly. We'd officially been set up. Anger at whoever did this surged from within. I would find out who. And once I did, it wasn't going to be pretty.

Lex held me tighter. After a couple of minutes, I set her down. She hugged me, tucking her face into my side.

Turning to Butch, I asked, "Can you tell anything from the letter?"

"The person is primarily dominant with their left hand. When they signed *Dad*, there's a slight lean to the left instead of the right, and the pressure of the pen changed minutely. It's nearly insignificant. This forgery would likely go undetected by many novice and intermediate forensic handwriting experts. It's most likely male due to the uneven, bold strokes. They appear to be natural versus forced. But I'm only about seventy-five percent sure of the gender."

Butch looked at the letter again. "Other than a left-handed

male, I'm not sure what else I can tell you."

That wasn't much to go on at all. And the likelihood of the forger living in Skagway was slim.

"Thank you, Butch. What do I owe you?"

"Nothing. Glad I could help." Standing, he put on his camo hat, which had been discarded on the desk while he'd studied the letters. It was something he wore every time I saw him.

It wasn't much, but I offered, "Beer's on me."

"Thanks, man. I appreciate it. That I will take."

I nodded. "Good."

"I best be headed out."

"Give Kane hell for me."

"Oh, I will."

We shook hands and Butch left. Lex sat on the couch, looking at her hands. When the door closed, I waited to see where her head was. And when she looked up, what I saw broke my heart.

CHAPTER
Sixteen

Drake

Her eyes were brimming with more tears. If only I could take away the pain. I stepped toward her, and she bolted upright and ran to me. Jumping into my arms, she cried, "It wasn't him." Her frame shook as she cried harder. "It wasn't my dad."

"No, it wasn't, baby. He wanted you happy. He wanted us together."

I brought her to the couch along the far wall of my office and held her until my arms grew numb. We would find our way through this. And whoever tried to interfere with our lives wouldn't be so lucky this next time around if I had anything to do with it. They would not succeed in coming between us.

Every so often, Lex squeezed me tighter. If this had fucked with *my* head, it was nothing compared to what it had done to hers. Life had been a whirlwind since she got back.

After a few more minutes, she pulled back, and I wiggled

my arms. Those damn tingles rushed down them.

"All that time I stayed away. All the time we lost. We'd be…" Lex trailed off.

Yeah, we'd most likely be married by now. Engaged, for sure. I rubbed my thumb on her chin. "It'll make us treasure our time together that much more now that we know what it's like to be apart."

She took an unsteady breath. "Who do you think did it? Why?"

"I don't know. But chances are whoever it was still doesn't want us together."

And that still made no sense to me. Who the hell would go through that much trouble just to fail? Unless it had simply been a power game to see if they could get away with it. "Have you heard from Raquel today? I saw the newsletter."

The Twiner sisters had painted our story as some kind of fairy tale. Raquel had not been so lucky. And they'd blown the lid off Chazz running for mayor. I was surprised no one had called me, but then again, I'd been off the radar for most of the day.

Lex shook her head. "No, Mom called a few times, but I ignored the phone calls and haven't listened to the messages. I imagine they aren't very kind. With everything else, I just didn't want to deal with the stress. And Raquel is probably plotting her revenge."

For a few minutes, Lex traced the letters of my faded Red Onion Bar shirt. She was still lost in her head. "Do you think Raquel did this?" she asked.

I blew out a breath. Regardless of the fact that Raquel was a bitch, she was still family. That wasn't just erased with a few mean words. This subject needed to be trod on carefully, yet truthfully. "I think she's a likely suspect."

"And my mom." It wasn't an accusation, just a statement. But this hurt my girl to the core. And I fucking hated that I couldn't do anything.

"It's no secret that neither of them likes us together."

Maybe it had all been to keep us apart and hurt Lex. Maybe it was Raquel's way of having fun, screwing with our lives. It wouldn't be the first time. When we were first dating, she'd planted the seed in Lex's head that I was on a date with another girl when I'd been out hunting with Kane and Hayden. She'd even had one of her friends lie and say she'd seen me. I'd been so pissed. So fucking pissed. When we'd started dating, Lex had been a little leery because she hadn't been sure if I was ready to date one person—for one, I was older, and two, I'd dated my fair share.

Knock. Knock. Knock.

Before I could call out or answer, Crete's muffled voice came through the door. "Drake, I need to talk to you. It's urgent."

This wasn't good. I didn't want to leave her, but she touched my shoulder. "Go. It sounds bad. And we don't need it to get worse. We have enough worse right now. I'll be fine."

After a moment's hesitation, Lex scooted off my lap. "I promise. I'll be fine."

Inside, I was torn, but she was right. "I'll be right back."

Nodding, she lay down and stared into space, obviously lost in thought. There was a blanket Mom had added to make the place a little more cozy. I laid it on her and knelt in front of her. "We'll make it through this. Me and you."

For the first time since Butch had arrived, she gave me a small smile. "I know we will. It's just a lot to wrap my head around."

I kissed her forehead. "I know it is. I'll be right back."

The best thing for Lex right now was probably to give her a little time to process everything, though it was the last thing I wanted to do. My instinct was to always rush to her, keep harm away from her. But I'd learned she processed better when she had a little time to herself.

She turned to look into my eyes. Each and every time she looked at me, I could get lost in them.

I headed out into the hallway and closed the door. "What happened?"

Crete had a hard look in his eyes. "I've got Randall on hold. He said he tried you, but it went to voicemail. He was going to pick up your liquor order for the ferry from Juneau tomorrow, but his boss told him to leave it."

"What the fuck?" That was the last thing I'd been expecting to hear. I'd honestly been expecting news of another fight between a couple of the regulars.

"Yeah, he's not sure what to do. He doesn't want to leave you hanging, but if he takes it, it'll cost him his job."

"Son of a bitch."

Randall and I had been friends since high school. He was a good man, and steady jobs weren't a dime a dozen in Skagway. There were tourist jobs, which brought a lot of people from the mainland, but day-in, day-out jobs that paid the bills throughout the winter were harder to come by.

"Tell Randall to leave it in Juneau and that there's no hard feelings." I had a few contacts I could call. Chazz was Randall's boss. That asshole would not pressure me to come crawling to him.

As Create walked to the front, he said, "Will do. Do you

know what's going on?"

"A sister with a vendetta."

Crete shook his head. "I saw the newsletter. People have been talking about it all day in the bar. It's rubbing them the wrong way after the dinner Chazz threw for Mayor Richards two nights ago."

"I would imagine. Tell Randall to stop by for dinner on the house. It'll be good to catch up with him." We'd tried to meet up a few times, but our schedules seemed to conflict.

"Will do."

People in our town were loyal. Chazz Hennington was still considered an outsider by many. And Chazz's latest move would spread through the town, alienating him more.

Crete walked away, and I cracked my neck. I should have kept my mouth shut to the Twiner sisters. This blowback was the last thing I wanted to deal with. I leaned against the wall to think this through.

My liquor came from Juneau. It had to be ferried to Haines first and then to Skagway. I loved my town, but it was hard as fuck to get stuff there. The delivery company I used was owned by Chazz. *Fucker*. There were rumors that Reeser, a longtime friend, was interested in expanding his warehouse business. I would call him, see what his thoughts were. If not, he might be able to recommend someone. With winter around the corner, delivery companies were doing their peak business. It was hard to get space unless you had a standing appointment.

I walked back to my office, thinking about solutions. Lex probably didn't want to hang out on the couch, so I'd take her somewhere more private, get her settled, and then come back here to get everything straightened out.

CHAPTER
Seventeen

Drake

As I stepped back inside my office, Lex sat up.

"Is everything okay?"

It was best to keep it straight and simple. I wouldn't want her to keep stuff from me. "The delivery company I use won't pick up my liquor in Juneau."

"Who do you use?"

"Hennington Express."

That said it all, and Lex's face dropped. "Oh no! Drake, I'm so sorry. I'll call Raquel and try to get it sorted out."

"No, that's what she wants. I'll find a way to get the liquor, and anything else I need, delivered. Hennington Express isn't the only game in town." I could tell there was a lot of turmoil within her. I framed Lex's face with my hands. "I mean it. I brought this on myself. It's fine; I'll get it worked out. I'm not worried."

And I wasn't. But man, it irritated me. Now, I had to sort

this out instead of being with Lex.

As she searched my eyes, I hoped she saw that I meant what I said. She looked at the clock. "We can meet at your parents' later."

There was no way I'd let her just leave by herself. If she really wanted to go to my parents', I would either drive her or follow her out there. However, there was another option, so I threw it out there. "Or we can stay at my place tonight."

It *would* be a hell of a lot easier. Lex hardly had to think about it. "Your place." She took a step forward. "I need to get my stuff out of my truck."

"You got your stuff today?"

Lex blew out a long breath. "Yes. I got a random text when I was leaving your parents'. Teagan put my stuff on her front porch if I wanted it."

"What?" *Who does that?*

Lex shook her head. "Yeah, she did. And she won't return my calls or my texts. I have no idea what's up with her."

We'd have to deal with Teagan later. She was still the same self-absorbed person I'd always known. "Let me walk you upstairs, and I'll go get your stuff."

"I can get it."

"I know you can. Humor me."

She leaned up on her tiptoes and kissed my lips. "Thank you."

It was hard not to say *I love you.* But it wasn't the right time—not yet. We needed to get away. Forget all this. I'd figure out how we could steal some time to ourselves after I got this other mess fixed.

I took her hand and led her out the back way. The town was quiet. The cruise ships had departed, leaving only the locals and those few tourists who were passing through town. Tomorrow was the night the ships stayed longer, which made everything busier.

As we stepped into my place, I saw there were a few things lying around. I picked up a shirt and threw it into the laundry. "Make yourself at home. I'll hurry."

"I may take a bath and relax. Try to sort my thoughts."

She was going to be naked in my bathroom. My dick hardened. Nothing would happen tonight, but I wanted her to fall asleep in my arms. "Yeah, I'll hurry."

She giggled. Outside the door, I waited until I heard the lock engage. Jogging down the stairs, I pulled out my phone to call Reeser.

He picked up on the second ring. "I was expecting your call. Sorry, man. That was a shitty thing for Hennington to do."

"I heard you were looking at becoming a distributor."

"Yeah, I've started small, and I'm pretty full. I'll beat Hennington's rates." Reeser was a good, honest guy.

"Sounds good. Can you handle my food and alcohol?"

"Yeah, I have the schedule. I'll have my guys pick it up when I grab another customer's load. We'll split those fees since there'll be full truckloads."

"Perfect. Thanks, Reeser. I'll tell the guys here."

"Sounds great. After this first round, if you're satisfied, any referrals would be appreciated."

"Of course."

I walked into the bar area. Crete was wiping down the dark wood counter. A couple of people sat at a table, drinking beers. Crete poured two beers from the tap and slid a mug my way. It was a local IPA that had a hearty wheat flavor.

"It's handled. Reeser will be our new guy."

"Good to know."

A man I'd never seen before sat at the bar. He was clean-cut and reminded me of Hollis. "Whiskey, neat. The most expensive thing you have."

Or not. Hollis was rich, but he didn't flaunt it like this man.

"Coming right up."

Without missing a beat, Crete poured the glass and slid it his way. The man downed it. "Keep them coming."

I liked to get a sense of the new people in town when they came into the bar. If this guy was going to drink himself into oblivion, then cause issues, I was going to stop it now. The last thing I needed was to go upstairs to Lex only to have to come back down. "Rough day?"

"Yeah, some days things just don't go your way."

"Hear, hear." I held up my beer. "I'm Drake."

"Drake Foster?"

It threw me off that he knew my full name. Visitors rarely did. "Yeah. I don't think I've seen you in here before."

He thrust out his hand. "I apologize for my lack of manners. I'm Dixon Hennington, Chazz's brother."

What the fuck? Chazz's brother was here, drinking. *Bold, cocky son of a bitch.* Before I could say anything, he continued, "Seems like I've stumbled into enemy territory."

I cocked an eyebrow, waiting to see if he said anything else. He was about five seconds from being cut off.

Grabbing his drink, he shook his head. "My tenacious sister-in-law may have mentioned you a few times today."

Tenacious was being kind. I took another pull, trying to appear unaffected. "Probably."

Dixon stood and threw down about five hundred dollars. Each drink ran about fifty dollars, so Crete would get a hefty tip tonight. *Good.* "I'll leave. Normally, Chazz meets me in California to conduct our business, but I decided to check out Alaska this time around." He shook his head as if the thought was a bad one. "I'm going to stay at the hotel tonight."

I set my beer down. It was best to take the high road. Maybe it would piss off the fucker more that his brother drank at my bar, where he'd refused to deliver the liquor. "Stay. I've never been one for petty shit. But I do need to go and get back to my girlfriend."

Dixon took a seat. "Thanks, I appreciate it. Raquel's sister, right? Alexa, I think I heard today. I didn't see her at the wedding in California."

"Yeah, that's her." I changed the subject, unwilling to give him any fuel. "How long are you in town for?"

"Was going to stay for at least a couple of weeks. I hired a hunting guide for a couple of days from now. But I may go home early."

It was hard to hide my smirk. "Kane? Is he your guide?"

"Yeah, he comes highly recommended. What they say is true… you really do know everyone in a small town."

"It's true. Kane's my brother. He's the best around here."

"That's what I heard from a friend in San Diego. We're flying inland to fish the first day."

When Kane flew places for a hunt, he refused to fly with anyone else but Hayden. In other towns, there were outfits similar to Hayden's, but he had the larger business. "You'll probably be riding with my other brother, Hayden."

He drained his second glass. "Well, let's remember that I'm not Chazz or Raquel."

Chuckling, I responded, "Duly noted." I rapped the counter three times. "Enjoy and stay as long as you want. Invite your brother in for a drink."

His eyes widened momentarily. So he knew what the fucker had done. "Probably not a good idea. I'm sure you've heard by now about what he's done."

"I did. But I'm not a dick, so feel free to invite him. Have a good night. Crete, I'll have my phone on if you need anything."

"Will do."

As I walked up the stairs, I called Kane. He answered on the third ring. "Yo."

"How's it going?"

He gave an agitated sigh. "Fine. They're in their tents with their blow-up mattresses. I mean, who the fuck camps in the middle of the damn woods with a blow-up mattress?"

"City slickers?"

"Damn straight. Even had some auto pump thing. I swear I felt like a pussy just being in proximity to it."

I gave a hearty laugh. "I'll order you one for Christmas."

"Ass. What did you call me for?"

"You taking a guy named Dixon out next week?"

He paused, thinking. "Yeah, one of the previous guys I took arranged it. He's Chazz's brother. Why?"

At least it was out in the open, which made me feel a little less wary of his intentions. "Just wanted to make sure you knew."

"It's been arranged for months. Shit, man, I'm sorry. I meant to tell you. Do you want me to cancel on him?"

That was Kane—loyal to the end. "Nah. He came into the bar tonight after Chazz refused to pick up my liquor in Juneau."

"What the fuck? Why?"

"I might have told the Twiner sisters about him running for mayor next election. Pussy move, I know, but fuck, Raquel pissed me off."

Kane chuckled on the other end. "I'll keep my eye on him. See if I notice anything."

"Thanks. He seemed nice enough, but you never know."

"Yeah, Hayden is flying us north for the day to fish. I'll fill him in."

I figured. "I appreciate it."

We hung up, and I walked up the stairs. Texting Crete, I checked on our visitor.

Me: *Dixon still there?*

Crete: *Yeah, he's pacing himself now. Chatting with Leroy.*

Me: *Keep an eye on him. Any extra he leaves over the booze, you take all of it.*

Crete: *Thanks, man. Much appreciated.*

I knew Crete would never keep that much cash, even though he deserved it. Hopefully, nothing crazy would happen. I just wanted to go home and wrap my arms around Lex.

I opened the door, catching the scent of the peach lotion Lex always used before bed. I felt like I was truly *home* for the first time in forever. She'd left the light over the stove on—the same way she'd always done when I was out late. I walked into the bedroom and stopped for a second. Lex lay in my bed, her blonde hair spread out on the pillow. It looked like she'd fallen asleep while reading a book. She took my breath away.

We definitely needed some time together. *Alone*. And if I didn't make plans now, something else would get in the way. There was something special I wanted to show her. We were ready.

I pulled out my phone.

Me: *Do you mind if I take Lex away tomorrow afternoon?*

Hollis: *Of course not. The medical equipment will be here the following day. I know she'll want to be there for setup.*

Me: *We'll be back by then. I'm going to take her to my cabin. It's a surprise.*

Hollis: *Do all Alaskans have cabins?*

I chuckled.

Me: *A lot do.*

Hollis: *Do Ike, Hayden, and Kane?*

I knew where this was going, and it was hard not to smile.

Me: *Yes, they do.*

Hollis: *I'll add it to my list. I need a cabin, it seems.*

Me: *You do that. I'll even help build it.*

Hollis: *Wait, you build it on your own?*

Me: *More or less.*

Hollis: *No offense, but I'll go with the less. I want a livable cabin.*

Me: *It'll be livable.*

Hollis: *If you say so. I'll see you guys tomorrow.*

I put my phone on the table and stared at my girl for a while. If I got into bed, I knew the movement would wake her, so I decided to let her sleep for a little bit first. She needed the rest. Neither of us had slept well the last couple of nights.

I stripped down to my boxers and went to the couch with my laptop. I wanted to research Montgomery—the lawyer—Chazz, Raquel, Irene, and anyone else connected to Lloyd. At the end of the day, Lloyd was the key to everything.

I just hoped he hadn't been involved in whatever had caused all this.

CHAPTER
Eighteen

Alexa

I woke up and stretched in bed. Expecting to find Drake's warm body, I was greeted with cold sheets. *That's odd.* I sat up and saw that the stove light was still on. Whenever he had to work late, I always left it on. When he came to bed, he always turned it off. *Did Drake not come to bed?*

I threw the heavy gray comforter aside and tiptoed into the living room. When I found him, I stopped and took in the man I loved with all my heart. He lay with his head tilted back on the couch, his computer in his lap. While Drake slept, he had a vulnerability to him that was less apparent when he was awake. A side only I knew. It was when his guard came down, baring his soul. His beard was more than a five-o'clock shadow, and his dark hair was slightly askew.

Checking the clock, I saw that it was a little past six, which was about the time I normally woke up. Curling up in a chair, I watched Drake sleep. After my bath, I'd fallen asleep reading a magazine. I hadn't realized how exhausting yesterday's events had been. Inside, I was still a mixture of emotions—relieved Dad hadn't written the note, mad someone had sabotaged my relationship with Drake, and scared they weren't done. Today, things felt a little less daunting. But I still had no idea where to begin.

I needed to find out who and why.

Drake shifted and woke up, turned his head toward the clock on the wall opposite me. When he saw the time, he whispered, "Oh man."

If I'd had to guess, I'd say he'd wanted to join me in bed last night but fell asleep on the couch. I loved how he wanted me close to him. He sat up, and his eyes met mine. His devilish grin was my greeting. "Morning."

"Morning. How'd you sleep?"

"Like shit. I meant to join you last night." Irritation flashed across his face. We'd been apart for so long, and I'd hoped to wake up cuddled next to him. I knew he felt the same. Maybe things would progress further than yesterday. I wanted to feel him inside me, have him claim me in a way no one else ever had. Drake had been my first, my only, and hopefully, he would be my last.

For a few seconds, Drake watched me. He always was clued in to how I was feeling.

"I want to know who it was. I want to understand why."

He put his laptop to one side and scratched his chin. "I was up late, looking into anyone I could think of."

My heart stopped. "Did you find anything?"

"A year ago, Montgomery had a heart attack and died."

"What? He was only thirty, maybe a year or two older."

"Yeah, his housekeeper found him at home in his office."

Dad had used a lawyer from Juneau, which was a ferry ride away. There weren't any lawyers in Skagway. The total population was over thirty thousand in Juneau, but here, we had fewer than nine hundred people.

This news put me more on edge. "Did they say anything else?"

"The autopsy revealed nothing, but his parents were suspicious. Said he'd been a healthy, active man with zero heart issues."

The entire situation didn't sit well with me. A knot formed in the pit of my stomach. "What do you think?"

"I have no idea. I want to find something so much and figure out who it is that I'm not sure if I'm grasping at straws."

"Did you find anything else?"

Drake yawned and propped his elbows on his knees. "I dug into the Municipality Record of Deeds and found who Raquel sold the land to."

At one point, I'd asked Raquel, but she'd refused to answer. It wasn't something I had cared to look into. "To who?"

"To some business called Milano Incorporated that has zero online presence." He'd been up way too long looking into all this. "Did you keep any of the offers for your land?"

Shaking my head, I said, "No. The bank called me with an offer once. I didn't want to hear it and told them to reject any they got. That was the last I heard from them."

Drake's eyebrows pinched together. "Can you reach out to Morgan? See if she has a record of any offers received."

"Yeah, I'll reach out to her this morning. Any more thoughts about the letter?"

"It's likely whoever did this wanted you isolated. You said Montgomery told you Lloyd brought the letter to him a couple of weeks before he died?"

A sense of dread settled over me. Last night in the tub, I'd had similar thoughts and hadn't been able to fully process them. "Yes, that's what he said. I know where you're going with this."

Drake waited for me to continue.

"Montgomery lied and was definitely in on it."

"Yeah." Drake stared into the distance, thinking. There were so many moving parts it was hard to wrap my head around them.

It was hard to believe Raquel had sold the land that had been in our family for generations. There were contingencies in the estate setup that stipulated only blood relatives of the family could inherit the land. That was why Mom only got the B&B—Dad had purchased it on his own before they got married.

How could she? Why would she? It had to be money related. Maybe that was why Mom had received all the "upgrades" to the house.

Yes, Chazz was well off, but having that kind of cash would give Raquel the opportunity to do whatever she wanted, unchecked. Dad would have been so disappointed, and it hurt my heart. "Do you think Raquel knows who Milano Incorporated is?"

If she did, I was certain she wouldn't tell me.

"I don't know, baby. All I've got is straws to grasp at." Drake's phone vibrated, and he looked at it. "Fuck. It's Reeser. He's come into town to go over the contracts. He needs them for liability reasons before he can transport my inventory."

I stood. "Go. Take care of that. I'm going to take a shower and head to the clinic. Hollis and I were going to go over the last of the arrangements."

Drake pulled me into his arms. "I want some time alone with you."

"I want that, too."

Drake must have gotten the answer he was looking for, and he gave me a smile before kissing me on the lips. My lips wanted more. My body craved him.

Drake went to his room and came out dressed less than two minutes later. He looked good, really good. I was nearly salivating when he gave me a wink.

I was having a hard time keeping my hormones under control. It had been too long since I'd been in Drake's arms. We needed to find some time for us to be together.

"Bye, baby. I'll see you at the clinic."

"See you then."

He was off. And I needed a cold shower.

CHAPTER
Nineteen

Alexa

About an hour and a half later, I was dressed and ready to head out the door to the clinic when my phone vibrated with a text from Hollis.

Hollis: *You available to talk?*

That was strange. He always just called if he needed something. I dialed his number. "What's going on?"

"There's a woman named Morgan here. She says she's your loan officer and needs to talk to you immediately." There was a distinctly worried sound in his tone.

Oh shit, I forgot to call her. "I'll come right away. Did she say what it's about?"

He sighed. "No, she won't say a word to me since I'm not on the *paperwork*."

These types of mundane things aggravated Hollis since he had originally wanted to be on the mortgage. If I'd added him, this could have been handled quickly. He was used to being able to pay a price to make things happen. Getting medical equipment up here was cumbersome, to say the least, and it had been entertaining when Hollis asked for a confirmation on the delivery date. The slower pace was definitely an adjustment for him.

"I'm coming right away. We'll get it all cleared up. This is good practice for patience in domesticated life."

He huffed, and I heard footsteps on the other end and a door closing. "You know me so well. Are you still good with me buying the place?"

"Of course. We'll get it started when I get there." I grabbed my keys, locked up, and started down the steps.

"Good. And I need your help with something."

That sounded ominous. Cautiously, I answered, "What's that?"

"Did Drake mention I'm going to build a cabin?"

I almost stumbled at his words. "*What?*"

"Yeah, well, I'm not going to build it. I mean, hello, I can barely hold a hammer. But it seems all Alaskan men have cabins. It's like a rite of passage."

It was true, which made me laugh. "Well, not all Alaskans have them."

"Do all the Fosters?"

The Fosters had become Hollis's official benchmark for true Alaskans. *Heaven help us.* "All of them but Drake do. Hayden's is smaller and more of a bachelor pad. Kane's is bigger and up in the mountains."

There was an awkward pause. "Well, Drake needs one,

and I need your advice."

What was that about? Maybe Morgan had walked into the room as he was speaking.

"I can take you to my dad's if you wanted to see a medium-sized one. Hayden and Kane would show you theirs, as well."

"Oh, yes. I like this idea. I can see myself standing on the porch with an ax. It'll have a lumberjack feel."

I nearly choked but managed to say, "I'm getting in my truck. Be there in five minutes."

"Sounds good."

Hollis and lumberjacks were about as opposite as anything could get. This idea had disaster written all over it.

The drive over to the clinic took no time at all, and when I got there, Hollis was leaning against the porch rail, talking to Morgan. I was afraid to ask why he had on a plaid shirt and cargo pants. He must have thought it was some sort of Alaskan uniform.

Suppressing my laughter, I managed to say in an even tone, "Good morning. I'm so sorry I didn't call you back, Morgan. It's been crazy since I got back into town."

Morgan fidgeted with her dress. "Hey, Alexa. It's good to have you back."

We'd gone to high school together but hadn't really hung out. For the most part, I'd gotten along with all the kids but kept to myself. Raquel would always cause issues, so it was just easier to stay out of the drama. "How's Greg? I heard you guys got married."

"He's good. Really good. It'll be a year this December." Again, she fidgeted. "I'm sorry to have to say this, but the bank has called in your note."

It took me a moment to process her words. "What? They called in my loan?"

"Yes, someone purchased it from the bank. Your collateral mortgage had a demand clause in it. There wasn't a term call option added, so this can be done at any time. Since you didn't have an income, this was the only type of loan I could get you approved for."

I vaguely remembered us talking about it. Morgan had been shocked and unsure why this was the only type I qualified for. But I hadn't thought it would be done. "How long do I have?"

"You have thirty days to pay it in full or you'll be in default. At that point, the new lender would take ownership and can use the collateral against the property for the principal still owed if they aren't able to sell this property within a reasonable amount of time. I'm so sorry, Alexa. I tried to get you more time. I just don't get it. I've never had this happen before."

It still stunned me that someone had called in my loan, even if Hollis was about to pay it off. The whole situation rubbed me the wrong way. And from Morgan's scrunched eyebrows, I doubted it made much sense to her either. "Who bought my loan?"

"I'm not at liberty to say anything. It's why I called the other day."

I felt like I'd been sucker-punched. *Who would do that?*

Hollis got my attention and inclined his head toward Morgan.

"Oh, yes. Umm... Hollis is going to buy the place. He'll be paying the loan in full."

Morgan was at a loss for words for a second. "You're going to pay off the loan?"

125

In Skagway, it wasn't often someone had that much cash on hand. The Fosters might have. Raquel most likely would.

"Yes, I can have my bank wire the funds today. I'll need your ABA number and the payoff amount as well as any title change fees. Alexa's collateral won't be an issue."

Morgan smiled, apparently still shocked as she smoothed her hair. "I'm so glad this will work out. I know how much the property that your dad left you means to you. I remember you guys did a lot of work on his cabin."

Hollis's eyes grew wide, and he mouthed the words *See? Cabin.* I laughed.

"Yes, it does. Thanks, Morgan."

While Hollis got the details for wiring the money, my thoughts wandered to why my loan had been called in. It felt dirty, especially on the heels of the letter.

"You good with that, Alexa?" Hollis asked.

"Huh?"

"It'll be easier to pay off the loan, then title the deed over to me."

"Perfect."

The final details were arranged. Before Morgan left, she asked to use the restroom, and I showed her the way. On her way out of the bathroom, she commented, "This is such a wonderful thing you're doing for Skagway. The clinic is look-ing amazing."

"Thank you. Hollis is a wonderful doctor. We're very lucky to have him." As we made our way to the front door, I remembered what Drake and I had talked about this morning. "Hey, Morgan, I have a favor to ask."

"Of course."

"Would you mind seeing if the bank has a history of offers for my land?"

She tipped her head to the side for a moment before nodding. "Yes, we keep all those. Would you like a copy? It's not my department, but I can get them for you."

"If you don't mind. You can email them to me."

At the door, she paused. "Are you thinking about selling?"

"No, not at all. Just curious."

On the front porch, Morgan picked up the folder of papers she'd left. "Welcome back, Alexa. Thank you for coming to our town, Dr. Fritz."

We said goodbye, and Morgan left. When I looked at the time, I realized that somehow, another hour had passed since I'd arrived. Part of me was just drained. But almost everything at the clinic was done, and now we waited until the equipment arrived.

Hollis took a call while I walked inside. It looked like a whole new place. The floors had been sanded and stained. The walls were a delicate light gray. New fixtures had been ordered, but the current brass ones would do until those arrived. The office furniture would arrive the day after the equipment. I ran my hands along the chair rail in the reception area. Soon this would be a place of healing... a place of hope. I was filled with pride at how much we'd accomplished.

I walked back outside as Hollis was ending his call.

"Why would someone call in your loan?" Hollis asked, bringing my concerns to the surface. It felt too coincidental.

I shook my head. "I don't know. If they'd done it yesterday or today, it would make sense because of Raquel and Chazz. I'm sure Chazz could make that happen. But Morgan tried to reach me the day I came back to Skagway. It had been called in before all the newsletter drama."

Hollis's eyebrows pinched together. "And your father's land was the collateral? Why would they need collateral on a mortgage?"

"The whole thing feels off to me. Even the type of loan the bank approved."

Taking out his phone, Hollis looked at something. "Does Milano Incorporated mean anything to you?"

I froze, and he tilted his head. "It does, doesn't it?"

"Why do you ask?" I asked hesitantly.

"That's who called in your loan. When Morgan left to use the restroom, I snooped through her papers."

My mouth dropped open. That wasn't like Hollis at all.

He shrugged. "What? We needed to know. People just don't call in loans for the fun of it. What do they want?"

"Milano Incorporated bought Raquel's land. It seems a little odd they would go through the trouble to call in my loan, which was guaranteed by the land I inherited from Dad."

"Have you ever heard of Milano?"

"Not until Drake found them last night." I filled Hollis in on everything Drake and I had talked about. I tried to think of anyone Dad may have had an issue with but couldn't. Dad loved his land. His belief was land was a priceless commodity. You couldn't make more. What we had here on Earth was it. Apparently, someone else wanted it, too.

"Raquel got some as well. Mom got the land the B&B was on. We were all surprised her name wasn't on the deed. Dad bought the place before he married Mom and never added her to the deed. The piece I inherited has been in the family for over a hundred years. It's about three hundred acres. Raquel got the piece our grandparents had bought. Those two parcels of land can only be passed down to blood relatives. It's why Mom only received the B&B in the will."

At that point, Drake's truck pulled in the driveway. He was freshly showered. But I could tell by the way his mouth flattened he knew something was up.

"You guys look like you're in deep thought." Drake gave me a quick kiss before putting his hand in his pocket and leaning against the rail.

Hollis nodded at me, and I explained to Drake what we'd talked about.

Afterward, he was quiet. "I don't think it's a coincidence."

"Me either," I responded. "But why—" I stopped talking as a shiny new black sports car with dark tinted windows pulled in behind Drake's truck. This place was becoming Grand Central Station by Skagway standards.

Who's that?

"Fuck, when it rains, it pours," muttered Drake.

That put me more on edge, and I straightened up. Drake put his arm around my waist protectively, which wasn't a good sign. It only heightened my anxiety as I waited for the car door to open. The flashy car wouldn't be very useful in the winter. Or the fall. Or the spring, for that matter. It made no sense to have a sports car in Alaska when there was snow on the ground most of the year.

When the door opened and I saw my mother, my stomach dropped. "Oh no," I said under my breath.

"Who is that?" Hollis murmured.

"My mother."

CHAPTER
Twenty

Alexa

Hollis and Drake stood on either side of me. I felt like I was being flanked when I was totally capable of taking care of myself. But, at the same time, I was glad they were there.

Mom dabbed her face with a handkerchief and looked at the clinic as if the mere site of such a place distressed her. There was still no landscaping, but that would come in the next few days or so. Other than that, it looked like a new home. If possible, her nose angled up in the air more than usual, and I felt like she was looking down on us even though we were higher on the porch.

"Alexa, I've been trying to reach you. Can we talk in private?"

Her entire attitude rubbed me the wrong way. And I was at my limit today. Why couldn't she greet me with *"Wow, what have you done with the place? I'd love a tour."* Or *"I've missed you so much. What can I do to help?"*

Instead, I got a raised eyebrow. I was tired of this song and dance. Irritation lurked underneath the surface, just begging to be unleashed. "Mom, I'd love to show you everything we've done around the clinic. But if you've come to lecture me about what happened with Raquel, please don't. Raquel and I will work it out if she would just grow up."

Without paying me any attention, Mom continued, "Seriously, Alexa, I'm disappointed in you."

She was always disappointed in me. Always. I could find the cure for cancer, and Mom would still have something to gripe about. I bet even if rainbows shot out of my ass, there would be something wrong with one of the colors. Nothing I ever did was good enough. Nothing.

Beside me, I could feel the annoyance rolling off Drake in waves. Hollis was more stunned than anything. Even his mom wasn't *this* cold.

I tried again to be pleasant. "Would you like to see the clinic?"

She shook her head, about to say something, when her phone rang. "Pardon me. Hi, sweetheart. Yes, I know. Oh, please don't stress yourself out. It's not good for your singing voice. It needs to be strong for the dinner tonight. There's a chance Dixon's friend will go back to Los Angeles and tell someone about your talent. I know Alexa is sorry. She told me so. Yes, I'm on my way."

It took everything I had not to roll my eyes. When she hung up the phone, she gave me a tight smile. "Where are my manners? You haven't introduced me to your sweet Hollis."

Drake's jaw tightened, and his fingers dug into my hip. There was only so much he was going to take before he spoke up. "Mom, this is my *friend,* Dr. Hollis Fritz. And, of course, you remember Drake. We're dating again."

Mom stood still with the same bland smile I remembered her giving Dad when he would say something she refused to acknowledge. *Oh boy.* This wasn't going to end well.

Drake took a step forward with his hand outstretched. "Good to see you again, Irene."

When we'd first met, he called her Mrs. Owens, which hadn't gone over well. *Irene* wasn't much better. Mom preferred to not have any interaction with Drake at all. It was honestly a no-win situation.

"Drake. How's Macy?"

Macy? Who's Macy? At this point, I'd reached the end of my rope. Dropping her name was most likely a ploy to plant a seed of doubt in my mind. At one time Raquel had done that when Drake had gone out of town hunting. I'd been crushed, thinking he was cheating on me. One thing I'd promised him that night was that I would never doubt him until I'd had a chance to hear him out. But hearing his name associated with someone else sent jolts of jealousy through me.

He let out a deep breath and shook his head. "I'm sure she's good. You'd have to ask her. She hasn't been in the bar for about five months—since I turned her down for a date." Drake crossed his arms over his chest and took a step forward. "Listen, I get that you'd rather Lex be dating Hollis. I think that picture has been painted pretty clearly. But I'm back in Lex's life, and I'm here to stay. I'd like things to be civil between us, Irene, but I won't tolerate you putting doubt in Lex's mind. Nothing happened with Macy, and nothing will be happening with Macy."

I knew it! My fists balled at my side. This was my mother.

But no matter how angry she made me, dumping a bucketful of water on her like I had with Raquel wasn't acceptable.

A loud truck engine drew our attention to the driveway, and we watched Ike and Amie pull in. Nervously, I glanced at Drake. The last thing I wanted was for his parents to be caught up in this drama. The way my mother treated me was embarrassing. That was why I was never seen with her in town or invited her over to the Fosters' for dinner.

With a stiff nod, Mom smoothed her new baby blue outfit into place. Amie got out of the truck in jeans and a long-sleeved T-shirt. Our mothers were complete opposites of each other. "Irene, it's so good to see you. So you've heard the news about our kids finding their way back to each other? We're so glad Alexa is back in our lives."

Mom gave a nod. "Yes, yes I heard. And I'm sure you are."

Whoa. The tone she was taking with Amie was completely uncalled for. I took a step forward. Mom may not have agreed that it was happy news, but there was no need to be disrespectful to Amie. "Mom, please."

She waved me off. "I need to go see your sister. Have a good day, Amie. Ike. Hope to see you for dinner, Hollis."

Without another glance at me or Drake, Mom left. She had grown colder to me since Dad died. So much colder. I remembered at the cemetery, I'd wanted her to wrap her arms around me the way she'd done with Raquel to show me that unconditional love only a mother can provide. She'd never once asked how I was doing. Not once. Amie and Drake had held me as I mourned the loss of my father. Not my mother. My mother would never love me like Raquel. And it hurt.

I watched as Mom drove away, wishing things were different.

"Ike, why don't you and Drake show Hollis the plans you drew up for the cabin. I'm going to have Alexa show me around the clinic." Amie's sweet voice brought me out of my thoughts.

Drake looked like he wanted to protest. When Amie raised her eyebrow, he followed his Dad to the truck. I wasn't sure what to do.

With an arm around my shoulders, she ushered me to the door. "Come, let's go inside. I want to see what's been done since the last time. And I have fabric samples."

We'd barely made it into the house when I felt her squeeze me. "I'm here, sweet girl. If you ever need anything, I'm here."

Furiously, I wiped at the tears that were coming too fast to stop. "Sorry. Let me show you around."

She walked me over to the bottom of the stairs instead. "Nonsense. I just wanted to check on you, see if you needed someone to talk to. I know Drake wants to be everything you need, but sometimes a girl needs another female to talk to. I may not be your mother, but I consider you one of my children."

I shook my head as more tears slid down my cheek. "I don't get why she acts like this. When Dad was alive, I think his presence made her less harsh, less severe. Or not. I don't know."

Amie hugged me, truly hugged me, and I clung to her like my life depended on it. It had been so long since I'd been comforted like this. "Thank you."

Pulling back, she gave me a smile. "I'm here anytime you

need it. I know Drake is, too. Lord knows my boy is head over heels for you. He has been since the first day he saw you. When he came home that day, I could tell something had changed." Amie had never told me this before. Gently, she wiped one of my tears away.

"What do you mean?"

"Since he was a little boy, Drake had never been afraid of his feelings the way Kane and, to some extent, Hayden were. Drake is more like me in that sense. Even though you guys have known each other since you were kids, the day Drake changed your tire, he saw you. I mean, *really* saw you. He walked through the front door in a complete daze. I thought he was supposed to have a date. He told me he canceled it, and he started asking about you. I knew, in that moment, he'd found his other half."

I smiled at the memory. "Since I was a little girl, I always thought Drake was so handsome and strong. But he was older, so I never gave it much thought. Then he showed up at my house with flowers the day after changing my tire. I just couldn't believe he was there to see me. And I nearly ruined it."

"It'll make you guys twice as strong."

"I hope so."

"I know so."

CHAPTER
Twenty-One

Alexa

Amie and I finished looking through the fabric samples she'd brought for the curtains in the clinic and Hollis's residence that the quilting circle were going to make. I loved this town. They'd welcomed my friend without any hesitation. It wasn't always that way, though. Sometimes newcomers remained on the outskirts of the community for a while. Chazz had been here for nearly two years, and I doubted he'd received the same welcome.

There would be a more rustic theme downstairs to go with the furniture we'd chosen. Upstairs, I'd chosen grays and creams to go with Hollis's furniture, which would be arriving from New York soon. We'd picked it out before we left. Hollis had debated selling his dad's house, but I thought it might be a little rash until he decided if he wanted to make Skagway his permanent home. Even then, he might want to keep it. I understood needing a fresh start. But doing that without regrets was equally important.

Outside, the men's voices grew stronger as they approached the building. I strained my ears to hear them clearly. They were talking about breaking ground. Once Hollis made a decision, it was rare for him to ever back away.

Amie leaned against me as they laughed. "I like your friend."

"He's a good guy on top of being a great doctor." But her words meant more to me than she'd ever know. I wanted Hollis to be accepted.

Drake opened the door cautiously. "Is it okay for us to come in now?"

Amie patted my leg, and I was able to give her a true smile. She said, "Yes, of course. Did you guys discuss the cabin?"

The men entered the room, and Hollis said, "We're going to break ground on my cabin in the spring. I just need to find some land."

I laughed. "I'm sure we'll be able to find you something." Changing subjects, I pointed to the fabrics spread out on the floor. "The quilting committee wants to make curtains for the clinic. Amie brought the fabric swatch book from Arlene's shop. Here's what I think you may like for downstairs and maybe your residence, based on the furniture we picked out in New York."

Hollis walked over to the book. "That's very kind of the quilting circle, but I'd like to pay for their time."

Standing, Amie waved him off. "Nonsense. It's what we do here. This clinic means a lot to all the families in Skagway. We want to be part of this."

"Thank you."

It was rare, if ever, that people in Hollis's world did things simply to be kind. I could tell he was touched by everything our little town had done for our clinic. He seemed lighter, happier. He wanted to make a difference. And I knew he would.

"What do you think of the fabrics?" I said as I pointed to the swatches.

Hollis leaned forward, and I wanted to laugh out loud. Ike and Drake were like ducks out of water when it came to fabric swatches. "I like the lower colors. For the upstairs, I think I want a change."

"What kind of change?"

"Something more macho. Alaskan macho."

I laughed. "But that won't go with the furniture you ordered."

"Ike's going to make my furniture. I'll figure out what to do with the furniture I ordered since it's already shipped."

Oh, he's serious. Offhandedly, I added, "I bet Kane could get you some sort of animal head for your walls or take you hunting to get your own."

His eyes lit up like Christmas lights. Kane might kill me. *Ha!* There was no *might* about it; he was going to kill me for suggesting this.

Drake's smile grew bigger. "I bet Kane would love that. I'll let him know."

"Now we're talking." Hollis replied. "He'd probably prefer to leave me out in the woods, tied to a tree. But killing the only doctor in town would not be good. I'll take those odds to get some beast up on my wall."

I gave Hollis a sideways hug. My friend knew how to keep things light. "Very Alaskan."

"I thought so."

I picked up a different book of fabric. "We can look at these swatches. They're probably more like what you're looking for."

"I think you have plans to be somewhere right now."

Wait. I do? I thought back to my plans for the day—I'd cleared my calendar to finish tidying up this clinic. "No, I don't."

"Yeah, you do."

Is he seriously arguing with me about my schedule? "No, I really don't."

"Yes, you really, really, *really* do. Top three reallys."

What's wrong with him? With a smug smile, he inclined his head toward Drake. On cue, Drake picked me up, and I squealed. "I'm kidnapping you for the day. See you guys tomorrow."

Hollis called after me, "See, I was really, really, really, *really* right."

"I guess you were," I called back. As Drake carried me to the car, I swung my legs ever so lightly, feeling more carefree by the second. "Where are we going? What do you mean you're kidnapping me?"

"You'll see." Drake looked at me with love and happiness. It was as if no time had passed between us. I wanted him. And by the hunger in his eyes, he wanted me, too.

He leaned down, and his lips grazed mine. "You're mine for the night."

Those words held a lot of promise. Tingles erupted over my skin, and anticipation pooled in my stomach. He was kidnapping me so we could spend some time alone together. Drake's eyes darkened with desire and I knew it meant I would have the closeness I craved from him soon.

He set me in the passenger seat of his truck, and I looked over to see mine still in the clinic driveway. "What about my truck?"

"We'll be back tomorrow. Hollis is sleeping here tonight. My parents are going to help him bring in an extra bed from the shop along with a few other pieces until Dad can make his furniture."

I felt guilty leaving my friend, but Drake shook his head. "It's okay. I asked Hollis if he wanted us to stay. He's good. Promise. And Hayden is getting back today. He's going to help out."

"Looks like you've thought of everything."

"Let's hope."

There was so much promise in those words.

CHAPTER
Twenty-Two

Alexa

D rake went around the front of his truck. He looked at the ground as he walked, the look on his face intense, as if he were thinking hard about something.

When he got in the truck, his eyes met mine. He was definitely nervous about something; his breaths were deeper and slower than usual.

I wondered where he was taking me, but I knew he'd never tell.

We needed this time alone. There were moments when it felt like we still tiptoed around each other without saying what we meant. But then another part of me was afraid we were moving too fast. *No, we're not.* Fate was correcting a wrong— we should never have been apart. Our souls were meant to be entwined together.

In town, Drake pulled into the post office parking lot, and handed me my silky pink sleeping mask.

"Put this on."

"Did you get this out of my bag?" I cocked an eyebrow in question.

He winked. "Maybe."

If he'd gotten it out of my gray duffel bag, there was a chance he'd seen my vibrator. Heat surged to my cheeks. I'd never had one when I lived here—I hadn't needed one. Biting my lip, I asked, "What else did you see?"

"Nothing."

His response was too quick. I knew he'd seen my vibrator. "Are you sure?"

In response, I got another wink, and he held out the blindfold. "You ready to get going?"

With a giggle, I took it and put it on. A few seconds later, I felt the truck move forward. It was time for a little fun. "Can you tell me just one thing?"

"Depends."

"Were you gentle with the bag? There's something very important to me in there."

He paused for a second, and then his voice grew deeper. "How important?"

"Off-the-charts important. It's given me some of the best memories ever. Life altering."

There was a muttered curse word, and I smiled. Drake was very well endowed, but he was also possessive of my pleasure. When Drake had found out I was a virgin after we started dating, he'd started to take things slower. I thought back to that moment.

Drake's lips had grazed mine as he kissed me. I could kiss him for hours. We'd been together two months. And on that day, I'd been allowed to go out to dinner with him. That had been a condition of my dad allowing me to date Drake. I had to be eighteen for dinner dates. Dad had been a little cautious about us dating because Drake was two years older.

Leaning me back, Drake hovered on top of me. His hand crept under my shirt, and our eyes met. "You are beautiful."

Drake's words warmed me as his hand slid up my shirt. This was as far as we'd gone. When I brought his head down to meet mine, he knew I was telling him to keep going. My nipples hardened, needing to feel his strong hands on me.

Drake gave a deep rumble of satisfaction when his hands brushed the stiff peaks of my breasts for the first time. I arched my back as the sensations spiraled through me. He rolled one nipple through his fingers.

"Fuck, your body is so responsive."

I shifted my hips, looking for some kind of relief. One of his hands trailed down my stomach.

As his tongue commanded my mouth, I moaned.

"Fuck, I want you."

"Me, too." But then I stiffened. *Are we ready? Will it hurt?* I'd never had sex before.

Drake immediately sensed a change within me, and he pulled his hand back. "What's wrong?"

I felt foolish, so I remained silent. It was no secret that Drake was more experienced than I was. I'd seen him take girls out on more than one occasion. I tried to pull him back to me, but he sat back on his heels. "Lex, tell me what's wrong."

"I… uhh…"

As I stalled, his face grew more concerned, and his brows knitted together. I made sure my shirt was pulled down and sat up. "Why don't we head home."

"I'll take you home. But I want to know what happened."

Drake put his hand on my cheek and rubbed my jaw. "I just want to know if I did something wrong, Lex. You know you're different."

"Different?"

"More. You mean so much more to me. More than anyone else has, which I know is sappy as shit, but it's true."

The confession I'd been holding was making me feel raw. I was scared he'd think I was a child. Closing my eyes, I whispered, "I'm a virgin."

I drew in tighter, more embarrassed than ever. When he said nothing, I closed my eyes. "Will you take me home now?"

"Lex. Look at me, please."

I opened my eyes, and Drake's eyes were on fire. "You mean to tell me you've never slept with anyone before?"

"No. Drake, you were my first kiss."

His eyes grew wide, and he practically attacked my mouth. In the next second, he pulled away. "I'll be all your firsts when it's time. I'll be yours, always."

Drake's voice interrupted my thoughts. "What are you thinking about?"

"The day I told you I was a virgin."

He inhaled. "Best fucking day of my life. You are the most amazing thing that has ever happened to me."

"You made me wait almost six months," I groaned.

It was true. When Drake realized I had never done anything before, he'd gone out of his way to make sure each step we took was special and well thought out. I had felt cherished.

His warm hand lay on top of mine. "What you gave me was a gift. We needed to be sure."

A lump formed in my throat. I loved him so much. Wherever we were headed, I hoped he planned on us being together.

I needed him more than I needed the air I breathed.

"Can I take the blindfold off?" I wanted to look into his eyes.

"Five more minutes. I want this to be special for you."

I let out a deep breath. Those words confirmed what I'd hoped for. *Patience. Soon we'll be together.*

The truck came to a stop, and I asked, "Can I take it off now?"

"Not yet. I'll come get you."

Waiting for Drake to come get me only amped up the anticipation. He came around, opened my door, and lifted me from my seat. Only silence and the smell of the woods greeted us. From the lack of noise—other than the chirping of birds—it was obvious we were far from town. Of course, it only took about five minutes to leave town and be in the wilderness.

Gently, Drake set my feet on the ground. The heat of his body pressed against my back. I shivered when his warm breath tickled my neck. "You are my world, Lex."

"And you're mine."

He pressed his lips against my shoulder, and I leaned to the side, exposing my neck to him. "I still want the life we dreamed of having together."

"I want that, too. More than anything."

I leaned back against him, needing more contact.

He trailed kisses up my neck. "Take off the blindfold."

For a moment, I froze, so caught up in Drake's touch. Then I slid it off my head, opened my eyes, and let them adjust to the light.

The image before me took my breath away. It was exactly like I had dreamed so many times with him. *Where are we?* My eyes shot around as I tried to place our location. I hadn't remembered a cabin like this. But we'd talked about it so much. *Is this his? Did he build this place... for us?*

I turned in his arms and looked up at him "Is this...?"

"Yes. Down to every detail we discussed."

I gasped. We'd planned to build a cabin on Drake's land where we'd live after college. While we were apart, he'd gone ahead and built it. *Did he know we'd find our way back to each other?* I'd been so lost, I never dreamed of being back in his arms. "Why?"

"It gave me hope that we'd live here together someday." His thumb brushed my chin. "You're it for me, Lex. And I knew if I ever got you back, I wanted to have this place for us. I love you, Lex. Always have. Always will."

With those words, it felt like the final barrier lifted between us. Throwing my arms around him, I pulled him closer to me. "I love you, too. So much, Drake."

"There's something else I need to show you."

What else could there possibly be? As we walked up the stone path that led to the front porch, I tried to take it all in. The railing was more of a half wall to help keep the snow from accumulating in front of the window. There was a fire pit on each side, surrounded by handmade wood furniture. I stopped, recognizing the pieces that—once upon a time—I'd helped craft. My hands shook as I reached out to touch the smooth wood. I knew the answer, but I had to ask. "Are these...?" My voice shook.

"Yes, they're your dad's. I managed to get them at the auction without Irene knowing by having a few friends bid on them. I wanted to be sure they weren't lost to you. I know how special this furniture is to you. Our cabin has other pieces from the bed and breakfast, as well. I got it all, baby."

My throat tightened. I had a piece of my dad back. I ran a hand over the arm of one of the rocking chairs. The wood was so smooth from hours of sanding. This chair had been my favorite place to sit when Dad told his nighttime stories.

"Drake... I have no words." I turned to face him. "You... I...." It was too much, and I started to cry in earnest. I wrapped my arms around his waist. "I love you."

He always took care of me in every way possible. *If I could marry this man tomorrow, I would.*

A chilly breeze blew, and I shivered.

"Let's go inside," Drake said.

I wanted nothing more than the promise behind those words.

He opened the door, and before I could step over the threshold, he picked me up and stepped inside. It was just as we'd drawn it together. There was a stone fireplace on the left side of the cabin. The living room, kitchen, and dining space were combined in one open space.

"Are the two bedrooms down this hallway?"

"Yes, just like we discussed—with a joint bathroom."

This was home. *Our home.* The dream we'd always shared. The rooms were for the kids we wanted in the future. "And down that way?"

"The office and master bedroom."

I was drawn to the bedroom, and I rushed in that direction. Drake followed close behind me. As I walked around the bedroom, I couldn't believe Drake had done all this. The bedroom was warm and cozy, with rustic, dark wood furniture.

I ran a hand along the wood. "Your dad?"

"I helped. It was something I did on the side."

"I did the same thing, too. Busied myself with anything

and everything. If I sat still for too long, it was hard. My thoughts always drifted to you."

"Mine, too, Lex."

He leaned down and captured my lips. When we broke apart, I whispered, "Make love to me."

He walked me back to the bed, lay me down, and hovered over me. "I love you, Lex."

"Love you, too."

Drake always made me feel like the most cherished woman in the world.

CHAPTER
Twenty-Three

Drake

That was, hands down, the best night of my life.

I poured myself a cup of coffee and leaned against the counter to stare out into the forest. Being here with Lex was better than I'd ever imagined. Just thinking about it had my cock hard to have her again, but she needed the rest. I'd woken Lex four times through the night. It was like a dream I was afraid to wake up from. Afraid I'd be without her again. And as she'd clung to me while I moved inside her, I knew she felt the same way, too.

The thought of her legs wrapping around my waist had my dick hardening. My damn boxers looked like a tent. I couldn't get enough of her.

I checked the time; it was almost eight. *Shit.* We'd have to leave here in a couple of hours but I wasn't ready for our time away to end. Last night, I used a condom every time. We'd been together two years before I entered her bare. I didn't want to rush through the steps this time. It was imperative every single step we took, sexually, was taken with care. When I'd found out she was a virgin, I wanted to wait until she graduated high school. Hell, the woman tempted me time and time again to make love to her sooner. But it was important in case she ever changed her mind about us. I never wanted to be on her list of regrets.

I reconsidered waking her up, but I took a sip of my coffee and focused on the burn instead. I knew she'd be sore. She'd been tight, so fucking tight, last night. Every inch of her beautiful body was mine.

Every. Single. Inch.

The thought had the Neanderthal in me coming out with a need to possess her very being. I knew she could handle herself, but, hell, I wanted to slay every demon in her path.

Yesterday, I asked my dad to look into Lloyd's accident. Dad was good friends with Roy, our local sheriff. Something about the timing of his death and the letter bothered me. Either Montgomery had gotten the letter two weeks ahead, which meant someone knew Lloyd was going to die, or they'd had the letter written in less than four days. That was hella fast to obtain someone's handwriting, hire a professional to forge it, and get it into the lawyer's hands.

What if it had been premeditated?

My fist clenched at the thought. For now, I wasn't going to share my thoughts with Lex. Until I knew more, there wasn't any reason to bring it up. Thinking your dad was murdered only brought on more unanswered questions. I'd share everything with her after Dad got back to me. The last thing she needed right now was more worry. And I knew she'd do the same if our roles were reversed.

I was taking another sip of coffee when I heard her soft footsteps on the kitchen floor. Her arms slipped around my waist, and she pressed her face into my back.

"Morning."

That sweet, sexy, fresh-out-of-bed voice wasn't helping my resolve to leave her alone until this evening. I didn't immediately turn around, knowing when I did, it was going to be hell. Morning sex with Lex was out of this world. Well, it was amazing any time, but there was something about being together before the day started. That was why I'd left the bed when I woke up.

"Morning, baby. Did you sleep good?" I took another sip and focused on my coffee. It was either that or I'd have her bent over the counter.

"Mmm-hmm. I missed waking up next to you."

"Me, too."

Lex let out a little giggle, probably knowing why I got up at the ass crack of dawn, and tightened her arms around me. I savored the moment.

She let out a contented sigh. "I love it out here, Drake."

"Me, too." I adjusted myself and turned around, and she snuggled into my chest. She was wearing one of my flannel shirts—no doubt she'd done that on purpose. I'd always had a weakness for her wearing my stuff.

"How often do you come out here?" she asked.

"About once a week to check on things. Last night was the first night I've stayed here."

She pulled back, shock evident on her face. Her blonde hair was pulled up in that sexy-as-fuck messy way. She'd only fastened a few of the buttons, which left her cleavage on display. *Hell, I'm in trouble.*

Her hand settled on my chest, and I waited for her to ask the question I knew was coming.

"Why?"

I laid my coffee cup down. "Because it wouldn't have been right if you weren't here, too. I wanted our first night here to be together."

She jumped into my arms and rained kisses down all over my face. "I love you so much. So, so much."

"I love you, too, Lex. More than life itself."

Lex flexed her hips, and her pussy rubbed against my stiff cock. Yeah, she knew what that did to me, and she was doing her damnedest to seduce me. She nibbled on my lip, and I put her down. I was only so strong.

I took a deep breath. "You're too sore."

The lip I wanted to devour settled into a full-blown pout. "Morning sex is the best with you."

I cracked my neck back and forth. "Tell me you're not feeling it this morning."

"Please."

I scrubbed a hand down my face, feeling myself losing this battle.

"Lex." I could hear the hesitation in my voice. And from the smile on her face, she did, too.

She took a step back, her hands on the button right below her breasts. Slowly she unbuttoned it. "So... you're sure I'm too sore?"

Hell no, I'm not sure. But I nodded anyway.

As she walked backward into the living room, the next button exposed her flat abdomen. Like a puppy, I followed her.

Yeah, I was going to fuck her. We knew she'd win this battle. She'd already won. But I would hold out as long as possible.

She lay down on the rug in front of the fireplace, where I'd started a fire to ward off the chill in the air. My eyes were riveted to her movements as she rubbed her legs together, keeping her pussy from view.

Her eyes dropped to my dick. "I think he likes what he sees."

"Yeah, he does. A whole hell of a lot."

She let out another sexy-as-sin giggle.

There was still one button on her shirt to go. She played with the button with one hand while tracing her lips with the other before finally slipping a finger in her mouth and sucking on it.

"Fucking hell," I muttered. I was about two seconds from pouncing on her.

She shifted ever so slightly, and the shirt slipped a little farther open, exposing her breasts.

As if sensing where my thoughts were, she moved the hand that had been at her mouth inside the shirt to play with the rosy pink tip of one breast. "What about a compromise?"

I was captivated by every movement.

"Drake?"

"Yeah."

"What about a compromise?"

"I'm listening."

She arched her back ever so slightly. "What if you just touch me? Then I'll suck you off."

The words were barely out of her mouth before I was practically on top of her, and she squealed in excitement. I tore the shirt open and heard the button bounce on the floor somewhere. But then I had to pause and stare at her. She was pure perfection. And she was mine.

I moved my hands along the outside of her breasts, teasing her as I worked down her body. I kissed the inner part of her thigh, and she moaned when I gave it a small bite. I was going to tease and torment her, have her writhing beneath me.

When I got to her core, I licked up all the sweetness she had to offer. I sucked her clit, and she ground down on me, looking for more friction. Right before she was about to come, I slowed.

"Drake. More," she groaned in frustration.

"Not yet."

I kissed my way back up her stomach while she used her feet to push my boxers down, springing me free. When my lips made it to her nipples, I sucked each peak into my mouth while my cock rubbed against her. She moved her hips against the head of my cock. *Hell yeah.*

"Drake. Please. I need you inside me."

I gave her nipple a small bite before soothing it with my tongue. "Let me get you off, then you can suck me off before we soak in the tub. You're too sore."

She writhed underneath me. "Kiss me, Drake."

My lips found hers, and she ground her sweet pussy harder against me. I was lost in her when she pulled back. I moved to her neck, savoring her taste. I swore she tasted like peaches.

"Drake."

"Mmm-hmm."

Her legs wrapped around my waist, lining my cock up right at her entrance. I had to hold back to keep my hips from thrusting forward and feeling her. The one thing I craved more than anything was to feel her without any barriers.

Leaning up a little, her mouth found my ear, and she

traced the rim of it with her tongue. "What if there were no condoms this time?"

Her hips moved, and I slipped just barely inside her. "Oh, fuck."

This was heaven on earth, and my dick screamed for more. "I'm still on birth control. Please. I want you to come inside me."

Her feet pulled on my ass, and I slid all the way in, willingly.

Our eyes locked as I slid out and pushed back in. She was still tight and greedy for my cock.

Everything felt right in my world when we came, together.

Lex walked into the kitchen, fresh from a soak in the tub, and sat at the table where I placed a plate of bacon, eggs, and toast. She winced a little when she sat. *Yeah, I'm going to need more self-control.* She glanced at me and knew I'd seen her flinch. In response, I got a sheepish grin. "Don't even think about it, Drake. I'm not a fragile china doll. I'll be fine."

"I don't want to hurt you."

Taking a bite of bacon, she winked at me. "Just think. Every time I move today, I'll be reminded of you inside me."

Okay, I liked that. I smiled behind my coffee cup.

Lex, of course, caught on and gave me a beautiful smile. "When did you stock the place?"

"Before I picked you up. My meeting with Reeser wasn't as long as expected."

"Best surprise ever. I wish we could stay longer." She

looked around the cabin, her voice wistful.

Hell, I'm going to go with it. I'd wanted this since the moment she stepped foot back into town. If I were honest with myself, before she even came back. "Well, we can start staying out here at night if you want. But if you're not—"

"I would love that." She thought for a second before adding, "I'll contribute to the expenses."

As far as I was concerned, this was *our* place. The only thing hindering that was a technicality. And it was one I wanted rectified as soon as possible. But I'd settle for this... for now.

The clock ticked closer to time for us to leave. It was going to be a long day at the bar with the tourists in town, and I needed to be there. "Do you want to join me for dinner at the Red Onion? After it slows down, we can come back here. If you don't want to hang at the bar, you can hang at our place there."

She got a goofy grin on her face when I said *our.* That was one thing I loved about her. She never took things for granted.

"I'd like that. I may reach out to Teagan, she if she wants to join me for a drink. Things seem really off with her. And I want to feel her out, see if she knows anything."

Teagan was definitely on my list of suspects. It would be good to have her close and see if I could find anything out. And at least they'd be at the bar. "Sounds good."

Lex finished her breakfast and took her plate to the dishwasher. "Let me know what I owe for my part of the bills. I can pay half of both places."

"Okay." I wasn't going to, of course, but it wasn't a fight I wanted to have right now.

She watched me carefully. "Drake. I mean it."

"How do I get out of accepting your money without pissing you off?"

"That's an impossible task." With a smile, she gave me a kiss. "I'm not a freeloader."

Yeah, I wasn't going to argue. I got that it was important to Lex to pay her own way. We'd figure out something. She looked at her watch. "I probably should head in soon. Most of the equipment is coming in within the hour."

"Are you excited?"

"Very. It's a dream come true. I wish Dad was here." Lex grew quiet. "What should we do about the letter?"

Early that morning, when I'd been holding Lex in my arms and watching the sun come up, I'd given that some thought. Only one option seemed viable—keep investigating. Somewhere along the way, the person behind this had to slip up. No one was perfect. "I thought I could talk to Hayden. See if he's heard anything about Milano Incorporated."

Since Hayden flew everywhere, he knew a lot. Well, the people he knew, knew a lot. The people he flew around were generally well off, so it was worth a shot.

"If you don't mind."

"Not at all. Let's head into town. The sooner we get done, the sooner I can have you back in my arms in our bed."

CHAPTER
Twenty-Four

Alexa

A week later, I pulled into the clinic and smiled at the sign, fritz medical. We'd been officially open for three days. Thank goodness it was Friday. I took a sip of my coffee and just enjoyed the moment. We'd done it. And the town was overjoyed. I swore the majority of Skagway had booked an initial visit with Hollis. We needed to hire someone for the clerical work at some point.

It was a success, and my heart couldn't have been happier.

Hollis had offered twenty-dollar initial visits, regardless of insurance coverage. He was also working on some cash discounts for those who didn't have insurance. People were responding and interested. And they were also plying him with food. He had received more jelly, canned vegetables, and cakes in the past three days than he could eat in a month. I was so proud of my small town.

Mom and Raquel hadn't stopped by. Not that I'd expected them to, but still. And Teagan had also been a no-show. I'd sent her a few texts, called a few times, and got nothing. I'd driven by her place several times, but her car hadn't been there. It was odd. While I was thinking of Teagan, I sent her another text. My heart hurt for her. It was probably why I remained friends with her for so long.

Me: *Getting worried. Let me know you're okay.*

Of course, there was no response.
My phone did, however, vibrate with a text from Drake.

Drake: *Just wanted you to know I love you.*

Me: *Love you, too.*

We hadn't found out anything else regarding the letter, and I was starting to think we never would. Drake and I had decided to keep moving forward with our lives. And if the past wasn't supposed to be unearthed, we'd leave it buried. It still frustrated me, though. Raquel and Mom were at the top of my list, but they'd never confess. And I didn't want them to know I knew the letter was fake. They weren't supposed to know what the letter said... unless they wrote it. It was all a very twisted web.

Hollis walked out of the clinic and waved to me. Ike had loaned Hollis some of the extra furniture he had until his order was done. I think he'd only finished the bed so far.

By the look on his face, he wasn't in the best of moods. Yesterday, Hollis had been a bear and a half to deal with. I'd come to find out he was irritable because of the lack of decent coffee. His current coffee maker was not cutting it. Apparently, according to Hollis, it produced sludge. So he was sweet as could be with the patients but grumpy as hell with me. He'd ordered a new, top-of-the-line unit, but of course it was going to take a couple of weeks to arrive.

At one point, he'd made me so aggravated I threw a book at his head. Anything I did, he snapped at me. Anything. He was a little perturbed at how I used the paper clips. Or the stapler wasn't sitting just right on the counter. The supplies weren't stored in the alphabetical order he thought they should be. Grumpy with a capital G.

When Drake had picked me up, Hollis had muttered something about flying books and attitude adjustments and headed upstairs. If he was the same today, I might drug him. Kidding. Maybe. Not really.

My peace offering had to get him back on track. The local jewelry store in town had a Starbucks. Only the tourists really stopped there, and it had slipped my mind until Drake mentioned it the night before while we made dinner together at our cabin.

I held up the cup as I got out. "I come with a peace offering in the hope that you'll be less irritable."

Hollis's eyes grew wide. "Where in the hell did you find a Starbucks?"

"Jewelry store."

He slapped his head. "Of course. A jewelry store. Why would it be anywhere else in this town?"

Okay, he was still a little grumpy. "Do you want it or not?"

"Does a bear shit in the woods? I mean, yeah, they do and

apparently in towns, too."

Yesterday, Hollis had read the Twiner sisters' newsletter about a bear being spotted on the outskirts of town. That had led to a whole rant about something that had made no sense. I still had no idea what point he was trying to make.

He reached for the cup, but I held it back. "If I give this to you, no more grumpiness."

"I won't need to be aggravated because I'll have a decent cup of fucking coffee."

I kept it just out of reach, and I swore I saw steam start to come out of his ears. "Hollis, I need you to promise me. Otherwise, I'm contemplating medicating you."

He gave me a grunt. "Promise."

Oh, man, he's on edge.

I handed it over. He took a sip and sighed. "Soy milk latte with a hint of vanilla and chocolate with a double espresso, I have never missed you so much." He took another sip. "I thought I was going to have to fly back to the mainland for one of these to tide me over until my new machine arrived." Then he pointed an accusing finger at me. "You withheld this on purpose."

I put my hands on my hips. "I will carry through with the threat. You better turn that finger around and point it at yourself. I forgot we had a Starbucks. Only the tourists drink it. That's why it's in the jewelry store. The cruisers come to port and trade diamonds while sipping their Starbucks. It's not very Alaskan."

Narrowing his eyes, Hollis knew I'd backhandedly called him a tourist; he'd otherwise abandoned all those things in favor of being a true "Alaskan."

He took another sip. "We all have our downfalls. I don't

have to be a full Alaskan on my coffee."

I laughed. "Come on, Dr. Fritz, you've got a busy day ahead of you."

We were filled with appointments for the next month. Plus, we had to keep some appointments open for the walk-in patients or those who needed emergency care.

Before the first person arrived, I busied myself with making sure the charts were as I left them the night before. At some point, we would need to hire a receptionist, but for now, I could handle it. Keeping the office in order, charts pulled, appointments made was difficult on top of my duties as a nurse.

"Ready for today?" he asked.

"Absolutely. It's a great day. There's pep in my step. And someone is bringing you another coffee in about two hours."

He squeezed me hard. "You are the best of friends."

Yeah, I'd be bringing him coffee every morning for the foreseeable future.

"That's not what you were saying yesterday."

He waved me off. "Yesterday is in the past."

"If you say so." I laughed.

We got to work, and the day flew by in a blur. A walk-in had arrived with an infection from an untreated cut, which put us behind. Hollis was in with the last patient while I worked on getting the paperwork completed before I left. After a day like today, I was glad I could sleep in tomorrow. At one point, we'd talked about opening the clinic for a half day on Saturdays, but we decided it was best to not start that.

Devney, the high school music teacher, was currently with Hollis. She was a year older than Drake and a year younger than Hollis, and she taught music on the side. The kids loved her. She'd always been quiet when I was around.

The door opened, and she stepped out. "Thank you, Dr. Fritz. Welcome to Skagway."

Hollis had an interesting look about him as he said goodbye. It was odd—like he was in a trance. I put my pen down and watched.

As she walked by my desk, her cheeks were flushed and stood out against her otherwise pale skin. Her dark hair was pulled up, and it looked like her neck was a little red, as well. "Goodbye, Alexa. Welcome home."

"Thanks, Devney. Have a good weekend."

She left, and Hollis stared after her for a full minute before he turned my way. "Do you know her?"

Yeah, he was taken with her. Completely and utterly taken.

"Yes, she graduated with Drake. We've never hung out, but I've heard great things about her. She's the music teacher at the high school. Why?"

Hollis blushed like a kid caught with his hand in the cookie jar. "No reason. Why would you ask? Can't I ask a question about a member of the Skagway community?"

It was hard to keep a straight face. Calmly, I stated, "Because we've seen twenty-two patients today, and not once have you acted goofy like this. Did something happen in there?"

Hollis looked at me like I was crazy. "I can guarantee that nothing happened in there."

I teased, "Did you want something to happen in there?"

He stood straighter and blinked a few times. "You need some rest, Alexa. I'm not acting *goofy*, as you say. And... you're delusional."

"Or I'm totally on my game and see that the good ol' doc

has been bitten by the lovebug."

Hollis rolled his eyes at me. He was protesting too much for this. Normally, when I was wrong, he shrugged and moved on.

"Skagway is too far north for lovebugs to reside. The southeastern United States is as far north as they're typically found. I believe your diagnosis is wrong, Ms. Owens. The weather is not conducive to the lovebug species."

I giggled. "Sometimes you're too smart for your own good. You know that's not what I meant. Metaphorically speaking, the lovebug got you. Admit it."

Shaking his head, he replied, "I'm too tired for this nonsense. I'm going to head up to my place to read the medical journals that arrived." He stopped and looked at the time. "No, I'm going to go get another coffee. That's what I'm going to do."

"And hope you run into a certain music teacher?"

That got no response. He stomped upstairs to get his keys. "Lovebug my ass. You know the threat of medicating me… it goes both ways."

On his way back down, he looked at me, and I smiled before making a kissy face. He mumbled, "Sometimes I feel bad for Drake."

"Night, Hollis. I've heard that asking someone out cures the lovebug."

He said nothing. Yeah, he had it bad. We'd revisit the Devney topic the next time he irritated me, which was likely the next week. When he got to the door, I asked, "Do you want to come to dinner tomorrow night at our place? You could see the cabin and start thinking about what you want to do for yours. I'm going to make your favorite dessert."

"You're trying to bribe me."

"Maybe. Is it working?"

"Count me in," he said as he walked out the door.

I finished the filing and got prepped for Monday. When I was just about done, the door opened again, and Hollis came back in and hugged me. "On a serious note, thanks for convincing me to come here, Alexa. It really has been what I needed all along."

I hugged him tighter. "Thank you for coming. It's turned out better than I could ever have imagined." Not only was there regular medical help, but people had a better chance of survival when there was an accident.

He raised his eyebrow. "But we need a receptionist."

I began to agree, but he cut me off. "Seriously, I need you with me in there. We'll never make it as a fully functioning clinic if we're not doing what we were each trained to do. You're spending too much time on administrative tasks."

We were on the same page. "Okay, I'll look for someone. Maybe we could start off with a part-time position."

"Just get someone trustworthy. Part-time, full-time—it doesn't matter. And we'll pay whatever is fair for here."

"I'll start looking."

Satisfied that reason had prevailed, Hollis said goodbye. He was right, of course. Things would be less stressful if I were able to actually focus on the nursing aspect and not have to check in patients, schedule appointments, and deal with insurance.

After locking up, I went to my truck. It wasn't as late as I thought, and I'd beat Drake home by a few hours. Maybe I would make lasagna and start a fire. An easy night home sounded blissful.

As I reached my truck, a car pulled into the driveway, and I groaned. As terrible as it sounded, I hoped it wasn't a patient who needed to be seen. I was beyond tired. The car stopped, and I realized it was Teagan. *Great.* I was still sore about how she'd left my stuff on her front porch and hadn't bothered to return any of my calls or texts.

She rolled down her window. "Hi. I came to apologize for how I've been and see if I could take my best friend to dinner."

I almost turned her down, but she pleaded with me. "Please, Alexa. I need to talk to you. You're the only friend I have."

There were dark circles under her eyes, and she looked almost gaunt. *Did she lose weight?* "Are you okay, Teagan?"

She shook her head. "Not really. I was hoping we could talk. You're the only person I can turn to. I've been waiting for you to come out."

I shut my truck door and walked over to her car. "What's going on?"

She looked around nervously. "Can we go somewhere to talk? Please? I know I don't deserve a second chance, but I'm asking anyway."

"Sure."

Never before had I heard Teagan sound desperate. And I couldn't deny someone who was asking for help. I'd never been able to. I grabbed my purse and got in the passenger seat of her car. My heart hurt for Teagan. All the years we'd been friends, I'd always had a soft spot for her.

She let out a sigh. "I'm sorry for not returning your calls."

"What's been going on?"

Her hair was greasy, and her clothes looked dirty. "Let's go to the dock and talk."

"Okay."

We turned left, and Teagan scratched at her arm, which pulled up her sleeve. She had sores forming on her forearm. Suddenly, I had a bad feeling about what she'd been up to. *I should have driven.* Her knee bounced about ninety miles an hour. And the signs I hadn't noticed before started to connect. I shifted uncomfortably in my seat, wondering how I should handle this.

Don't do anything drastic.

Stay calm.

Let Drake know where you're at.

There was a definite tremor in my hands when I grabbed my phone from my purse. Teagan scratched more viciously at her arm.

I pulled out my phone and went straight to Drake's number. An overwhelming queasiness settled in my stomach. I needed to get out of this situation.

"What are you doing?" she asked, her voice a little too loud in the quiet car. The wheel jerked at the same time.

Shrugging, I tried to hide my shaky voice. Being alone with her at the dock was not a smart idea. "Letting Drake know I'll be home later. I was supposed to meet him for dinner. You know how he is. He'd have a search party out for me."

Her movements became even more jerky. "Yes. Good idea. Text him right now." I started to text. "Now! Text him NOW!"

"Okay. I will. I am."

Me: *Hey, I got in the car with Teagan. I have a bad feeling. Where are you? Don't call.*

Drake: *At the Red Onion. Heading to my truck. Where are you headed?*

"What's he saying? Tell ME! What is he saying?" She wiped at her nose, momentarily taking her hands off the steering wheel.

Maybe I could talk her into stopping the car. "Why don't we pull over and let me get a drink?"

"WHAT DID HE SAY?" She was becoming more agitated by the second.

I took a deep breath. "Told me to tell you hi and to have a good time. Where are we—"

Her phone beeped, and she picked it up to read it. "I need to stop by my place. Then we'll go to the dock."

"Okay. Sounds good." We were close to her place.

Teagan scratched her sleeve up farther, and I could see the track marks up her arm. My heart hammered in my chest. I knew how unpredictable drug addicts could be. If provoked, she could swerve the car and crash. Drug addicts couldn't be reasoned with logically.

Drake: *Where the fuck is she taking you?*

Me: *Her place. Then the dock. Hurry. I think she's on drugs.*

Drake: *I'm on my way. But when she stops at her place, if I haven't made it, get out of the car.*

Me: *Okay.*

I'd missed the signs. Somehow, I'd missed all the signs for who knows how long. I was trained to see this, and I'd completely overlooked it. But it now made sense.

We pulled into the parking lot of her apartment complex. "Be right back. Then we'll be on our way." She went to close the door but then reopened it. "I missed you, Alexa. I really did."

Teagan left the car running and ran into her building. Her movements were awkward and lacked fluidity. In a panic, I opened the car door, but I paused when I saw her cell phone in the seat. The text app was pulled up. When I heard Drake's truck pull into the parking lot, I decided to look at her text. It was from an unknown number.

Unknown: *I know what you need. Meet me at your place.*

My heart nearly stopped in my chest, and I glanced at the apartment door. Before I could get out of the car, Drake lifted me into his arms, and I dropped the phone. He wrapped his arms around me tightly and walked swiftly to his truck.

"You okay? Are you hurt?"

I was still a little shaken and couldn't quite form a sentence.

"Lex, speak to me."

"I'm not hurt." It all felt like a dream. I shuddered, remembering what she looked like. "I think she's on heroin. I saw the tracks up her arm. She wasn't herself."

Within a minute, I was in Drake's truck, and he whipped out of the parking lot. His jaw was tense as he watched his rearview mirror. His knuckles were white where he held onto the steering wheel, and his eyes were tight as he focused on the road. The vein in his neck pulsed. This wasn't good. "You seem agitated."

"No, Lex, I'm fucking pissed."

CHAPTER
Twenty-Five

Drake

I focused on calming myself down as we drove out to our cabin. Damn it all to hell, Teagan had crossed the line that night. *Drugs.* And she'd had my girl with her. Lex knew better. She fucking knew Teagan was bad news. Always had been. But this was the first time it had gone too far.

"Drake. Calm down. I'm okay."

That was it. I pulled the truck onto the side of the road. "*This* time you're okay. This time. Drugs, Lex. Come on. You're a nurse. You could have ended up in an accident. Or worse."

She let out a breath, and I could tell she was getting frustrated, too. *Welcome to the club, baby.* From the moment I got her text, everything had moved in slow motion. Things could have gone drastically wrong. I'd even called Hollis and asked him to be on standby in case something happened.

"I'm okay, Drake."

Okay. There was that damn word again.

"No more Teagan."

She held up her hand, and her eyes flashed fire. *Well, step up to the plate, baby, because I'm not backing down.*

"You do not control me."

"No more Teagan."

Her eyes narrowed. I knew I was being a jackass. But my concern for her won over any common sense I may have possessed at that moment. Her lips thinned. "It's amazing I somehow survived the two years we spent apart."

It felt like she slapped me, and I shook my head. This could escalate out of control fast. I knew she was scared. But Lex had a heart of gold, and it was bleeding for her friend. If we kept going on the way we were, one of us was going to say something we'd regret.

So I held up my hands. "First, I'm not questioning whether you can survive on your own. You're very capable. And don't make me sound like some overbearing boyfriend. You were scared, or you wouldn't have texted me. What happened tonight... If I'd lost you, or something had happened to you, Lex... I can't lose you." The thought was almost too much to bear.

She touched my hand. "But you didn't."

"But I could have." I took a deep breath. "I get that we need to try and help Teagan. But the key word is *we*. If Donnie's involved, and you're there by yourself... Fuck. I don't even want to think about what could happen."

"Drake, I get it."

I needed to calm down. My phone rang through the connection in the car, and I hit reject, wishing I could punch the screen.

"Do you? Because I plan on marrying you, having kids with you. It's my job to protect you. I fucking *love* you."

"Whoa. That's a little deep for me. But by the way, I don't want to marry or have kids with you. And telling me you fucking love me is a little weird." Hayden's voice boomed through the car speakers.

Lex's eyes went wide. This was not the time for Hayden. He had no idea how serious this was.

"Damn it all to hell. What do you want, Hayden?"

"Is Lex okay?" He must have picked up on the fact that something was wrong.

I exhaled. "Yes, Teagan was driving her around. We think she's doing drugs. Maybe heroin."

"Fuck. Lex, you can't be doing that. You could have been seriously hurt."

Well, maybe I can let Hayden intervene for a minute. It made me feel a little less of an ass. When I looked over at Lex, she was nervously chewing on her lip. "Hayden, I'll call you back."

I made sure to disconnect the call this time. She fidgeted with her hands. I closed my eyes and took a deep breath. "Lex, I'm sorry. I shouldn't have yelled like that. Can I hold you?"

She unbuckled her seat belt and crawled into my lap. This was the fear coming out. Earlier had been a knee-jerk reaction. One thing I knew about Lex was she didn't like being controlled. I tried to explain further, which I hoped would help. "When I got your text asking me to hurry, I died a thousand deaths. I could tell from your text you were scared. So I ran both stoplights to get to you. I just can't ever lose you again."

"I know. I'm sorry for what I said." She sniffed and pulled back to look at me. "Teagan showed up at the clinic and said she wasn't good, that she needed to talk to me. I missed all the signs. All I saw was a shell of a friend who needed someone."

"We'll get her help."

"She needs help now, Drake. She's in bad shape."

The worry was clear in her face. This was more than Lex making a bad choice. She'd wanted to help her friend. I couldn't stand in her way. I'd stand by her side the entire way, instead. "What do you need?"

Leaning in, she kissed my lips, and I knew we would be okay.

"Can Hayden meet us there? I'll call Hollis, too. I'm not sure if your dad's available. Drug addicts can become irate. But I have to try."

"Okay. But please don't ever ride with her again."

"I promise. I was scared, too. And Drake?"

"Yeah, baby."

"I want all those things, too."

The ring I'd bought for her was now burning a hole in my pocket.

CHAPTER
Twenty-Six

Drake

We pulled into the apartment complex with Dad, Hayden, and Hollis following behind us. They'd come from the clinic together. We thought it would be good to have two vehicles, just in case.

One of the two cop cars in Skagway pulled into the lot, and Roy—the older of the two police officers in town—met us on the sidewalk. We thought it was better to have him there just in case.

"If she doesn't answer the door, we can't enter without probable cause."

Lex looked shocked. "We can't get in there?"

"Not unless we have probable cause."

Closing her eyes, Lex took a deep breath and reeled herself in. "Okay. Let's see if I can get her to open up the door." She looked around the parking lot, scanning the cars. "Donnie's truck is still here, too."

Great. There was still the unknown number that had me on edge.

Knock.

Knock.

Knock.

"Hey, Teagan, it's Alexa. I wanted to see if we could talk now."

She listened for any sound. We waited. But there was nothing.

Knock.

Knock.

Knock.

"Teagan, open up."

Still, there was no answer. Again, Lex called out to Teagan. And again. But there was nothing.

Roy was about done. "I'll keep an eye out for her, Alexa."

She shook her head and muttered something under her breath. Roy turned to speak to Dad, and Lex narrowed her eyes at the door. I recognized the look of determination on her face. Silently, she turned the knob.

"Oh, look. The door opened."

Roy spun around, his eyes flying open in surprise. "What?"

"I think I heard someone call my name to come in."

A foul smell wafted out the open door. I took a step forward and extended my arm. "Roy, do you want to go in first?"

"Yes." Walking inside, he called, "Teagan, this is Sheriff Bolton with the police department. Did you open the door?"

Roy knew damn well the door hadn't been opened by someone on the inside, but I guess he had to cover all possibilities. After Roy entered, we followed him. There was an overpowering smell about the place. Trash was everywhere. A box with a half-eaten pizza with bugs crawling in it sat at our feet. *How can anyone live like this?*

Hollis stayed with us while Dad and Hayden followed Roy further into the apartment.

"I was here just twelve days ago. It's like I've walked into another world," Alexa said.

From the back of the apartment, Roy called out, "Dr. Fritz, Alexa, we need you in the left bedroom."

Hollis hurried back with Lex following behind him. Lex slipped into professional mode, and suddenly she was all business. When we crossed over the threshold of the bedroom, I wasn't prepared for what we'd find.

Donnie was lying on the bed in a pool of vomit. Teagan lay unmoving on the bed, her arm flung out to the side with a needle still in it.

Hollis immediately sprang into action. "Check his pulse."

Lex felt for a pulse, but I knew he was gone. His skin was a pale blue and his eyes were open and unmoving. Nevertheless, Lex kept searching for signs of life.

On the other side of the bed, Hollis was working steadily on Teagan. "I have a pulse, but she's not breathing. Get me a syringe with one milliliter naloxone."

Lex dug into Hollis's bag. With a steady hand, she filled the syringe and handed it off.

"Stay with me, Teagan. Don't let this nasty stuff beat you." Hollis continued to do chest compressions, and after every tenth, he squeezed the bag over her mouth to supply oxygen.

Lex injected the needle into Teagan's bony arm and released the plunger of the needle on Hollis's command. Hollis kept working. Lex kept her fingers on Teagan's wrist. "It's still weak."

"Get another dose ready in case we need to repeat."

Time slowed down as Hollis continued to perform CPR on Teagan.

"Another milliliter of naloxone."

Lex injected it in her upper thigh this time.

There were more compressions. Another squeeze of the bag. Hollis wasn't stopping. "Come on, Teagan. Fight. You want to live. We can get you help. Fight. Damn it. *Fight.*"

Hollis was urging Teagan on, fighting for her. He'd never met her, but he cared. We all held our breath as we waited for her to breathe.

For what seemed like an eternity, we watched, silently cheering her on.

And then, suddenly, Teagan gasped for air.

"Good girl. All right, let's get you to the clinic."

She wasn't coherent, but at least she was breathing.

CHAPTER
Twenty-Seven

Alexa

What a night.

Teagan was sleeping peacefully in a hospital bed. Hollis sat on the couch against the wall, reading one of his medical journals. Drake sat beside me as I watched Teagan's weak body fight to come back from an overdose.

We were in the back of the clinic in a room we'd set up as a hospital room. Across the hall was another room we would use for surgery. The operating room would need to have multiple upgrades come spring. We'd simply run out of time.

The beeping of the machine filled the silence.

From what had been found at the apartment, it had been determined that Teagan had been using heroin. Unfortunately, I'd been right. Donnie had overdosed and had already been dead when we got there. The police were handling the arrangement to transport his body to Juneau, as per his parents' wishes, where the closest funeral home was.

Hollis estimated time of death as sometime that morning, which meant Donnie had been dead when Teagan arrived back at her apartment. The police had interviewed me regarding everything that had happened today. I mentioned the text from the unknown number, but so far, no one had found her phone.

I should have given up on Teagan a long time ago. But maybe, just maybe, I was meant to remain in her life in order to help her. Earlier, when Drake and I had been fighting, I'd actually agreed with him. I'd been scared to be in the car with Teagan.

No more Teagan.

I'd be there for her, but I knew I couldn't take the risk of being in the car or alone with her again.

The solid pressure of Drake's hand on mine sent warmth through me. He'd dropped everything to help me, to help Teagan. Sometimes I felt like I didn't deserve him.

Marriage.

Kids.

He'd mentioned both of those things. And I wanted them. I wanted it all with him. This wasn't the time or place to talk about that, though. So, I focused back on Teagan's breathing. Hopefully she'd get better and start a life somewhere. Maybe find happiness and love.

I wondered how long she'd been doing drugs and how she'd managed to hide it. We'd emailed from time to time when I was in New York. In the beginning, maybe once or twice a month. But lately, it had been every other month, at most.

I took a deep breath. Life was a delicate balance. And I wanted to make sure I lived mine to the fullest.

Movement at the door caught my attention. Hayden stood there, staring at Teagan while he ran his fingers through his hair. Something like this would rock the town to its core. The news of what happened would spread like wildfire. Things like overdoses rarely happened in Skagway. The townspeople would be wary of Teagan now. They would love her through it, but I don't know how they'd ever trust her again.

After a few minutes, Hayden motioned for Drake to meet him in the hallway. At our insistence, Ike had gone home to be with Amie, but Hayden had stuck around. The police were stopping by at regular intervals to check on Teagan. Our concern was what would happen when she awoke. She might be docile, or she could be violent. If it was the latter, Drake and Hayden would be able to help manage her if Hollis and I had to sedate her.

Drake sat up. "I'm going to speak to Hayden. You want to come?"

He must have known what his brother wanted to talk about if he asked me to join him. This only increased the unease I was feeling.

Hollis was still engrossed in his journal, so I had to interrupt him for a second. "I'm going to step into the hallway if you're okay with it."

"Mmm." Without looking up, Hollis continued to read and make notes. The journal on genetics must have been the most interesting thing in the world.

"Hollis?"

He glanced up at me. "I'm fine. She's not going to wake up for at least another hour or so."

"Okay. I'll be right outside."

Drake and I took a step out into the hallway, where the

bleach smell still lingered from when Teagan had vomited ear-lier before she finally passed out.

Hayden held the back of his neck. "How is she?"

"Stable. But the hardest part is yet to come. Hollis has her on methadone. When she wakes up, that should keep the with-drawal symptoms at bay while we talk to her. She just won't have that high feeling. But maybe it'll allow us to reason with her."

He shook his head. "This is just so hard to believe. Mom called a little while ago. She's bringing over breakfast. The quilting circle is going to bring lunch. They also wanted to know if there was anything Teagan needed."

I shouldn't have been surprised. This town pulled together for the people who were part of it regardless of who they were. They always had. "Tell them thank-you. I'll let you know."

"I will." There was some sort of silent communication be-tween the brothers before Hayden spoke again. "I was flying with one of my buddies yesterday. I asked if he knew about a Milano Incorporated. Said he'd had an offer from them he was seriously entertaining."

"Where's his property?" I asked.

From his raised eyebrow, I had a feeling I wasn't going to like the answer. "Butts up to your place. You know the Ewings from Anchorage?"

"Yes. That land has been in their family forever." I was pretty sure their family had owned that land for almost as long as mine had owned ours.

"It has. But he said they were offering over the market price. It's hard to walk away from that kind of money. Busi-ness has been hard."

Drake nodded. "Yeah, at our quarterly business meeting,

he talked about being down double digits. Wanted to know if anyone else had the same issue."

Drake was part of a group of other businessmen. They touched base four times a year to see how business was going and what could be done to help each other.

It wouldn't matter how much this Milano Incorporated offered. Some things weren't for sale. My head spun as I wondered what was going on.

Drake asked, "How have they been communicating with Ewing?"

"Through the bank. He thinks it's Chazz, and that's the only reason he's not selling yet. But the bank confirmed the offer was valid."

To me, it just sounded shady.

"Thanks, Hayden. I appreciate it," Drake said.

Why would someone work so hard to remain anonymous? Secrecy in this sort of transaction generally wasn't a good thing.

Drake's phone rang, and he looked at the number, his finger hovering over the Ignore button. It was the Red Onion.

I touched his arm. "Go ahead and take it."

The last week of normalcy had felt like a reprieve as issues had begun to stack up against us. There was still a sense of dread lingering in the air, like we were waiting for something else to happen. Stepping away, he took the call, keeping his voice low.

Hayden asked, "How are you holding up?"

"Okay. I had no idea how far gone Teagan was. I mean, I sensed something was off, but it's always been that way with her. I don't know. My head was a mess being back here, too. I had only been there to sleep, really. And she hadn't been home."

"Hang in there. What you and Hollis did tonight was impressive. It's because of you two she has a fighting chance."

I gave a sad smile. An overdose wasn't how I envisioned our first emergency. "Thanks. I just hope she wants to be saved. Once she's stable, we can't keep her here if she doesn't want help. And we're not an addiction-treatment facility. It's not going to be an easy road for her."

And Donnie was dead. That alone could be enough to send Teagan spiraling to the point of no return.

Drake returned from his phone call. "That was Crete. News of Teagan and Donnie is spreading. Everyone's talking about it. The Twiner sisters sent a newsletter."

I groaned. "Why can't they just wait?"

They'd already sent out three newsletters this week about how marvelous the clinic was. They'd even posed in their gold-digger uniforms on the front porch. These ladies were exhausting at times.

"The focus of the newsletter was Raquel. Apparently, she called Elvira with her new anti-drug campaign since Skagway now has a growing drug issue."

Anger flared within me. *How dare she? How dare she turn this into something about her?*

A person's—a very sick person's—life hung in the balance, and Raquel wanted to turn the situation into something it wasn't. If Teagan chose to fight to get better, it would nearly be impossible for her to stay here. Raquel would do everything she could to make Teagan feel uncomfortable, which was the worst combination for a newly recovering addict. The negative often outweighed the positive in an addict's mind.

Closing my eyes, I took a deep breath. "I'll deal with her

later. I'm going to check in on Teagan and keep Hollis company."

Drake started to follow, but I put my hand on his chest.
"Spend time with your brother. I need time to cool off before I
take a baseball bat to Raquel's car. Stupid cow."

About twenty to thirty minutes later, Teagan stirred. She rolled
her head to the side, and I stood beside her bed, waiting for
any further reaction. Hollis opened the door to the hallway
where Drake and Hayden sat. "She's awake."

Drake and Hayden came in for support. At any moment,
she might become violent or unmanageable.

Softly, I said, "Hey, there. You're at the clinic. We found
you in your apartment—you overdosed, Teagan."

"I did? That can't be right." Her eyes were glazed. She
cleared her throat, and I brought a wet sponge to her lips.

"Suck on this." She gave it more of a lick, but at least she
got some moisture. So far, she seemed calm. "Dr. Fritz is going to a check you for a few things. Do you care if I hold your
hand?"

She gave another weak cough. "Will it hurt?"

Hollis already had on white surgical gloves. "Not at all.
May I call you Teagan?"

"Sure."

With gentle movements, he touched the inside of her
wrist. "I haven't had the pleasure of officially meeting you, but
I've heard so many nice things."

To that, she gave no response.

Hollis checked the basics, explaining everything he was

doing as he was doing it. From the lag in her responses, it was possible the drugs had created an adverse effect on her, neurologically. My heart hurt.

With a nod from Hollis, I asked, "Teagan, when did you start using heroin?"

She took a deep breath, still a bit out of it. "I don't know. While ago. He gave me all I wanted."

He? I waited for her to continue, but her eyes drooped a little. "Who is *he*?"

"My boyfriend."

"Donnie?"

"No."

Hollis put his hand on my shoulder. I knew I was getting too intense. Teagan began to shift more, becoming restless. Changing the pace, Hollis took off his gloves. "So… I've been looking at treatment options. There are some amazing facilities you can go to."

"Expensive." It hurt to hear how defeated she sounded. But it gave me hope that she might want to get better.

"Yes, they are. But I'm going to cover all the costs. We need you better so you can have dinner with Alexa and me. You and I can exchange notes on all Alexa's secrets."

She gave a weak chuckle and looked at me. "You've been a good friend."

I gave her a smile. "So have you. And you'll be better before you know it."

For a second, she closed her eyes and refocused on the doctor. "Am I on anything right now?"

"Methadone—to keep you from having severe withdrawal symptoms as you detox." Hollis kept it very level and matter-of-fact.

Everyone in the room waited to see what Teagan would say next. She asked, "When can I go?"

"The facility has an opening now. We could leave as early as tomorrow if everything continues on track, medically speaking. How much heroin were you using and how often?"

"No, I mean when can I leave here?"

It wasn't lost on anyone that she'd ignored the second part of the question. From the number of needles and heroin we'd found, it was probably a lot.

I reminded myself to stay calm. "Teagan, you need medical help to detox from the heroin. To get your life back."

She turned my way and moved her hand closer to mine. "But I don't want to. I wish you would've let me die. I've done things. Things a friend should never do."

This confused me. "Teagan, what are you talking about?"

"How long, doctor?"

Hollis looked torn. "Legally, I can't force you to stay. Medically, you're weak and need help. I'm not sure how much more your body can take."

This had to be her decision. She had to *want* to be clean.

Closing her eyes, she turned away from us. "I'll think about it."

CHAPTER
Twenty-Eight

Drake

Lex was passed out on my lap in the waiting area, exhausted from everything that had happened that day. I sat and thought about something Teagan had said that was bothering me in a major fucking way.

"I've done things. Things a friend should never do."

Was she behind the letter? Who is this guy she claims is her boyfriend? Lex had continued to try and talk to her, but Teagan had pretended to sleep.

Hayden handed me a cup of coffee. "What the hell was Teagan talking about? She's 'done things'? 'Things a friend should never do.' What kind of *things*?"

"I don't know. None of this sits right with me."

"Me either."

The likelihood of her seeking treatment seemed slim. "I think we need to follow Teagan discreetly when she leaves here. See where she goes. Maybe we can figure out who's behind this. The cops said there was over a hundred thousand dollars of heroin in her apartment. Where the hell did she get that kind of money?"

"I don't know, man. But I think we should watch her. We can take shifts. Kane's getting back this evening."

The one person who could track a person without anyone knowing about it was Kane. "I'll call him and ask. He said Dixon was a normal stupid-ass city slicker. What'd you think of Chazz's brother?"

I'd run into Dixon in town once. He'd been helping Elvira across the street with a heavy load. If it had been Chazz, he'd have walked past her without a second thought.

"He's different as day and night from Chazz. He's personable and seemed to enjoy himself. He wasn't a half-bad shot, either. And you could tell he knew his way around a fishing pole."

"That's good." So we were on the same page when it came to Dixon.

"Has Chazz caused you any more problems?"

"No, not since my liquor issue. He lost several customers, so I imagine that had something to do with him backing off."

At the quarterly business meeting, I'd confirmed it. Several owners had changed over to Reeser.

Lex shifted slightly in my lap. We paused our conversation to see if she was waking, but she took a deep breath and settled back to sleep. I brushed my thumb along her cheek and remembered that earlier, Dad had said he needed to talk to me. I wondered what it was about. Most likely the request to look into Lloyd's death.

After a couple of minutes, Hayden said, "I'm glad she's back. You're not quite the asshole you were while she was gone."

I chuckled. "I wasn't that big of an asshole."

"If you say so. Were you serious about what I heard over the car? Marriage. Kids."

It made me pause. *Oh, shit, he was on the phone.* But it occurred to me that it might be good to talk to Hayden. Get his thoughts.

"Yeah, as soon as I know she's ready, I'm going to."

"I'm happy for you. You can tell you guys have what it takes to make it. Mom's going to be excited when it does happen. Maybe it'll get her off our asses to settle down."

I took a sip of my coffee. "Mom isn't on your ass."

"She called me with the name of a girl she'd like me to take out. She's moving here, and Mom thought I'd be the perfect person." Hayden leaned back and blew out a breath. "I'm fucked up over a girl."

That got my attention. "What?"

"Yeah. There was this girl in Ketchikan. We were seeing each other when I came to town. It wasn't supposed to be exclusive, but it turned out to be. Fuck, I don't know."

"*Was?*"

He nearly drained his huge mug of coffee. "Yeah, she went back home. I texted her to say I was coming into town. Nothing. Then I find out she's gone back to Washington."

This was news. From the sound of it, Hayden was really messed up over this girl. "Have you tried calling her?"

"The number's been disconnected."

Oh, this was more serious than I'd thought. And now it made sense why he hadn't told us about his conquests, or should I say conquest, this summer. But now, Hayden was a little lost. "What are you going to do?"

"I don't know yet. But I feel like a fool."

I shook my head. "My advice? It's worth it. Every one of those feelings is worth it if she's the one. Don't give up."

CHAPTER
Twenty-Nine

Alexa

We made it through the night. After Teagan woke the first time, she fell back to sleep and didn't wake again. I slept for a bit in Drake's lap, but other than that, it was hit or miss. At the moment, I was sitting with Teagan while Hollis caught a couple of hours of sleep. Everyone was dragging that morning.

Amie had delivered freshly baked cinnamon rolls about an hour before. I'd put one on a plate, and I was going to see if I could get Teagan to eat. That day would be the day she'd have to choose—life or death. The choice was in her hands. But if she chose to continue using, I would be forced to cut all ties with her, personally. It was a boundary that had to be set.

In her sleep, she seemed a bit more agitated, which was to be expected the longer she went without the high she got from heroin. The methadone dose was still high, but not enough to fool her body into thinking it was getting the dose of drugs it was used to.

Teagan's eyes fluttered open, and I sent Drake and Hollis a text.

Me: *She's awake.*

Drake: *Outside the door if you need me.*

Hollis: *On my way.*

I'd asked for some time to talk to Teagan by myself that morning. They agreed on one condition—that they stay right outside the door. Hopefully, we could keep things calm.

As she grew more alert, her eyes searched the room.

"Hey there. Amie brought some cinnamon rolls. Do you want to try and eat something?"

Teagan stiffly nodded, and I laid the plate on the table and rolled it up to the bed. She was in desperate need of a bath. Her dark hair was matted and plastered to the side of her face.

"Mind if I sit with you?"

"No." Her tone was bordering on unfriendly. She haphazardly picked at the roll, but after two bites, she pushed it aside.

I sat next to the chair and tried to relax. This was my first time doing anything like this. *What if I mess up?* Thankfully, Hollis had walked me through the basics.

Cautiously, I continued. "You gave us quite a scare. How are you feeling?"

I was met with only silence.

This wasn't going well. "Can I get you anything?"

She snorted. "No."

I let out a long breath. *Here goes nothing.* "I don't know if you remember, but Dr. Fritz has offered to send you to a detox program. All expenses paid."

"He's a good guy." She wiped her nose with her forearm.

"Yes, he is. Last night you mentioned something about a boyfriend."

She paused and shifted a little as if she were uncomfortable. "He... uh... yeah. Where's Donnie?"

There was a knock at the door, and Hollis stepped inside. "The police are here to interview Teagan since she's awake. I've told them she needed to finish her breakfast first."

"Thanks."

Teagan took my hand. Her skin loosely hung on her bony frame, and she looked like a shadow of her former self. "I think I want to try and get clean."

This was good news. Very good news. I took her hand. "I'll be here to help every step of the way. Do we need to tell your boyfriend?"

She shook her head, her answer quick. Too quick. "No."

"I think your boyfriend would want to know you're okay."

Again, she shook her head. "Sam wouldn't like that. Not at all."

After a moment, it was obvious Teagan hadn't realized she'd given me a name. "Do you want me to call him so he knows where you are?"

"I'll text him later. He saved his phone number into my phone."

I tried one more tactic. "Do you remember the number? I could call him."

"No."

Okay. We were back to cold. The mood swings were normal. But I wanted to help her.

Hollis knocked on the door again. "Teagan, are you ready?"

Her eyes flew to Hollis. "Can I talk to you? Alone?"

"Yes."

I knew this was going to be hard, but I felt like Teagan wasn't a hundred percent in. I left the room. Roy, the older officer from last night, was outside with Skagway's other cop, Travis. They'd been partners for about seven years. Roy was older, about my dad's age, but Travis and Drake had graduated together. After Drake asked me out on my first date, Travis continued to run into me more than usual and strike up a conversation. It had pissed Drake off—he'd thought his intentions were more than friendly. And as it turned out, Drake had been right. After we'd been dating for a month, Travis asked me out. It had been a mess because Drake had overheard him.

"Hey, Alexa. Good to see you." Travis tipped his hat to me.

I kept it friendly. "Good to see you, too. How have you been?"

"Great. Better now that you're back."

Oh geez. I was too tired to deal with him. He gave me one of those smiles I'm sure made some women all gooey. *Not me.* I saw Drake stiffen behind him. When Drake had gone a bit caveman on Travis when we were younger, I'd gotten irritated. I could handle myself. If he had a problem trusting me, that was another issue. This time, Drake backed off and let me handle it.

Travis touched my arm. "How about we get a beer and catch up?"

"I'll let Drake know. The three of us would have a good time chatting, I'm sure."

195

I motioned to Drake to come stand beside me. He had quite the smirk on his face. "Hey, Travis. Sorry I didn't say hello earlier. We've been a little on edge with the Teagan situation."

Travis's brows pinched together. There had always been something off between Travis and Drake. I think it had something to do with a pool tournament in high school. *Stupid.* Ever since then, Travis hadn't been friendly to Drake.

"It's been awhile."

"Yes, it has." Then he paused. "How is she?" he asked softly, and I remembered that he dated Teagan in junior high. It seemed like he'd really liked her. Then one day, out of the blue, she broke up with him. Honestly, I think it was because he treated her well—like a boyfriend should.

Hollis stepped into the hall. "She requested to do the interview alone." He turned to the officers. "You guys can go in. Remember what we discussed."

They nodded and walked inside. The door closing felt like a death sentence. "Is that a good idea?"

Shaking his head, Hollis ran his fingers through his hair. Hollis had done some of his residency in the drug detox unit and had seen this all before. "Probably not. But she can technically leave here at any moment, so if you push her too hard, she'll run. And I can't keep the cops from questioning her."

"Do you think she's serious about considering the facility or just telling me what I want to hear?"

"I don't know. Let me get the paperwork ready in case she is serious."

I was exhausted. Thankfully, Drake put his arm around me. "After all this time, I finally understand why you never cut ties with Teagan."

Curious, I looked at him to continue.

"It's the same reason you built this clinic. You'd save the world if given the chance."

I smiled. "I would. Everyone needs someone fighting for them. The way I have you."

"And you always will." Drake kissed my forehead, and I leaned into him, grateful for his strength.

I could hear voices talking in the room, but I couldn't make anything out. Ten minutes passed, and one of the cops shouted Teagan's name. It sounded like Roy. Hollis and I looked at each other and bolted for the door. Any remaining sleepiness dissipated immediately.

"What's going on?" Hollis asked.

Both cops were knocking at the bathroom door.

"We began to ask her questions, and she said she needed to use the restroom. The door's locked, and she's been in there about ten minutes."

Hollis grabbed his key and unlocked it. "Teagan, I'm coming in."

He disappeared into the room but came back quickly. "She's gone. Out through the window. What did you say to her?"

Already heading to the door, Travis yelled, "Nothing. We never asked our first question. Stay here in case she comes back."

My heart sank. She'd been playing me all along.

Sometimes people didn't want to be saved.

CHAPTER
Thirty

Alexa

It had been a week since Teagan disappeared. Part of me worried about her, knowing she was one high away from death. Deep in my heart, I believed no one should be left behind. Everyone deserved a chance to be saved. Yet I couldn't save someone I'd considered a friend. For as long as I'd known her, I'd only had her best interests at heart. Yet... she chose to stay ill.

For the rest of the week, I'd been in a funk. I felt like a failure. But I knew I had to keep moving forward and focus on what I could do to help other people. At the end of the day, Teagan had to want to save herself first.

I imagined she was most likely somewhere dead or close to it. Her vitals had been poor. There was no way her body could take much more.

Yet I kept hoping.

As each day passed, a little more hope faded away.

Teagan hadn't been back to her apartment. No one had seen her. After the cops had cleared the area, Kane had come to the clinic and had been able to track her to a road on the other side of the woods. There he found a second set of tracks. It wasn't far—maybe a ten-minute walk at an easy pace. From there, the trail disappeared. It was likely the mysterious Sam had met her there.

But how did she know he'd be there?

I blew out a deep breath as I sat in my car outside the community center, unhappy about being there at all. I wasn't in the mood to socialize. But, I needed to be since Drake was on the city council. More people walked toward the balloon arch. Colored spotlights faced toward the building, nearly transforming our plain, white meeting hall.

Tonight was the local Fall Festival. It was a celebration of the end of the tourist season. Normally, I loved the event. The townspeople came together to enjoy an evening of socializing before the harsh winter set in. After this, everyone would be consumed with preparations before the temperature turned frigid.

But this year, Raquel had taken over. Normally, it was a simple town event. I had a feeling it wasn't going to be simple this year.

I got out of my car and walked to the entrance, smoothing the skirt of my simple black dress. The attire had said *formal*, but I couldn't imagine anyone showing up in a tux or a ball gown. That wasn't our town's culture.

A couple of times that week, I'd called Raquel to talk to her about her selling her land to Milano Incorporated. Each time, my call was sent to voicemail. On Tuesday, I invited Mom to lunch. When I was already at the restaurant, she'd sent me a text saying she couldn't come. Every subsequent text I sent went unanswered. It was like I was a stranger to my own family. An outsider to my own mother. At times, I felt like I had no parents left. When my dad had died, I lost everything.

It hurt.

A lot.

But I kept moving forward. I had no choice.

When I was halfway to the door, my phone vibrated.

Drake: *Last-minute meeting ran late. I'll be there in thirty. Need to stop by the Red Onion. It's been a hell of a day with this Fall Festival.*

Me: *I'll see you there. Love you.*

Drake: *Love you, too, Lex.*

Maybe we'd be able to leave the festival early. Hollis planned to meet me there after he finished installing his new coffee machine that arrived that day. The Starbucks was going to miss him. Or not. I imagined he would probably keep going to retain his gold status.

I waved hello to the Twiner sisters, who stood near the door and spoke into a recorder. They normally described what people wore and what they did. Then they sent out the Twiner newsletter, which made it sound like we held some sort of huge gala with celebrities, when in reality it was just a laid-back, hometown event.

Devney joined me on the sidewalk. I said, "Hey there. How are you doing?"

"Okay."

But she didn't look okay. I touched her elbow. "What's

going on?"

We stepped into the foyer inside the main doors. The weight of the world seemed to be resting on her shoulders, but she looked adorable in her flowery dress. "It's my mom. I just found out she has cancer. I'm going to get a second job to help with the medical expenses. She's going to move in with my brother, who'll take her to her appointments at the Mayo Clinic. He's helping significantly, but I want to, as well."

Devney and I weren't close, but it was obvious she needed someone to talk to. "Oh, Devney, I'm so sorry. Where have you applied?"

"Just about everywhere I could think of. But tourist season is over, so there aren't many jobs left. I thought coming here tonight would be a good idea, but now that I'm here, I think I need to go home." Her shoulders sagged with the weight of her troubles.

An idea hit me. "Would you consider being a receptionist at the clinic? The job isn't listed yet, but Hollis and I decided we needed help."

She grabbed my shoulders as her eyes lit up. "Are you serious? But I couldn't get there until noon. My classes at the high school end at 11:30. But I could move my music lessons to the evening." Devney was a part-time teacher at the school. Due to our low population, a full-time music teacher wasn't a necessity.

"Noon works great. The clinic is closed tomorrow for Labor Day, so when do you think you could start?"

Devney pulled out her phone, tucking her dark hair behind her ear with her free hand. "Do you think I could have a few days to get my music lessons rearranged? I might need this week if it's not too much to ask."

"Of course."

"I'll stop by Wednesday to get all the paperwork done, if that's okay. My schedule is light on Wednesdays."

"Perfect."

Devney hugged me. "Thank you, Alexa. Thank you." She walked back toward the door. "I'm going home. I thought I could do this tonight, but I'm not feeling up to it. I cannot thank you enough."

"I'm glad it worked out."

Before we could discuss pay, she was out the door. I couldn't imagine what she was going through. Oh, my heart hurt for her. I had to remember to tell Hollis later. That was going to be an adventure all by itself. Maybe I could get him to believe the lovebug had migrated further north than Florida.

I paused as I stepped inside the community center. Things were more over the top than I'd expected. The normal wood walls were draped with shimmery fabrics. Silver and black balls were strung up to the ceiling. A full string quartet played soft music from the stage. They'd had to be brought in from either Juneau or Anchorage.

This was not the Fall Festival. *Far from it.*

Ol' Man Rooster sat at a table off to one side, looking a little lost. Behind him was a three-tiered champagne fountain. He wore a suit jacket over his coveralls. He looked relieved when he saw me and waved me to come over. It was going to be interesting to get his take on this circus.

Raquel had gone so far overboard.

"Hey, Rooster. How are you?"

He grunted. "Starving."

His affronted tone had me chuckling. "Want me to get you some food?"

"Ain't no way I'm eating stuff I can't pronounce."

I looked around the room and located the food table. Some of it, from what I could see, was barely recognizable.

He huffed. "Is it too much to ask for moose chili and a beer?"

An idea hit me. "I've been meaning to do a welcome to Skagway party for Dr. Fritz. I'll ask the quilting circle to provide the chili, and I may have a connection for the beer." I gave a wink.

He stood and hugged me. "If you were a little older, I'd take you from Drake and marry you."

"I'd be careful saying that too loud. I met the other end of his fist once. And let me tell you, it's not something I want to be reacquainted with."

I turned to see Hollis dressed in slacks and a dress shirt. He held out his hand to greet Ol' Man Rooster.

Normally, Ol' Man Rooster was a little abrasive with new people in town. He wasn't a fan of change. So, I braced myself for what he'd say. "Where's your penguin suit?"

Hollis shrugged. "Never was a fan. It's one of the reasons I came here. Alexa assured me I would never have to wear one."

A slow, approving smile appeared on his face. "You might be an okay city slicker. I wasn't so sure when I saw you going into that fancy-schmancy coffee shop. I thought you might be one of *those* guys." Rooster nodded toward the front of the room where there were two men in tuxes. *Must be Chazz and the brother I've heard about.*

"It makes me a work in progress. Rome wasn't built in a day. I guess making me into an Alaskan is the same thing. Hopefully, you won't hold it against me too much."

Rooster let out a loud, gruff laugh. "Come. I want you to meet my granddaughter."

Hollis's eyes widened, and he looked to me for help. I gave a sweet smile and patted his shoulder. "Have fun. I'm going to take a close look at the food table."

"That stuff ain't natural, Alexa. Green and orange eggs." He shuddered. "Eggs are supposed to be white and yellow."

"I won't try the eggs. Promise." The thought of green and orange eggs wasn't appealing.

As they walked away, Hollis turned and looked back at me. I waved my fingers at him. This was payback for the week he'd been grumpy, almost insufferable, to me. As I made my way to the food table, I said hello to other locals. Everyone looked miserable. Everyone except Raquel, who stood at the front of the room, oblivious to the total flop.

Amie and Ike spotted me. "You look beautiful, Alexa. Where's Drake?" she asked.

"Thank you. You do, too." Her dark green dress made her eyes sparkle and flattered her blonde hair. "Drake texted me a little while ago. The city council meeting ran late, and he needed to run by the Red Onion first."

Ike was in jeans and a button-up shirt. It made me chuckle that the people refused to conform to Raquel's rules. Amie patted my shoulder. "This is definitely a change from the normal."

"Yeah. Ol' Man Rooster is fit to be tied. He's missing the moose chili. I thought maybe I could see if the quilting circle would make it for Hollis's welcome party at the Red Onion."

"Consider it done. I'll see if the church wants to do desserts."

"Perfect." The church usually did the desserts for the Fall

Festival. Hollis would be a hero— the town would be getting their normal Fall Festival food at *his* party.

Amie took out her phone. "When were you thinking? I have to make a note, or I'll forget to ask everyone."

I stopped to think about it. "Well, with the weather, we probably should do it soon. How does next Friday sound?"

Amie bumped my shoulder. "Good thinking. With this flop for the Fall Festival, Hollis will be the town hero."

"I was thinking the same thing."

Beside Amie, Ike grumbled, "I'm starving, and all this talk of moose chili is only making it worse." This event was far worse than I imagined it would be with Raquel in charge. I knew I was counting down the minutes until I could leave.

CHAPTER
Thirty-One

Alexa

The party dragged on. Seconds felt like minutes. From across the room, Jim Hathaway motioned to Ike. He was the owner of the logging company, and for years, he'd been my dad's boss. When he spotted me, he didn't wait for Ike to come to him. I felt a little uncomfortable. I'd always liked Jim, but it was his machine that had killed my dad. I pushed those thoughts aside as he approached me. "Alexa, it's good to see you."

It's not his fault.

I kept a smile on my face. "You, too, Jim."

"I know this is probably an inappropriate time, but I still have your dad's stuff. Your mother never answered me about picking it up."

His words were another knife in my chest. *Did my mom love my dad at all?* I wasn't sure anymore. Mom had gotten pregnant with Raquel, and they'd gotten married a few months

206

later. As time went on, it seemed they stayed together more out of obligation than love. My throat grew a little thick. "Yes, I'd love to get whatever you have of Dad's. When would be a good time?"

"I'll drop it off at the clinic next week when I come in."

"Perfect."

As Ike and Jim started talking deliveries, I excused myself and headed to the food table. My curiosity was piqued. When I arrived at the table, I wasn't sure if I should laugh or gag at the offerings there. As Ol' Man Rooster had said, there were tiny orange and green eggs arranged around some sort of foul-smelling brown stuff. *Is this stuff edible?* There was nothing recognizable on the table.

"You could at least look like you're enjoying yourself," my sister hissed in my ear, bringing me up short.

Putting on a pleasant smile, I turned to face her. "I was trying to figure out what the brown stuff was and why the eggs aren't the right color." It was childish, but I knew the comment would piss her off.

She smoothed her dark hair with a roll of her eyes. "It's paté with fish eggs as a garnish."

Yuck. That sounded disgusting. Ol' Man Rooster was right; moose chili sounded good about now. My stomach rumbled, but I'd wait until later.

The two men in tuxedos stood behind Raquel, both similar in features and handsome. Their blue eyes stood out prominently against the dark hair.

The one to the right extended his hand. "I'm Chazz Hennington, and this is my brother Dixon."

So this was my brother-in-law. It was an awkward introduction for someone who was supposed to be family. "Nice to meet you both." Stiffly, I stood there for a moment before I realized they were waiting for me to introduce myself. "I'm Alexa, Raquel's sister. Well, I guess I'm your sister-in-law. It's nice to finally meet you."

"You, as well. Raquel, darling, let's take our seats. I don't want you standing in your delicate condition."

Raquel and Chazz had begun to walk away by the time the words hit me. I grabbed her elbow. "Oh my gosh. Raquel, are you?"

Am I going to be an aunt?

For a second, I forgot our precarious relationship. However, my mom came up to Raquel and grabbed her hand, her eyes shooting daggers at me. "Come along, sweetheart. Let's get you seated."

"Hey, Mom."

"Alexa." Her eyes flicked down my dress, her frown disapproving. Next to Raquel's sparkling, beaded dress, I looked like a homeless person. "Come, darling. Let's get you some water and enjoy your party."

Her party?

They walked off without another glance my way. I knew I should be used to this, but I wasn't. I could become an aunt, but I might never know my niece or nephew. I wanted to have a loving family so badly.

"So, I take it you're not a paté fan?"

I turned to see Chazz's brother. He'd definitely dressed the part in his penguin suit.

Extending my hand, I remembered my manners. "Dixon, right?"

"Nice to meet you, Alexa." Conspiringly, he leaned in closer. "Between you and me, if you haven't tried the paté, don't. It's positively one of the most wretched things. And from the looks of things, the town agrees."

I chuckled. "The smell alone made up my mind for me. We're more of a crab, shrimp, and moose chili kind of town."

"I had the chili for the first time this last week. It's good. I can see why it's high up on the list."

One of the waiters came by with glasses of champagne on a tray. I took one, grateful for the temporary distraction while I got my emotions under control. After a moment, I asked, "How long are you in town for? I think I remember seeing your name in the newsletter."

"Word travels fast in a small town. I'm planning on going back to California in another two weeks. Our annual business dealings will be done by then, and I'll be ready to get back home. The hotel is nice, but I'm ready for a home-cooked meal. Or a well-cooked meal from my housekeeper, Mrs. O'Neal."

Dixon didn't seem like the type of guy who could do laundry or cook. But as I'd learned with Hollis, appearances could be deceiving. Well, Hollis could do neither, but he wasn't a stuck-up snob. "Maybe you should stay with Raquel some. She's actually a really good baker."

He took a sip of his champagne and let out a sigh. "Been there, done that, got the T-shirt. It was best to leave, if you get my drift."

"Oh, I do."

We laughed, and it was nice to let the earlier encounter with my family go. Dixon picked up one of the crackers with some sort of concoction on top and popped it in his mouth. "So, I hear you came back to open a clinic. Brought your friend from New York."

"I did. I'll have to introduce you to Hollis." I glanced around the room. He was still with Ol' Man Rooster, but they were now joined by four of Skagway's single ladies. Poor, poor Hollis. He was like fresh meat, which would be good for him. And I wasn't done paying him back yet. "He looks a little preoccupied. Maybe later."

Dixon laughed. It was deep and pleasant. "I kind of pity him right now. Samone and Jane cornered me earlier. They are quite... forward."

Yeah, they're "friendly" with the tourists.

"It'll make him tougher."

"Cheers to that." We clinked our glasses together.

Right then, I sensed Drake before I felt him. Little tingles raced across my skin in anticipation of his touch after being away from him for a while.

"Hey, Lex. Sorry I'm late."

He kissed my cheek, and I melted into his side. He was wearing jeans and a nice button-up shirt. Extending his hand, he said, "Dixon. Good to see you again. How'd the hunt with Kane go?"

So, they'd met. And he'd been hunting with Kane. That was good to know. From Drake's demeanor, he seemed to like Dixon. I imagined he'd already had him checked out.

"Fantastic. That brother of yours can track anything through the woods. We found what we were looking for each day. Most amazing guided hunt I've had."

Before Drake could respond, Chazz's voice filled the room through the sound system. "Good evening, everyone. If you would like to find your seats, we'll begin serving dinner in about fifteen minutes."

"That's my cue. I better join my brother. I think we're

having quail eggs with Haggis."

This was the oddest menu ever. It was as if Raquel had found the most unappealing sounding foods and served them in one evening. "It was nice meeting you, Dixon. I'm sure I'll see you around but enjoy your stay if I don't."

"Thank you." Leaning in, he whispered, "I don't think she's pregnant. It had something to do with vocal cords."

My shoulders relaxed. Of course I wanted Raquel to have children, if that was what she wanted, but knowing she wasn't pregnant helped ease the ostracism I felt. "Yes, the vocal cords have always been a concern for Raquel—and Mom. If you haven't heard, she's going to be famous once an agent comes this way and discovers her talents."

"I bet." With that he shook Drake's hand and headed to his table. Once, I'd asked why we didn't go to LA. Mom responded with, *"Only the people willing to go the extra mile will be worth Raquel's time."* I had given up trying to make sense of their reasoning.

Drake and I made our way to the back of the room. "What was that about?"

I shook my head. "Normal head games from Mom and Raquel. She said something about Raquel's 'delicate position,' and I thought she was pregnant. Dixon doesn't think she is."

He sighed, running his hands through his hair. "Well, it looks like the party is a hit."

The room had already begun to empty as people walked out before dinner was even served. I couldn't help but laugh. Everyone looked miserable. "What was she thinking?"

He sighed. "It's been a mess. Last week, she told one of the guys on the board she was changing the menu. He forgot to mention it because, honestly, who would have thought it would be to this shit. He thought she meant changing up a pie or cake. The townspeople aren't thrilled, to say the least. Since the festival started, we've received several complaints, which was why the city council had a quick meeting. This is going to turn into a shit storm. The people of Skagway look forward to the Fall Festival."

"Well, good news. We're going to have the quilting circle make moose chili and the church will do the desserts for Hollis's welcome party. I was hoping we could use the Red Onion next Friday."

"Done. You just made our lives a hell of a lot easier." He gave me a kiss. "I knew there was a reason I loved you."

Hollis walked in front of us and ducked. "I think my ass has been pinched twice by either Jane or Samone. I can't keep them straight. Ol' Man Rooster promised his granddaughter a date with me. The Twiner sisters want to do some sort of auction, which included the word *bachelor*. Alexa, you have to help me."

I tapped my chin. "I'll think about it."

"You have to. I'm serious. Payback is over."

Drake chuckled. "Good luck."

Hollis threw his head back and groaned. "Paybacks are a bitch. Even in Alaska." Then he looked at me. "By the way, is *surströmming* Alaskan? I can't believe I saw it on one of the *hors d'oeuvres* trays."

My stomach was turning as the smells of the different foods blended together. "I'm afraid to ask what that is."

"I'll take that as a no." Hayden dramatically wiped his brow. "I might have to leave Alaska if it was."

"What is it?" I asked.

"Fermented Baltic herring."

Fermented and *herring* did not sound like a good combination. The bile rose in my throat. "I think I just threw up in my mouth. When in the world did you try that? I might have to defriend you."

Hollis's face pinched up. "Some party I attended with my family in New York. It wasn't a... pleasant experience."

"No wonder you came to Alaska."

"The *surströmming* sent me right over the edge."

We smiled. Having Hollis here was such a gift. He was a true friend.

The community center grew even more empty. "Want to leave, baby?"

For a second, I almost objected, wanting to support my family, but then I remembered how badly Raquel and Mom had treated me. *What's the point of putting myself through that?* There was none.

"Let's go. Hollis, want to join us for dinner?"

"Absolutely. I'm not staying here by myself."

As we made our escape, I saw Ike and Amie getting in their truck at the same time Drake's phone buzzed. He read the text. "Mom and Dad just invited us to dinner. Hollis, too. She's cooking burgers."

"Sounds great." I slapped Hollis's shoulder. "Hollis, we can talk about how we're going to get you out of that date with Ol' Man Rooster's granddaughter."

"Wait. What about the auction?"

"You're on your own for that."

CHAPTER
Thirty-Two

Alexa

The next morning, I spent some quality time lounging on the couch. There was a chill in the air, and Drake had started a fire. I pulled the blanket in closer around me, soaking in this moment of utter perfection. Life was good… more than good, to be honest.

"I poured you a cup of coffee." Drake's deep voice drew my attention away from the crackling fire. I took a deep breath and was greeted with the aroma of fresh coffee. Drake was oh-so-delicious in jeans with no shirt.

"You are the best boyfriend ever." I reached out with gimme hands. He paused before handing me the cup. "What?" I asked.

"Nothing. I just like having you here with me."

That was a little odd. Not to say that the past wasn't still fresh in our minds, but he normally never brought it up.

I took a sip. "I love it, too. This place is more perfect than

I ever could have imagined."

"It is." He motioned for me to lean forward, and then he settled in behind me. I lay back against his chest. The fire crackled, and the wind blew the leaves outside. It was a moment in time I wanted to freeze and keep forever. "This is a perfect Saturday morning. What time do you have to leave?"

At dinner last night, Reeser had called Drake and asked if he could come to Juneau. At the last minute, Reeser had been invited to a business dinner with some influential Alaskan business leaders. Somehow Drake's name had come up, and they'd asked Reeser to see if he could join them. It was an opportunity Drake couldn't pass up. They were discussing the possibility of getting a group of business owners together to promote Alaskan-owned-and-operated businesses. Alaskans weren't typically fans of chains that took customers away from our locally owned businesses. We stuck together by keeping as much locally owned as possible.

He checked the clock. "In a couple of hours. Hayden's going to fly me there and then come back. One of the guys joining us, Rick, will drop me off on his way to Anchorage."

"I'm going to miss you."

He kissed my neck. "I'm going to miss you, too. Are you going to stay out here tonight or head into town?"

I'd given that some thought. I found the quiet isolation comforting. "Here. I'm going to soak in our huge tub and eat ice cream. Maybe read."

"I'm jealous of the tub." His hand crept up my thigh, and my lower stomach clenched in anticipation.

I set my coffee cup down and turned around to straddle his lap. The blanket was discarded behind me. "Well, I feel like I may need a bath now. I'm suddenly feeling dirty. Very,

very dirty."

In a flash, Drake stood and held me to his chest, his arms under my legs. My mouth found his as he walked us back to the bathroom. "I'm going to make sure you're squeaky clean before I leave."

His words held promise of what was to come.

"I'm going to miss you so much."

A light wind blew as Drake held me in his arms in the circle drive next to his truck. I pulled my jacket more tightly around me.

"Me, too, baby." His nose grazed mine. "Why don't we go away somewhere next weekend? After Hollis's welcome party. Just the two of us."

"I'd like that a lot."

Another truck pulled into the driveway. I recognized Jim and waved. It was wrong, I knew, but I dreaded seeing him. Seeing him reminded me of the loss of my dad.

With a white cardboard box in his hands, Jim got out of the truck. "Afternoon. I was in the area and thought I'd drop off your dad's stuff. I hope it's okay. I thought it might be easier."

My chest tightened as I took the box, knowing this was Dad's. "Thanks, I appreciate it. It is easier. Thanks for thinking of me."

Jim was a good man. He took a few steps back, probably knowing this was hard for me. "I hate to cut this short, but I'm meeting Ike for lunch."

Nodding, Drake responded, "Dad mentioned that last

night. Have a good one."

"Tell Mallory we said hello," I added. His wife was sweet.

"Will do."

As fast as he'd come in, he left. I was relieved. Maybe next time it wouldn't be so hard. I realized I'd forgotten to tell Drake about my conversation with Jim from the night before. "This is dad's stuff. Apparently, Mom never picked it up."

From his locked jaw, I knew Drake was refraining from saying anything. "You okay?"

"I will be. Promise. If I need company, I'll call Hollis or your mom. Maybe try to stir up some trouble."

I could tell Drake didn't want to leave, but he needed to go. And he knew this. I set the box down and stood on my tip-toes to give him a kiss. "Call me when you get to Juneau. Love you."

"Love you, too."

His phone vibrated, and he winced as he looked at it. "Hayden's threatening to leave without me."

"Go. I promise I'll be fine. You'll be back tomorrow afternoon. We'll hang out before you meet the guys at the bar."

I sensed he was ready to cancel his meeting. But it was important that we continued moving forward with our lives. I wanted to avoid being stagnant. That was how I'd lived for the last two years. It was something I needed to work on. "No canceling, Drake Foster."

"You win." Drake gave me another kiss. "Next weekend, you're mine."

"Absolutely."

He kissed me again. Hard. Then he gave me the gorgeous smile that made me weak at the knees, and he made his way to the truck.

Drake rolled down his window and waved as he pulled out of the driveway. My heart was full. I saw his brake lights, and not two seconds later, I received a text.

Drake: *Miss you. Love you, baby.*

Me: *Miss you, too. Love you lots. Be careful.*

At that, I headed back inside with the box and placed it on the table before closing the door and leaning against it. *What's in there?* It was full of Dad's things. Probably some of the last things he'd ever touched. All in all, there wasn't much of his stuff left other than the few things I'd taken after the funeral and the furniture Drake had managed to save. It felt like I was given a treasure, and a part of me wanted to open it immediately while the other part thought I should savor it—wait for a special time to reveal what was inside.

I stared at the box, unsure.

I grabbed my phone and looked at the time. By now, Drake should be at the airfield.

Me: *Do you think I should wait to open the box?*

Drake: *I think you need to do what you think is best for you.*

Staring at the phone, I wondered what to think about it all. Seconds later, another text came through.

Drake: *You don't have to come up with the answer right now. You'll know when it's time.*

Me: *You're right. I'm going to go soak in the tub.*

Drake: *You're making me hard thinking about how you slid on my cock earlier in the water.*

Me: *Maybe I'll find my vibrator. It's water safe.*

Drake: *Fuck.*

Me: *Yes, that's what I'll be doing to myself.*

Drake: *Baby, when I get done with dinner tonight, I'm calling.*

Me: *Oh, I like the sound of that. I'll be waiting.*

And just like that, Drake helped clear the stormy seas in my mind. He was my other half. I wanted to be Drake's in every way, including his wife. But for now, I left the box on the table and headed back to the bathroom to relax in the tub.

Several hours later, I was back in the living room, sipping a glass of red wine on the couch in front of the fireplace. The box called to me like a beacon. *What is in there?* Unable to stand it a moment longer, I brought the box closer to torment myself.

I took another sip of my wine. The sun had set about three hours earlier, which made it pitch black outside. Without Drake in the cabin with me, it felt a little eerie, so I drew the curtains. The only light came from the fire as it crackled in the otherwise quiet space.

I wish Drake was here. He'd made it into Juneau safely. Dinner had led to drinks at a local bar. Normally, I wasn't the clingy type, but everything felt off tonight. And I wanted to talk to him. I knew he'd take my call, but he needed to handle his business. This was an amazing opportunity for him. It occurred to me that not knowing what was in the box may have been the reason I was more on edge.

I kept staring at the white box, telling myself how ridiculous I was. *Thirty minutes.* If I didn't open the box in the next half hour, I was going to bed—it was nearly midnight.

Five minutes passed. Then ten.

My phone dinged with an email, and I checked it, thankful for the distraction. Time had slowed to a near standstill. The email was from Morgan, the loan officer.

Alexa,

I apologize for the delay. It's been a busy week, and I'm trying to catch up.

Per your request, I researched our records for all offers made on your land. In accordance with your instructions, we retained the information but did not pass it along to you. Attached is a list of offers received with the amounts and contact information. To each offer, Ms. Owens declined with no counteroffer.

All the best,

Morgan

The blood drained from my face when I opened the attachment. Milano Incorporated had been offering to buy my land every two months, increasing the price significantly each time. This had to be more than the property was worth.

Out of nowhere, a chill crept over my body.

Who are they? What do they want?

First, they wanted Raquel's land.

Then the Ewings'.

Then they'd wanted mine.

What other land did they want?

Creak.

I shot up on the couch at the sound coming from the front porch. My heart nearly stopped, and I froze, listening.

Creak.

My eyes were fixed on the curtain. *Is that a shadow?* My eyes might have been playing tricks on me, but deep down I knew better. The shadow moved closer to the window, as if someone were peering in. Time stood still, and my breaths became shallower. I lay stock-still until whoever it was backed away. There was definitely someone outside on the porch. My heart was hammering in my chest, and instinct kicked in. Grabbing my phone, I crept toward the study where Drake kept the guns. To survive in Alaska, you had to be comfortable with firearms and know how to keep your wits about you. The same applied for being a nurse. A level head was a necessity.

I thought about the news over the past week. A bear had been seen in town. Maybe it was a bear on our front porch. A bear would make noise. But a bear wouldn't peer in the window. *Would it? And wouldn't it be louder?* My mind raced as I tried to sort it out.

Remain calm.

Think.

Call someone.

Drake was out of town. I needed someone who was close. I dialed Hayden, knowing his place wasn't too far.

On the second ring, he picked up. "Hey there. What are you doing? Ka—"

"I think someone is outside on the porch."

He got serious instantly. "We're on our way. Where are you inside the house?"

Grabbing a gun and ammunition, I loaded the gun. I crept back down the hallway toward our bedroom. I was a complete mess inside, but I kept my breathing normal. Nevertheless, a slight tremor broke through my practiced calmness. "I'm in the hallway on the way to the bedroom. Let me stop and see if I hear anything."

"Ale—"

"Shh."

The revving of Hayden's truck was loud over the phone, so I pulled it away from my ear. Closing my eyes, I focused on listening. The distinct rattle of the front doorknob brought me up short. "Someone is definitely here. They're trying to open the door."

Bears can't open doors.

"Alexa, I'm with Kane. We are less than two minutes away. Keep going to the bedroom and lock yourself in."

There was another exit in the bedroom. I pushed forward though my feet felt like they were stuck in sludge.

Hayden kept talking. He was calm but authoritative. "Stay on the phone with me. If anyone walks through that door, you shoot the motherfucker. Kane is on the phone with Drake."

Drake.

I wish he was here.

I strained my ears to listen for anything, but the whooshing of my heartbeat was louder than anything else. With a shaky hand, I released the safety on the gun and took a deep breath to calm myself. The tremors eased as I remained focused on the task at hand the same way I did when a patient's life was on the line.

Remain calm.

Assess the situation.

React to what happens.

Think about what could happen.

Be prepared.

"We're a minute away." Hayden's voice brought me back from my thoughts. I watched the bedroom door. I was in the corner of the room where I could see the entrance to the bedroom and also the door that led to the private porch.

"I'm still in the bedroom."

A silhouette ran by the window, the footsteps heavy, and my heart raced faster. I raised my gun, prepared to shoot if I needed to. "Whoever it was just ran by the bedroom window."

"We're coming down the driveway. I'm going to come inside, and Kane's going after the son of a bitch. He's going to run by your bedroom. Don't shoot him."

They were almost here, and my voice quavered for the first time. "O—okay."

I had to go through the steps to calm down again before the fear consumed me.

Remain calm.

Assess the situation.

React to what happens.

Think about what could happen.

Be prepared.

I had to stay focused so I didn't make a critical mistake.

Hayden's truck screeched to a stop. There were thunderous steps as Kane ran by, calling. "Grab the scent, Mariah!"

With one bark, they were gone.

Hayden's voice came through the phone. "Alexa, I'm using the key Drake gave me. I'm going to hang up now and call him. When I enter the house, I'm going to let you know."

"Okay."

The door opened, and I heard Hayden call, "I'm in the house. Please don't shoot me. I have too pretty a face."

With a nervous chuckle, I pulled my finger away from the trigger and reengaged the safety.

The bedroom door cracked opened. "Alexa, it's me."

"Back here."

The door opened, and Hayden walked in with his gun drawn but pointed toward the floor. "Drake. She's fine. I've got her."

I raced into Hayden's chest. My breaths became more labored as I began to feel safe.

I'm going to be okay. I'm going to survive.

"Hey, we're here. You're okay."

My body shook as the adrenaline subsided. Someone had tried to break into the house.

The gun was removed from my hand. "Yes, Drake. She's just shaken. I swear. Hold on." He pulled back a little. "Hey, he wants to talk to you."

My hands were trembling as I took the phone. "Drake."

At his name, I couldn't hold back a sob.

"Thank fuck. Baby, are you okay?"

That broke the dam, and I let one sob out before I regained control. "Yes, yes, I'm okay. I'm just... they just..."

"I know, Lex. I know. What happened?"

"I was on the couch reading an email when I heard the creak. Then I saw someone outside. I called Hayden. Got a gun, loaded it, and waited."

I gave more details, recounting what I could remember as Hayden and Drake asked more questions. Everything was beginning to blur. We put Drake on speakerphone while Hayden kept watch and we went back to the living room.

"Lex, will you please stay with my parents tonight? Hayden and Kane are going to stay there, too. Just for tonight until I can get home to you. I'm working on that now."

The last thing I wanted was to stay in the cabin by myself. "Yes. No problem. I'll go."

"Thank you."

"I love you, Drake."

"I love you, too."

I felt calmer. Drake was working on coming home to me.

"Can I talk to Hayden again?" Drake asked.

"Sure."

I handed the phone back. Hayden took the phone off speaker but continued to scan for anything out of the ordinary. "Yes. No problem. Yeah, I'll sleep in my old room. No, he's not back yet. Yeah, when we stopped, Kane ran along the porch, telling Mariah to get the scent, and off they went. I will. Yes. Let me get Alexa to Mom and Dad's first. Yes."

He ended the call. "Where are the keys to your truck?"

I dug through my purse where it sat on the kitchen counter. I'd forgotten to bring it with me earlier when I'd gotten the gun. That was an error, and my heart sank. I should have known better. *If someone had broken in, how would I have gotten out of here?*

"Here they are." I could hear more of a waver in my voice, but I focused on holding it together.

Hayden walked into the kitchen and hid them in the drawer with the silverware. "In case someone comes back, I don't want your keys out in the open. I'll let Kane know where they are. You ready to go to Mom and Dad's?"

"Yes."

I picked up my purse, and Hayden handed me the gun I'd had before. "Stay close. This is just precautionary."

The white box from earlier caught my attention. "I need to take that box. It's my dad's stuff."

If someone came back and they took something from that box, it would be more than I could bear right now. "Engage the safety on your gun and put it in your purse. Put the strap over your shoulder." I swung my head around with a confused look. "This is just precautionary."

That made sense. If someone was out there and we had to run, Hayden wanted me armed. I did as he asked, then grabbed the box. I hoped when I returned, the place wouldn't be tainted. *Will I be scared to be out here alone?* Probably. Which meant I would have to make sure to stay here alone at some point in the future once we figured out what was going on.

The crisp night air hit my face as we walked to Hayden's truck, which was parked not two feet from the porch. Hayden locked the door. "Kane has a key to get in."

The truck ride was quiet as I tried to come to grips with what had happened. *Why did someone try to break in?*

And worse yet... had they known I'd be there alone tonight?

CHAPTER
Thirty-Three

Drake

It was a little after four in the morning when I walked into my parents' house. It felt good to be home. Just being in the same place as Lex calmed me.

Mariah gave a warning growl, signaling to Kane that someone was here.

"It's me, girl," I said.

Immediately, the growling stopped, and Kane flicked on the light. He looked as pissed off as I felt. Someone had tried to break into the house when Lex was there alone. I'd never felt so helpless and enraged in all my life. I wanted nothing more than to go upstairs and wrap Lex in my arms, but I needed to talk to Kane first without anyone else around. On the phone, when he'd gone back to my place, I'd sensed he'd only told me the absolute minimum. Some things needed to be discussed in person.

When I sat, Kane leaned forward. "I think there were two

people there tonight. I think the person at the house tried to get in the back door first and then circled around to the front. Alexa said all the lights were off because she was in front of the fire, but her truck was parked plain as day in your driveway. They fucking knew she was there."

My blood ran cold. "Why do you think there were two?"

"There was a pile of cigarette butts where the asshole took off. Someone was waiting."

An inferno ignited within me. Someone had fucked with my girl. Which meant they had fucked with me. I cracked my knuckles and gritted my teeth.

Kane continued, "I wasn't fast enough. It was dark, and they had about ninety seconds on me. As I got to the road, they were pulling away in a van. The license plate light was out. They could have been planning to take Alexa. I'm not sure. But I can't imagine a van would be their first choice as an escape vehicle without a valid reason."

"Fuck." *Kidnapping*? My heart was gripped by a fear I kept hidden. "Anything else?"

"I'm going to go back tomorrow, scope the rest of the place out. No way that was their first time at your place."

"Why?"

He scoffed. "Dark. New place. No way they would get to their vehicle that easily. No way. Mariah was on their trail. We never got lost."

Double shit. That meant they'd been out to my place who knows how many times before. Over the last week, Lex had often beat me home. If they'd gotten to her... I had to stop those thoughts. They hadn't. She was safe.

"What does Lex know?" I asked.

"That I couldn't get to them in time before the person

made it to the vehicle. I'll let you decide what you want her to know. But my advice? Less is more."

We don't keep secrets from each other.

Kane reacted to my silence. "Drake, someone wanted something from her. Who the hell knows what. I think they've been watching your place for a while. Does she really need to know that? She's tough, but come on, knowing someone wants to kidnap you could do a number on anyone."

He had a point. "You're probably right. But I won't lie to her."

"She may not want to know the whys and hows. Let her guide you on what you say."

I stared at Kane, wondering who he was. This wasn't his normal *modus operandi.*

"Listen, I can imagine how pissed off you are. She's like a sister to me, and I'm ready to tear the bastard apart. But we have to be smart about this."

That was definitely true. "I agree. Less is more. But if she asks, I'll let her know."

"I wouldn't lie to my girl either—if I had one."

That was the first time Kane had ever alluded to even having a girl, but I was too tired and stressed to give him shit. I rolled my neck and said, "Lex called Hollis. He said nothing happened at the clinic. If someone were looking for drugs, that's where I think they would start."

I sat back in my chair now that the heavy part was out of the way.

Kane responded, "Yeah, I agree. They weren't after the drugs."

Which meant they wanted something else. For a moment, the ticking of the grandfather clock was the only sound in the room.

Kane asked, "Do you know why someone would want her?"

"The only connection is the land. It's all I can think of."

After she'd gotten settled, she told me about the offers on the land the bank had received from Milano Incorporated. And Dad had an update on Lloyd's accident. He'd called me when I landed in Juneau and asked if I could swing by the house and chat when I got back. That wasn't good. Fuck, details were stacking up against us.

"My guess is mineral rights," Kane said.

That had been my thought, as well. "Oil. And Lex's family still has the rights. I imagine Ewing's does, too."

"I bet Ol' Man Calgary has received an offer, too. His land is on the south end of Alexa's."

"If that's true, then they're putting together a puzzle. Raquel's piece gets them access to the water. If they piece enough together, they could have a straight shot from inland to the ocean. There would be no stopping them."

"We'd be surrounded by logging and oil fields. Literally surrounded. They're obviously becoming impatient."

For now, I needed to get to Lex and hold her in my arms while I thought about it all. "I'm going to head to bed. Thanks for all you did. I appreciate it."

Shaking hands, Kane said, "Night, dickhead."

"Night, asswipe."

Some things never changed.

After talking more, we decided to not get the police involved. *What could they do?* They'd found no clues since Teagan had disappeared. Sometimes it was best to keep the cards close to the vest until there was some sort of proof. So far there were no leads, only conjunctures.

At the bottom of the stairs, I slipped off my boots before heading up to my room. The last thing I wanted to do was wake the whole house. For the next couple of hours, I just wanted to hold Lex in my arms.

I opened the door and saw her on the bed, her hair spreading out on the pillow with the light of the bathroom casting a glow that made her look like an angel.

Quietly, I shut the door and just watched her. She was my entire world. Everything I'd ever wanted, and I could have lost her that night. I touched the ring box burning a hole in my pocket. I wanted to ask her now, but somehow, I needed to make it special.

I slipped off my shirt and took off my pants, leaving the ring in the pocket, before I scooted into bed. Lex shifted closer to me and draped her arm over my chest.

"Hey, baby."

Sleepily she raised her head. "Drake. You're here." Before I could respond, she buried her face in my chest and clung to me. "You're here."

"I am."

"How?"

I hated how scared her voice sounded. This had shaken her to the core. But she was a survivor and wouldn't want me to make her feel helpless. "Rick Stocks. When he heard what happened, he offered to get me home tonight instead of tomorrow."

She snuggled closer to me. "I'm so glad you're here."

"Me, too. How are you doing?"

"Okay. Better. At least I'm not one of those girls in scary movies who loses her mind and just runs outside."

I gave a small chuckle. "You're one hell of a tough woman."

She yawned. She had to be tired. "Let's try to get some sleep."

Snuggling in closer, I let exhaustion claim me.

CHAPTER
Thirty-Four

Drake

I woke and grabbed for Lex, but she was gone. I jerked upright, on alert, but then relaxed. We were at my parents' house. Everything was okay. I rubbed my eyes. Man, I was wiped. *What time is it?* It took a few seconds for the red numbers on the clock to become clear. Shit, it was after ten in the morning. I grabbed my phone and checked my messages. Only the normal—city council notes, statements, and some additional applications for the position I posted two days ago. Being gone from the bar so much lately made me realize it was time to get Crete some help.

I threw some clothes on and headed downstairs to look for Lex. After what happened the previous night, I needed to see how my girl was doing. At the bottom of the stairs, I heard laughter in the living room. That was a good sign, which helped me relax some.

At the doorway, I watched the two most important women in my life smiling as they talked.

I leaned against the doorframe, unnoticed. Well, maybe Lex sensed me; her mouth twitched a little and her smile grew.

Mom asked, "So tell me how you're doing. Not how you want people to think you're doing."

"I was shaken last night. But when Drake came home and held me, it eased my fears a lot." She sighed. "I know that sounds archaic, but just his touch calms and centers me."

As I listened to her, I knew she would be okay. Today she sounded strong and ready to keep moving forward.

We would survive this.

Mom said, "No, it doesn't. Ike does the same for me. I get it. And I know you do the same for Drake. It's what makes you each other's soul mate."

"He is mine, for sure."

Those words affirmed it for me.

Slapping me on the back, Kane said loudly, "Well if the princess hasn't decided to wake up."

"Don't be an ass."

Mom sighed. "I swear, I did not use enough soap in their mouths when they were younger. If you have a boy one day, Alexa, and he takes after the Foster men, use lots of soap."

Her beautiful laughter filled the air. "Will do."

Our eyes locked, and I knew what she was thinking. *Kids. Our kids.*

Mom stood. "Do you want some breakfast, Drake?"

"I'll get some in a minute, Mom. Thanks."

She waved her hand. "Don't be silly. I'll warm up some leftovers."

Hayden walked in from outside as Mom disappeared into the kitchen. Hell, I *was* the last one up. "Oh, look who's up.

Morning, Drake."

"He prefers to be called princess this morning," Kane said smugly beside me.

Hayden smiled. "Yeah, I like the sound of that better. Morning, princess."

I shot them both the bird. "Fuckers."

Lex stood. "Play nice. I'll go help your mom with your breakfast." She walked over to me and got on her tiptoes to kiss me. "Morning."

"Morning." I smiled against her lips.

Mom called from the kitchen. "Eloise called this morning. She was wondering if one of you boys could stop by to help her."

Eloise was one of the neighbors. We helped her out from time to time, especially in the winter. She was a bit of a wild lady, at times. One who liked to think of herself as a cougar. I called out, "Kane said he'd love to help. Let Eloise know."

"Oh good. She loves Mariah. I'll text her now."

That earned me a shove. "Not funny."

"Yeah, it was, *Prince Charming*. Let me know how Eloise's ass grabbing goes."

He muttered a few curse words. Eloise was a character, and she loved Kane. When she was around him, somehow, her hands ending up "accidentally" in the general vicinity of Kane's ass. Hayden was her second favorite. That was why, most times, I ended up over there.

Kane nodded for us to follow him outside. From the chill in the air, it was clear that fall was definitely upon us. Fuck, I wished I had some coffee—my head was pounding like a freight train was coming through.

"So, I went to your place this morning and set up some

game cameras. We'll know if anyone steps foot on the property. From what I can tell, someone had walked a lot of it, probably figuring out the best way to get to and from the place. Some of the tracks were a week old, I'd estimate. So they've been out there a lot."

"Fuck."

Kane ran his hands through his dark hair. "Yeah. But no one came back last night. I set a few things in place before I left, and none of them were disturbed. Same with your place in town. I've got cameras on the doors to monitor there, too." Knowing Kane, after I'd gone to bed, he'd probably started setting things up. "What's your plan, Drake?"

I thought for a second. "Hayden, can you call Ewing and ask how long Milano has been offering?"

"Sure. Let me check really quick." Hayden walked a few steps away, his phone to his ear.

Mariah sat at Kane's feet, and my brother looked at me, waiting for the plan. I started with the obvious. "I need to flush this bastard out. It's not just letters and bank offers. They came to my house. For Lex."

"How are you going to do it?"

Hayden walked back to us. "Ewing said he's been getting offers for about three years. Until about six months ago they weren't worth entertaining."

"That would have been when Lloyd was still alive." I needed to find Dad and see what he had found out. "Do you know where Dad is?"

Hayden said, "He's in the shop out back. He mentioned he wanted to speak with the princess when he woke up."

I shoved my brother, and Kane chuckled, adding, "More like the *pissy* princess, if you ask me."

INTOXICATED BY YOU

As I started to the back, I shot them both the birds again. *Mature, I know.* But that was all I had at the moment. *I mean, come on... prissy princess?* We still acted like we were right back in high school. Some things never changed. I called over my shoulder. "You guys might want to hear this if you're done being immature assholes."

They caught up with me, and I explained. "I asked Dad to look into Lloyd's accident."

"You think it might not have been one?" Kane asked. The fact that he hadn't made a joke about it told me he probably agreed with my thoughts on the subject.

Glancing back at the house, I saw Lex at the window. She waved and gave me a smile.

Kane hit me on the back of the head. "You're an embarrassment to the Foster name. Stop getting that stupid-ass grin on your face, or I may have to disown you."

To really aggravate him, I put my hands in the shape of a heart then pointed to Lex. I could see her laughing in the window. Kane muttered and stalked off to the barn. Hayden just shook his head. I said, "I can't wait till that dipshit falls for someone. I'm going to make so much fun of him."

"Yeah... me, too." We'd walked a few more steps when I asked, "You thought any more about that girl?"

"I've tried not to." Hayden's entire demeanor changed. If anything, he probably hadn't been able to *stop* thinking about her. There was a new intenseness about him.

Of course, I had to press on. "And how's that working out for you?"

"Not good. I got an address for her."

Whoa. That was a serious step for him. "And..."

"I don't know."

This time I shook my head, wanting to bang his head against the wall. I had been in this miserable purgatory not too long ago. And I should have gone after Lex. It would have saved us a lot of heartache. Instead of reminding him of that, I went at it from another angle. "Well, she must not be that great considering how much *thinking* you're doing. Was probably just a piece of ass to tap for the summer."

In the next second, I was ducking to keep Hayden's fist from connecting with my face. "Don't say that about her," he spat.

"That's what I thought."

That made Hayden stop, and he stood there with his fist cocked, ready to deal another blow. "What?"

"My advice? Go after her before it's too late. You obviously care about her. Don't deny it. Just don't get into a situation like I was in with Lex. You can't go back in time. I should have gone to her and talked things through when I was in New York. Not just assumed she was with Hollis. We wouldn't have spent the last two years miserable if I had. And if something had happened to keep us apart forever, I would have spent my life regretting it and wondering *what if.*"

His mouth opened and closed a couple of times. And I kept walking. "Think about it. But don't think too long."

We made it to the shop, Hayden still deep in thought, his brow creased. Hopefully he wouldn't dick around.

Kane had left the door wide open and was sitting on a chair, looking at blueprint plans. "Are those the final ones for Hollis's cabin?"

"Yeah, it looks simple enough. We'll be able to knock it out in no time."

Dad was standing at the table, measuring some wood for

some piece of Hollis's furniture. "Hey, Dad."

"Morning. How's Alexa?"

"Good. Better today. We'll see." I was still worried how this was going to affect her. Considering she left the bed this morning, I assumed she wasn't ready to talk in depth about it. And I understood her needing time. She had always needed time to process things.

He nodded to himself. "I think that's about all that can be expected." He set aside the freshly cut cedar and took off his work gloves. "I talked to Roy. I assume you brought your brothers up to speed?"

I nodded.

Dad finger-combed his hair, displacing some wood shavings in the process. "Well, I told Roy we were working on safety manuals at the lumber yard and forgot the details of Lloyd's accident. I thought that wouldn't raise suspicions. When he went to locate the file, it was gone."

"Gone?"

Dad nodded, his face solemn. This wasn't sitting well with him, either. "Gone. No record of the digital or paper file. It's got him poking around now."

Shit. That wasn't good. "So… Lloyd's investigation mysteriously disappears. Someone is hiding something."

Dad's eyebrows were drawn in concern. "I agree with you. I honestly didn't believe it to begin with. But it gets more suspicious. After Jim left your place, we had lunch. We'd planned to meet up after we talked at the Fall Festival. He told me about dropping off the box for Alexa. So, I asked nonchalantly what had ever come of the investigation into Lloyd's death. I remembered that one moment his office had been swarming with investigators, and the next, his name had been cleared."

"What'd he say?"

"They'd been combing through his files, making sure everything was in order. Things like whether the machine had been serviced properly or had any of the men been over their allotted hours. The normal. One thing in particular they'd focused on was the maintenance. Jim couldn't understand why. The next day, they came in, packed up shop, and closed the case."

"That seems abrupt."

"Jim thought so, too. But he figured they realized he'd followed all the laws and exceeded any requirements. The guys told him the machine had been out of oil and seized up. He figured there'd been a leak in the line somewhere."

A machine that size would have left a sizeable puddle if the oil had been leaking. Lloyd would have noticed it. "Did Jim think it was odd?"

"Son, when you've been in the industry as long as he has, you understand that machines stop working. It was a logical conclusion. Why would he think someone might be after anyone? When those people packed up and left, he probably thought *good riddance*. A guilty man wouldn't share that type of information. He'd sidestep the question."

Maybe.

But none of this was sitting well with me. And by the looks on my brothers' faces, they agreed.

CHAPTER
Thirty-Five

Drake

Kane and Hayden left to head to their houses, and I sat on the back porch, trying to organize my thoughts. Mom walked out on the back porch with a plate of food and a cup of coffee. She handed both to me. "Hey. Mind if I join you?"

"Not at all. Thanks, Mom. I needed this bad."

"Alexa thought you might."

I smiled into the cup as I took a drink.

She took the seat beside me. In the distance, I could hear the saw in the shop as Dad kept working on the furniture. It was oddly comforting since it was a childhood sound I'd heard all my life.

"So, how are you doing?"

I took a deep breath. "Honestly, Mom, I feel like I'm barely keeping my head above water. It seems like trouble is coming from all angles."

"Well, I've given the same advice to Alexa. Make sure you're making time for you."

I sat back, pinching the bridge of my nose. "I'm trying."

"I know." She placed something on my knee, and I opened my eyes. *Shit*. The ring. I'd forgotten about it last night. "I went into your room to do a load of laundry and found this. I didn't think you'd want Alexa to find it." She paused, and I turned to face her. "Don't waste a lot of time waiting for the perfect time. Do it when it feels right."

I stared back at the ring. It felt like a beacon on my knee. I wanted nothing more than to give it to her. But I wanted the moment to be something that she would cherish for the rest of her life. And with all that we had going on, nothing felt like that moment.

"Drake, why don't you take a walk, clear you head? Just take some time to breathe."

My head was a mess. Maybe some normalcy would help clear it. But I couldn't leave Lex. I stood and gave Mom a kiss on the forehead. "Thanks."

Walking into the house, I found Lex in the kitchen sifting flour. I slipped my arms around her waist.

"Hey." She sweetly greeted me with a kiss.

"Hey, how are you doing?"

"Good. Better than I thought I would be. I've been baking to help with the church cookie walk this week."

As I stared into her gorgeous eyes, I didn't see any signs of distress. Lex squeezed me tighter. "I promise I'm doing okay. I mean I'm not to the point where I want to stay at our place by myself, but they didn't get to me. And we'll just have to be smart while we figure this out."

My phone vibrated in my pocket, but I didn't take it out.

Lex raised an eyebrow. "Check to see who that is. Make sure that you're not missing something."

I checked my phone. It was from Moochie.

Moochie: *Impromptu card night at my house. You in?*

I must have taken too long because Lex asked, "What is it?"

"Just Moochie wanting to know if I'm going to play cards. I'll let him know I'm not coming."

One of her eyebrows raised. "I think you should go."

I gawked at her. "I'm not going."

"Oh yes, you are."

There were times I thought she was certifiably insane. And the determined look on her face had me stopping this in its tracks before it started. "Lex, last night someone tried to break into our house."

"*Tried.* They didn't. And I'll be here with your parents tonight." She took a step away from me. "Drake, you need to go. I'll be fine."

It was then I realized it wasn't *me* she needed to convince. I saw it in her eyes. There was some fear there, but she was trying to face it, to *believe* the words she was telling me.

"Okay, how about a compromise. I'll play a couple of rounds of cards, but I'm not staying late."

Leaning up on her tiptoes, she gave me one of those sweet kisses I could never get enough of. "Good. Have fun. Win lots of money."

"I will, baby. Love you."

"Love you, too.

I grabbed my keys and headed out the door. As I walked

to my truck, I got another text from Moochie.

Moochie: *You coming?*

Me: *I'm on my way.*

Moochie: *Good. Bring beer.*

I took another sip of my beer, pacing myself to make sure I could drive home. Moochie and I sat on the back porch, shooting the shit. His wife, Amber, had gone to Ketchikan with their two kids. The rest of the guys hadn't been able to make it. As it turned out, Mom and Lex had been right. This had helped clear my head and get my thoughts back on track.

Moochie held his beer to mine. "So, you and Alexa still good?"

"Yeah, it seems like we were able to pick up where we left off."

"Good. I'm glad. You guys always seemed good together."

I tossed my bottle in the trash. "Thanks. I better be going. Next card game is at my place."

"Perfect. I'll let the guys know."

In my truck, I rolled down the windows and headed back to my parents'. Tomorrow, we'd try to get back to our normal lives; me at the Red Onion and Lex at the clinic. It was going to be tough being away from her. Somehow, we'd have to work out a system that gave her independence but let me know she was safe at the same time.

I pulled into my parents' driveway. My brothers were

there, too. It felt good to have us under the same roof, united against whoever was out there.

I walked in the house and followed the sound of a movie coming from the living room.

Lex turned around from her spot on the couch. "Hey. We're watching *Die Hard*. Your mom and I were outvoted."

Hayden threw popcorn at her. "You wanted to watch *Pretty Woman*. No way in hell."

"Might as well take my manhood away before I watched that sh—stuff," Kane added.

I chuckled, joining Lex on the couch. "I've got to say, I would have voted for *Die Hard*, too."

"Traitor," she teased and gave me a quick kiss as she snuggled into my side. This was perfect. Through all the craziness, we could still find our normal.

But I knew the darkness wasn't far away.

CHAPTER
Thirty-Six

Drake

I t had been a hell of a long day. I swore, everyone I knew came into the bar to talk about the recent Fall Festival de-bacle. Hell, the entire city council was up in arms about the complaints. Thank goodness, we had Hollis's welcome party to diffuse the situation.

I dragged my feet up the stairs. So far, Lex hadn't asked much about what Kane had found, so I hadn't volunteered the information. We did agree that for this week, I would follow her to work and Hollis would follow her home. And the fol-lowing week, we'd reevaluate the situation. It was a joint agreement to help keep us all living our lives but being cau-tious at the same time.

I opened the door to find Lex sitting on the couch with a glass of wine. Tonight, we were staying at my apartment over the Red Onion. "Hey, honey, I'm home."

"Hey, how was your day?"

"People were bitching about the Fall Festival. You are my hero for suggesting the welcome party. Otherwise, I think all the council members might be in trouble."

She chuckled. "Yeah, the patients complained to me, too. Since I'm Raquel's sister, I guess they think I have some sort of sway over her. But then they hugged me and Hollis for saving the town."

This town and the Fall Festival. *Who would have thought?* It was then I noticed the white box that had been in my room at my parents' house now sat on the ottoman. "You still debating?"

"No, I don't think so. I'm going to open it tonight. I feel ready, but I wanted you to be here with me."

This got my attention. The last time Lex wanted to read something from her dad she did it alone, which had led to a whole mess of issues. This time, we'd face it together.

I joined her on the couch as she lifted the lid from the box. On top were several framed pictures. Picking up the first one, Lex smiled. "Look at this."

She turned it toward me. It was a picture of the three of us fishing on the dock. "That was a good day."

"It was."

It had been the first decently warm day of spring. We'd gone fishing on the dock on the piece of land Raquel had inherited. It had been a day full of laughter. That night, we'd eaten fresh fish cooked over an open campfire and just enjoyed each other's company.

With her index finger, she traced the image of her dad, her breath growing a little shakier. I remained silent, allowing Lex to guide the conversation. She set the first picture aside and picked up the next one. It was a family photo, which she quickly put down. As was the next, and it was put down immediately. The rest of the box held awards Lloyd had won. At the bottom of the box was a file folder.

She opened the folder and began to read, and I waited to see what she said. Her eyes grew wider and she gasped. "Why does he have *this*?"

"What is it?"

She showed me the paper. The first page held test results. Paternity test results. Alexa's name was written on the top.

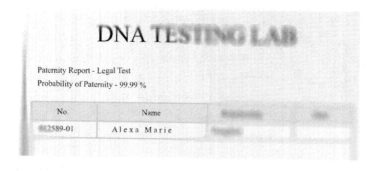

"He did a paternity test on me? Why?" She took the paper back and continued to read. She turned to the next page. "It was from a hair sample. A hair sample? When did he take a hair sample from me? I was in college when these were done."

"A hairbrush would have samples they could use."

Lex stared at the paper, her expression unreadable. "Why would he doubt I was his child?"

"What does the rest of the paperwork say?" Hopefully there were answers. *What in the hell had Lloyd been thinking?* It was obvious she was his, considering how much Lex favored him, physically. An uneasy feeling settled in the pit of my stomach.

She kept flipping the papers and suddenly stopped. She let out an audible gasp, and her hand flew up to her mouth.

"What is it?"

"Raquel isn't Dad's. If I'm reading this right, he's not her father."

She handed me the paper. On the top, Raquel's name was printed just like Lex's had been.

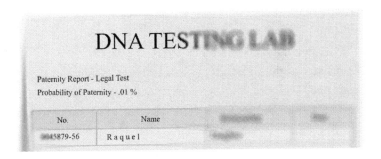

The date on the report was four weeks before the accident. "Did you notice the date?"

Her eyes blinked a little more rapidly. "Yes, mine was two weeks after Raquel's."

"So your dad tested Raquel and then checked you?"

"Yes. This makes much more sense. So much more."

The pieces were fitting together for Lex, but so far, she wasn't filling me in. I let her work through it. At some point, she'd clue me in.

She shook her head. "Remember when we were on the dock, I told you how Dad hadn't been acting right the last few weeks before he died? It felt like he was keeping something from me. That was why the letter was so believable."

"Yes."

She shook the paper in front of me, and it all fell into

place for me. "He had realized Raquel wasn't his."

Son of a bitch.

Raquel wasn't Lloyd's. He'd married Irene because she'd been pregnant.

We stared at the paper, waiting for said information to sink in. After a few minutes, Lex whispered, "Do you think my mom knows?"

I waited for Lex to look at me. This wasn't going to be easy to say, but I wasn't going to lie to her. "To be honest, your mom may not have known for sure, but she would've had to have known the possibility existed."

I hated seeing that sadness that turned her mouth downward. "She would have. There are times I can't stand the fact that she's my mother. How could she do this? I'm going to have to confront her about this."

"I know."

"Thank goodness I'm Dad's. I just don't know if I could take it if I wasn't." She paused as if the next thought had just occurred to her. "Raquel's only my half sister."

"Yes, she is."

Though Raquel was a piece of work, I wasn't sure what Lex thought about this news. It had to hurt to know her mom deceived her, which shot Irene straight to the top of my suspects list.

She took a deep breath and looked through the rest of the papers. Something caught her attention, and she paused to read it intently.

I looked at the heading.

Last Will and Testament

"Drake, this is Dad's will."

I waited as Lex kept scanning the pages.

She stood abruptly, and I barely caught the wineglass before it toppled over. "He changed it. He changed it all. This isn't what was read to me in the lawyer's office."

"What does it say?"

"I get it all. Raquel's land. The B&B. All of it. Dad had bought the B&B before he married Mom. Remember? The title was never moved into her name."

Oh fuck.

She handed me the paper and began to pace. The anger was clearly starting to build. "Drake, what am I going to do?"

"You don't have to decide today. What else is in the folder?" I pointed to the open folder.

The only thing remaining was an envelope. Lex pulled it out, saw her name printed on the envelope, and dropped it like it was on fire. She stepped back, her hands up. "Drake, the last time I read a letter I thought was from Dad, it nearly destroyed me."

She backed almost to the wall, and I picked up the envelope. The word *Alexa* was printed on it in neat handwriting. The sense of déjà vu was overwhelming.

"You don't have to read it. But it might give you some closure."

Chewing on her lip, she took a step closer. Then two more. After a few minutes, she was sitting in my lap and staring at the envelope in my hand. Her fingers traced the letters. With the way her hand trembled, I knew she was feeling it, too. "Can you read it to me? I don't think I can do it."

"Sure, baby." The room grew deathly still. I flipped the envelope over, opened it, and began to read.

"Dear Alexa, if you're reading this, I've gone on to my next adventure. This news may come as a shock to you. I've given a lot of thought to how to handle the fact that Raquel is not my daughter. And if you're reading this, I didn't know how to tell you or anyone else. This is still a shock to me. Maybe I'll change my mind, and you'll never read this letter. No matter what, I'll never regret what happened because it gave me you. You are the best thing that has ever happened to me.

"You've blossomed into a beautiful woman, and I'm so proud of you following your dream. I can't wait to see you open up your clinic. And I know Drake will be beside you the entire time, supporting your dreams. He's your match, Alexa, and he loves you. A father always hopes his daughter will find a man who will put her first in all things. Drake is that man. Giving my blessing for you two to be married was the easiest decision I've ever made. I love you more than life itself. Dad."

As I finished the letter, Lex held onto me and sobbed. This was the letter she should have gotten. This was how everything should have gone. Lloyd had approved of us, and any doubt that had lingered in our minds vanished. Forever.

Thank you, Lloyd. I will love your daughter forever and always.

CHAPTER
Thirty-Seven

Alexa

Sadness.
    Anger.
    Frustration.
Sorrow.
Betrayal.

All these feelings coursed through me simultaneously. I'd told Drake's family what we'd found and showed them the paperwork from my dad's folder. They hadn't known what to say. Then I called Hollis, who came over. He got hold of his lawyer, who looked at the will. Apparently, there was nothing that could be done. I thought about what he'd said.

"The will is out of probate, and the statute of limitation has expired. Challenging the will is out. One option you have is to go after the law firm for negligence since they provided the wrong will. However, the lawyer who executed it is deceased. Unless we can find where it was filed with the law

firm, it won't hold any weight in a court of law. It can also be a lengthy and expensive process. The moment they realize what we're doing, it will become nearly impossible to get the information."

"How could she? How could she do this?"

Drake stood off to the side as I vented. I'd been ready to hop in my car and find my mom, but Drake had suggested that I calm down a little. Spending the night in jail wasn't on my to-do list.

My mom had lied. She'd lied. To me… Dad…

Does she know Dad figured it out? Does Raquel know?

And it all felt too coincidental—the land offers, the paternity, Dad's death. Drake shared with me what he'd found out about the accident. All the paperwork was gone. Just gone. *Are the cops in on it?*

How? Why? Who?

I grabbed my phone and dialed my mom. Voicemail. "I can't believe she sent me to voicemail! I'm her daughter!"

That was it. I'd had it. I took the paternity test results and the will to Drake's computer and scanned them in.

"What are you doing?"

"Giving the Twiner Tellings a red-hot newsletter."

"Do you really want the whole town involved?"

I stopped what I was doing and sank into the chair. Drake leaned against the doorframe. That's what he did when I was so mad I could see red, gave me space.

"I'm just saying—once you put it out there, you can't take it back. You'll lose any element of surprise. I get that you're pissed and hurt, but what will this accomplish? If you want to talk about it, I would suggest confronting Irene and Raquel to their faces. Then you'll know if they knew."

I pulled my legs onto the seat. "Do you think my mom was involved in Dad's accident somehow?"

"I'd like to think not, but…" He let it hang out, obviously unsure how to finish. The sad thing was, I wasn't sure how that sentence ended either. The whole situation made my mom look suspicious.

I leaned my head back and stared at the ceiling. "I wonder if it's Chazz or Raquel. But that seems so obvious. Do you think Raquel knows?"

"I don't know. Do I think Raquel knew when you lived here before? Maybe, but it seems doubtful. Is it a possibility now? Yes."

"I want to talk to her. And Mom."

"You sure about that?"

"Yes. I need to know if they knew."

The B&B was a bust. Mom wasn't home. Next up was Raquel's illustrious home on the side of the mountain. The house was completely out of place for Skagway. This was the first time I'd been there.

The lights were on, and Mom's car was parked out front. Of course she hadn't taken my call. I balled my fists as I thought about what I'd found.

"You sure you want to do this?" Drake asked.

I appreciated Drake trying to be the reasonable one in all this, but I wanted to see their faces. I needed to know if they knew. Keeping my voice steady, I said, "Yes, this isn't me acting irrationally. Maybe scanning the results to the Twiner sisters had been, but now I just feel numb toward them. I want them out of my lives forever after this."

"I get it, Lex. I do."

Honestly, family was good to have. But I would be glad to be rid of them.

We got out of the truck and headed to the massive, ornate front door. It was like approaching some sort of castle. *Ridiculous.* The stone exterior looked cold. When I pushed the button, some fancy tune played. We waited, and I got even angrier as the seconds ticked by. I refused to leave until I saw them, so I pushed the button again. And again. As my finger headed toward the button for a fourth time, the door opened. A woman wearing a black-and-white uniform answered, "Hello, how may I help you?"

"I'm Alexa Owens, Raquel's sister. I want to see her and my mother for a minute. It's urgent. Please let them know I'm not leaving until they see me. And they're going to want to see me. If not, I'll go to the Twiner sisters."

And I would. The woman looked surprised. "Just a moment, ma'am."

The door closed, and we waited. Within a minute, the door flung open. "What are you doing here?" Raquel screeched, crossing her arms over her beaded dress. *A bit over the top for casual dining, I'd say.*

If only I could wipe that arrogant look off her face. It always drove me mad. *Did she know?* I softened somewhat. *What if she doesn't know?*

But then Raquel snarled at me, "Are you deaf? What do you *want*?"

And I'm done with this. "I need to talk to you and Mom."

She crossed her arms again. "What about?"

Turning, I looked at Drake. "This is a waste of time. Take

me to Elvira and Sylvia's. They'll be interested in what I have to say."

We turned and took a few steps to the car before Raquel said, "Fine, come in. But take off your shoes. I don't want you dirtying my floors."

We followed Raquel, leaving on our shoes. Normally, yes, I would've taken them off, but treating us like we were barnyard animals was unacceptable. And quite frankly, I couldn't give two flying fucks about her—or her fancy floors —right now.

Chazz sat on the sofa, sipping a drink. "Alexa, Drake, what brings you to our home this evening?"

He wore one of those red silk dressing robes you see in movies paired with black pants. Honestly, he looked ridiculous. This whole scene, including Mom in her ball gown, sipping wine while the fire crackled, seemed fabricated.

Chazz motioned to us. "Would you like to take a seat? I've been meaning to ask Raquel to have you over. It's a shame the first time we met was at the Fall Festival."

"Thanks, but I'll stand. We won't be long." I turned to Raquel, who looked like she was going to blow a gasket. Plus, her fancy hairdo made her look like she had two dark horns sprouting from her head. "Why'd you sell Dad's land to Milano Incorporated?"

She rolled her eyes. "Because I wanted to."

I took a deep breath. "How much did you get for it?"

"Enough to say yes."

Bitch. I wanted to smack her right upside the head. "Dad wouldn't have wanted you to sell the land. It was supposed to go to his grandkids."

Raquel rolled her eyes again. I was about two seconds

away from decking her. Drake put his hand on my waist, and I unclenched my fists. The movement helped center me. "Do you know who Milano Incorporated is?"

"No, they offered me through the bank."

Chazz leaned forward, and for the first time, I saw some sort of human quality in him. "Is something the matter, Alexa?"

"No, nothing is the matter. I just wish someone would've told me."

During this exchange, my mother didn't say a word. "Mom, I've been trying to call you."

"Sorry, darling, I've been busy." She patted her hair into place. I swore, she and Raquel were two peas in a pod, and I was glad I looked more like my dad.

Tired of the charade, I took the photocopies from my jacket. Mom and Raquel obviously weren't going to give me any additional information. Now I needed to know if—or how much—they knew. "So… I got Dad's work stuff from Jim."

Raquel and Mom looked at each other. Their eyes widened for only a second, but then their expressions shut down again. Mom sighed. "He didn't have any work stuff."

I held up a finger and took a step forward. "Oh, but he did. Jim said he contacted you several times to pick it up, but you couldn't be bothered."

Again, they shared another look. *Okay.* It was time for the grand finale. "Anyway, I found something interesting in there. Paternity tests."

Mom's face contorted with rage. "Alexa, I'm warning you."

"*Warning* me? About what? What I found? That I'll tell the town what you did?"

Seething, she stepped forward, her hand raised.

Drake shot out in front of me. "Irene, I would suggest you take a couple of steps back. You lay a hand on Lex, you'll have me to deal with."

Drake would never hit a woman, but the threat was enough to make Mom retreat. However, I had my answers. I turned toward Raquel, who didn't seem the least bit fazed. "So you knew, too."

She said nothing

"That's why you sold the land. Cash out while you could."

Still, she said nothing.

"Don't you have anything you want to say? How long have you known, Raquel?"

And still, nothing.

Chazz stood. "Would you mind clarifying what you're talking about? I'm a bit lost."

For a second, I studied him to see if he was lying. His brows were drawn, and he appeared to have been kept in the dark. *But who knows?* "Raquel isn't my father's daughter."

"You're sure?" He stared at me in disbelief.

I tossed the copy of the paternity test results on the table. "Yes, I am. Raquel and I would be identified as only half sisters. Here's a copy for some light reading."

Chazz studied the paper. Raquel cleared her throat. "I believe it's time for you to leave."

"I was just thinking the same thing." I shook my head. "I don't know you, Chazz. But if I were you, I would get out while the getting is good. I've seen that you're close with your brother. This is how my family treats people when they aren't useful. I hope you never become obsolete, or you'll be standing where I am right now."

And with that, I turned and left.

As Drake started his truck, I felt the door to any relation-ship with my mother and sister slam shut. Mom hadn't stopped me when I walked out. She didn't care if I was in her life.

And that hurt most of all. Now I was parentless.

CHAPTER
Thirty-Eight

Alexa

Wednesday afternoon, Hollis was finishing up with a patient while I tried to catch up on the filing. It wasn't an easy task; my mind was going in all sorts of directions. A small part of me had hoped my mom or my sister would reach out and want to talk about everything. I couldn't imagine how lonely Dad must have felt when he found out the truth about his wife and daughter.

The front door opened, and Devney walked in wearing her glasses, her light hair up in a loose bun. She looked every bit the high school music teacher. "Hey, Alexa. I hope now is a good time."

"Yes. Yes, of course it is." I shook my head to try and clear the cobwebs. In all the chaos, I'd forgotten Devney was coming in today. *Oops.* Hollis would be surprised. "Here's the paperwork. You can start filling that out in the back office, if that's okay."

That would give me a chance to break the news to Hollis. With everything that had happened last night, Hollis had been so good to me today. He'd greeted me on the front step with coffee, brought in my favorite lunch from the Red Onion, and listened to my more girly music rather than the classical, boring stuff he liked to play during breaks.

Devney took the papers. "Perfect. Thank you again for this opportunity."

"Thank *you*." I indicated the stacks of papers that needed to be filed. "We need the help, as you can see."

The papers weren't as organized as we liked to keep them. The clinic had felt like a madhouse today. "That will be no problem."

I showed Devney to the back office and explained the different forms. For legal reasons, she had to sign confidentiality agreements.

The exam room door opened, and I said, "I'll be right back."

"No problem. I'll keep filling everything out."

Mr. Hortishire came out of the room and waved goodbye. This was my chance to give Hollis a little warning.

He handed me the chart. "I notated Mr. Hortishire had elevated blood pressure. I gave him a few suggestions to see if we could get it back in the normal range. I'd like to schedule a follow-up in a week."

I scribbled down the notes. "Consider it done."

"We really need someone to help out around here."

Clicking my tongue, I knew this was the perfect opportunity. "Well, you see, we may already have the positioned filled."

"We may?" Hollis tilted his head at me like I was crazy.

I laid down the chart. *Just rip the Band-Aid off.* "No, no, we for sure have someone."

"Okay, am I missing something?"

"Well, our new employee is in the back filling out her paperwork. I need to know what the position pays."

Hollis considered that for a second. "How about twenty dollars an hour?"

"She'll be grateful. That's perfect."

"Alexa, I have the paperwork."

"Coming!"

Oh shit, I thought I would have a few more minutes to tell him. Damn, Devney was fast.

Hollis's face froze. "Is that—I... she... you..."

I clapped him on the shoulder. "Deep breaths, Hollis. I thought you weren't attracted to Devney." Giving him a wink, I walked back into the office and took the papers from Devney.

"I just confirmed with Hollis; the pay is twenty dollars an hour."

"Oh my! I was only expecting half that. I appreciate it. This will help immensely. Thank you so much." Her eyes turned to the doorway, where I was sure Hollis had joined us. "Dr. Fritz, thank you again."

"You're... welcome. I'm—" Hollis started fiddling with this stethoscope. "I'm glad to have you..." Somehow in the next second, the stethoscope was wrapped around his neck. "Damn it. This thing is trying to kill me."

He tossed the stethoscope across the room, and we all watched it land. The clank of the metal hitting the ground was the only sound to be heard. "Well, that's one way to get it off," I said.

Devney gave a small giggle but then remembered herself.

An awkward silence filled the room. I was about to speak when Devney said, "I had lunch with Marlena today. She's excited."

"Excited?" Hollis asked, perplexed.

Devney's eyes grew wide, and she looked at me. I had no idea what she was talking about. "Umm about your date this Friday?"

"What?" Hollis's volume had us jumping. "What date?"

Devney looked to me for help. She probably thought that Hollis was a crazy loon. Sometimes he didn't have the demeanor of a doctor. The last time she was here, he'd shut his hand in the drawer. Now he'd nearly strangled himself with his stethoscope and was screaming questions.

"I... uh... I'm going to be heading out now. Thank you, Dr. Fritz. I'll see you Monday, Alexa. Thank you again."

I waved, saying, "Bye, Devney."

The door closed behind her, and I turned to Hollis. "You may want to make her feel a little more welcome. You might have scared her."

"What? I didn't... damn it." Hollis took off toward the front door, nearly tripping on his own feet. I heard him say, "Thanks for taking the job, Devney. We're looking forward to Monday."

That was a little better. Now he just sounded like a stiff. I wondered if he liked her more than I'd originally thought. Hollis was affected by her in a good way.

Back inside, Hollis leaned against the wall. "Is it hot in here? I thought we lived in the frozen tundra."

Yeah, he looked a little out of sorts. I poked at him a little more because it was exactly what he would have done. "Or it's the lovebug."

He ignored me. "She starts Monday?"

"Yep."

"And the entire town thinks I'm going out with Marlena?"

"Yep."

He dragged his hand through his hair. "You Alaskans are crazy. And by association, I'm becoming crazy."

"I thought you wanted to be one of us except—for the coffee."

"Only on the manly front. All this other stuff... I'll stay a New Yorker."

I put my arm around his shoulder. "Let me go make you a soy milk latte with a hint of vanilla and chocolate with a double espresso. We don't have another patient for thirty minutes."

"You might have just redeemed yourself as my best friend."

Well, I was probably about to un-redeem myself. On the way up the stairs, I asked, "Do you want me to call in sick on Monday?"

"Why?"

Oh, man. This was as easy as taking candy from a baby. "I figured you might want to play doctor with Devney?"

"Make it a triple espresso and bring me my hammer. I need to feel Alaskan."

I laughed as we entered his kitchen. Yep, Dr. Hollis Fritz had been bitten by the lovebug. Hard.

CHAPTER
Thirty-Nine

Drake

The welcome party was a hit; people relaxed and enjoyed the good food and the company of friends. I waved goodbye as all our friends cleared out. The city council had congratulated me on saving the day. People were happy that we'd been able to redeem ourselves after the Fall Festival. The party had been all about being part of the community and just enjoying the company.

Because of this, it looked like my reelection was in the bag. What had started off as a way to distract myself from losing Lex had turned into something I actually enjoyed. Skagway was important to me, and keeping our sense of community was something that would always be close to my heart.

Of course, Irene and Raquel hadn't shown up. Neither had Chazz. But I think Lex had worked through a lot of it. They'd never truly been her family, though she'd held out hope in the same way she had with Teagan. At this point, I believed

Teagan had been missing so long that all we'd find was a body. No way could she survive this long. And I knew it bothered Lex she couldn't save her.

Regardless of how nasty the person was, Lex wanted to help them.

So far this week, nothing else had happened. Kane was in the back, reviewing the tapes from the cameras he'd set up. Anything to get out of socializing.

Lex came up and bumped my hip. She'd been helping serve at the bar since I'd given Crete the night off to enjoy himself. "Poor Hollis."

In the corner, Hollis was sitting at a table, surrounded by girls. He looked like he wanted to get the fuck out of there.

Devney approached the bar. I noticed she glanced over her shoulder nonchalantly before looking our way. "It was a great party. Thanks for inviting me. Can't wait to start Monday."

"Neither can we," Lex replied, giving her a sweet smile. "You're going to be a great addition to the team."

Again, she gave another glance. Yeah, she liked Hollis. Lex had been right. Fidgeting with her hands, she nervously asked, "Will you tell Hollis good night for me? I don't want to interrupt him."

"I'm sure he'd love to be saved from that mess if you wanted to say goodbye. He's probably going to kill me because I left him over there with Samone and Jane."

I got a genuine smile, then she winked. "Have a good night. Don't make him suffer too long. We don't want a grumpy boss on Monday."

"You're probably right," Lex replied. "I've had a grumpy Hollis on my hands, and it resulted in me throwing a book at his head."

"Oh my." Devney's eyes were wide as saucers. "Well, I'll leave the book-throwing to you."

Lex laughed. "Deal."

As Devney left, I rapped on the bar three times and said, "Last call!"

When that happened, more people cleared out until there was only a handful left. Ol' Man Rooster approached the bar, strutting like a proud granddad. "Looks like I may have Marlena married off soon."

Uh. Oh.

Lex was apparently at a loss for what to say, so I asked, "What do you mean?"

Putting his hands in his overall pockets, he gave a shit-eating grin. "Oh, you can tell by the way your doctor fellow is looking at her that he's smitten." He tapped the counter. "My work here is done. Night, guys."

"Night," we called out in unison.

I glanced over to Hollis, who looked anything but smitten as he stood. Marlena waved her fingers before walking toward her grandfather. Lex looked at the door, then at Hollis again. Oh, I knew where this was going. I put my hands around Lex's waist and brought her a little closer. "I can see the wheels spinning."

She gave him an innocent look. "Whatever could you be talking about?"

"I wonder."

Before Lex could reply, Hollis was at the bar, pointing at Lex. "Why didn't you come save me?"

I busied myself putting a few beer glasses up.

"You looked smitten as a kitten," Lex said with a giggle.

Hollis glared, but I noticed he kept looking around the room as if searching for someone.

"She left," Lex said.

"Who?" Hollis put on the worse fake innocent look. Yeah, he liked Devney. He and Hayden should get together and compare notes on what not to do. And the first was not to let the girl slip through your fingers.

Lex countered, "Well, who are you looking for?"

"I don't know what you're talking about. So, Drake, ice fishing?"

Oh, hell. I was being brought into this. Casually, wondering where he was going with it, I asked, "What about it?"

There was no telling with Hollis. For all I knew, he wanted his own ice hole. I wondered if the guy had ever been fishing before, much less ice fishing.

"I think we need to get a group together. You know—be Alaskan men in an ice hut. Catch fish. Drink beer. I don't know... be manly."

I chuckled. This guy grew on me more and more every day. You'd never know he was a doctor just from talking to him. "Well, I go every December with my brothers. Want to join us?"

Hollis slapped the counter. "Count me in. I'll order the gear. Night."

I waved goodbye. Only one person remained at the bar. I did a double take, surprised to see Chazz sitting there. *When did he slip in?* He was watching us, and it was obvious from the way he tracked our movements that he wanted to talk to us. Lex stiffened beside me. *What the hell kind of game is he planning?* I put Lex slightly behind me before I said, "Sorry, man. I'm closing up."

"Understood." He looked around the room, not moving an inch. Apparently, he *didn't* understand. I was about to say something when he said, "Alexa, may we talk?"

"Whatever you have to say to me you can say in front of Drake." Her voice was cold, distant.

Chazz adjusted his suit jacket, then his cuff links, taking his time. He was about to get booted out, forcefully if needed. "Very well. How shall I put this? The information you recently received—what do you plan to do with it?"

Lex took a step toward him, and I moved, too. "So far I don't have any plans. Why?"

"I'm prepared to pay a sizeable amount for your discretion."

Asshole. I had to grit my teeth to keep from saying anything. This was Lex's fight, and she was strong enough.

She shook her head. "I don't want your money, Chazz."

Her words were met with only silence. *Fucker.* He was trying to intimidate her, but it wouldn't work.

He steepled his fingers and asked, "Then what do you want? There must be something."

"The B&B," she said without hesitation. Lex was trying to piece her father's land back together and get what was rightfully hers.

He let out a breath. "Anything else?"

"I wouldn't mind the piece of land Raquel sold."

He laughed. "That's not happening."

The door opened, and Dixon walked in. They were like night and day. Chazz looked like he was ready for an executive meeting while Dixon was casually dressed. "I just picked up dinner. Are you ready?" He looked up at us. "Drake. Alexa. Good to see you guys again."

We greeted him back.

Chazz continued to stare at Lex, and I wanted to punch him.

Dixon prompted, "Chazz?"

"Coming." Chazz nodded to himself before looking Lex straight in the eye. "I'll get your B&B back for you, but I don't want you to ever reach out to your mother or Raquel again. We're moving to Ketchikan, and I have objectives I'd rather not have thwarted this time."

"Then make sure they stay out of my business, too."

Chazz looked me in the eye for the first time. "You let you *girlfriend* do all the talking?"

"Lex doesn't need me to speak for her. But I will say this." I stepped closer to the counter and leaned in. I towered over him. "Don't fuck with her, me, or my family. Or there won't be a place in this state you can hide."

I felt Lex's hand on my back, but he needed to understand where I stood. There was only so far he could push me.

"Is that a threat?" he scoffed.

"No, it's a fact."

I dared the motherfucker to say anything else. He adjusted his cuff links again. "Well, your boyfriend's little stunt may have just cost you the B&B, Alexa."

She pulled out her phone. "Funny, that threat may have my finger twitchy to send something to the Twiner sisters along with another piece of information you haven't even seen yet."

That's my girl.

Chazz gave a snort. "I'll be in touch. Good evening."

And with that he left. Beside me, Lex threw her bar cloth on the counter. "He's such a... turd bucket. Ugh, he and

Raquel deserve each other."

"*Turd bucket?*" I couldn't help but chuckle.

"Whatever, you get the point."

She was so damn adorable as she scowled at the door. Truth be told, she was probably itching to send the report to the Twiner sisters regardless of what Chazz said.

Sighing, she flexed her fingers. "I may get the B&B back."

"Let's hope."

Kane came out from the back. "I just got done reviewing all the footage. There's nothing new."

Hayden was with him. I imagined at some point during the party, he'd gone back to give him shit.

"That's good." Whoever it had been was staying away from my place, which meant from Lex, too.

Beside Kane, Mariah gave a low growl, and the hairs on the back of her neck stood up. Kane knelt down and asked, "What is it, girl?"

Her growls became a little more intense, and she touched Kane's hand. I swore those two spoke some kind of secret language.

He stood. "The asshole was here tonight."

Shit. The entire town had been there tonight. "Think she can get the scent outside? Figure out which way he went?"

"Yeah."

The door opened, and Chazz walked back in. My eyes shot to Mariah, but she stood still and only watched him. "My apologies. I forgot my coat."

At that point, Dixon stepped into the doorway.

Mariah's low growling increased. *Dixon?* Kane looked over at me and nodded. He gave some sort of gesture, and Mariah settled.

I cleared my throat. "Listen, why don't we all have a drink? I heard Dixon was leaving in a couple of days. I know we've had our differences, but maybe we can put those aside."

Chazz stopped. "Sure."

From the tightness in Dixon's eyes, it was clear he didn't approve.

Well, too fucking bad. It was about time for him to face the music.

CHAPTER
Forty

Drake

The first thing I needed to do was get Lex out of there. Just in case. I needed to make sure she was safe. *Think of a reason.* I grabbed a few glasses and a bottle of my top-of-the-line whiskey. From the scowl on her face, I could tell she wasn't pleased about Chazz and was probably looking for an excuse. *Just give me a few minutes, baby. I'm going to get this sorted.* Kane and Hayden struck up a conversation with the Hennington brothers.

That was my first priority—getting Lex away. I put my hand on her shoulder and whispered, "Would you mind closing the books for me? I need a few minutes to sort something."

She glanced at me in confusion, and I widened my eyes. "*Please,*" I mouthed.

Even though she was confused, she said, "Sure. I'll get that taken care of."

Turning to Dixon, she gave him a genuine smile. *If she only knew.* "Night, Dixon. Be sure to stop by before you leave town."

"Will do."

Kane excused himself. "I left my phone in the office. I'll be right back."

No one suspected anything or caught the small, almost indiscernible gesture he made. Mariah stayed and stared almost unblinking at the brothers.

Dixon chuckled as he took off his coat. "That's an intense dog. She's amazing. But I wouldn't want to be on her bad side."

"Yeah, she gets it from Kane," I replied.

He shook his head. "Yeah, those two are tight."

Hayden held up his glass. "Man, it's not every day I can talk my brother into breaking out the good stuff. Cheers."

"Yeah, it's only when I'm feeling exceptionally good about something. Cheers." We clanked glasses and sipped.

Kane came back from the office. "Pour me some of that shit. I'm feeling good, too."

Hayden obliged, and with another surreptitious gesture, Mariah moved to the front door. Hayden took a seat at Chazz's side, and Kane sat next to Dixon. These assholes were effectively caged in.

Kane threw his drink back and said, "Good shit."

I took another sip and sat the glass down. "So, I have a question."

"Shoot," Dixon said.

Looking him straight in the eye, I said, "Tell me why you were at my place the other night, Dixon? You nearly scared the shit out of my girlfriend."

The glass he held stopped for a split second on the way to his mouth. It was enough of a pause, and I could see his wheels racing to buy some time. "What are you talking about?"

I scoffed. "You know exactly what I'm talking about. I'm going to ask again. Why. Were. You. At. My. Place?"

"I wasn't. I think it's time we go, Chazz. It appears we've outworn our welcome."

Dixon stood, and Kane's hand shot out to grip his shoulder. "I think you're just fine in your seat. My brother asked you a question. It's rude to not answer."

Begrudgingly, Dixon lowered himself into the seat. I folded my arms over my chest and stared. Chazz looked like he might be sick. He hadn't tried to move, but Hayden was ready for him. "Now, now, buddy. I think the same goes for you."

Chazz's eyes flew open and he looked uncomfortable as hell. Dixon was trying to remain cool and unaffected, but he knew he'd been caught. When the silence was so thick the tension could be tasted, I went on to say, "There's one of two ways I see this going down. One is you tell me why you were at my place. Or two..."

Kane picked up where I left off. "We take a nice trip out to the woods."

Dixon tried to push away from the bar, but Kane was faster and clamped down on his shoulder. Mariah growled, her teeth showing, and inched closer to the bar in warning. Dixon looked back and commanded, "Call her off."

Tsk-tsking, Kane said, "Nah, I don't feel like it today."

In one swift move, I jumped over the bar, taking them by surprise. "Get his wallet. I need to ID him and make sure he's twenty-one."

Roughly Kane brought Dixon out of the chair. "Hand me your wallet." Dixon didn't move. "I'm not asking again. Mariah is one command away from tearing into you. I suggest you cooperate."

Hell, Kane is a scary motherfucker. Dixon pulled out his wallet and Kane tossed it to me. I pulled out his driver's license. "Looks like you're legal, Dixon Samuel Hennington." He said nothing. The Samuel part stuck out to me. "Samuel? Sam? The same Sam who supplied Teagan with drugs?"

"You can't prove anything," he spat.

Chazz shifted, and Hayden put his hand on his shoulder. "Let's stay comfy in our chairs. We have front-row tickets to the show."

I decided to bluff. "No, I can't. But the witnesses at Teagan's apartment can. They identified a man who seems to resemble you quite a bit."

With a sinister smile, the calculating man reappeared. "You have no such thing. There are no witnesses."

Asshole. He was good, but I was better after hiding my feelings for two years. "You sure about that? Think really hard; there wasn't one time you might have slipped or left something behind?" I turned to Chazz. "You'll go down as an accomplice."

Chazz held up his hands. "Let's be reasonable. We can work this out. Dixon needs the land."

"Shut up, you idiot," he yelled.

Chazz turned to him. "I am not going down for this. You promised."

"They have nothing. And shut the fuck up!"

"You sure about that?" Kane crossed his arms over his chest, and Mariah inched closer. "I hear prison isn't very fun. They don't do that froufrou food you had at the party. More like Spam, I would guess."

Chazz looked so aghast it was almost comical. For the first time, I saw hesitation in Dixon's eyes as he scanned our faces. Chazz grew more fidgety. Dixon took a step back, and Mariah snarled.

"I wouldn't piss her off. I don't think she's had dinner," I said.

"What are you going to do? Take me out to the woods and bury me?" He laughed. "This is getting ridiculous."

I pulled out my phone. *We're not getting anywhere.* It was time for another approach. I dialed, and Roy picked up on the third ring. "Well, this can't be good. Normally you don't call me late at night unless there's been a disturbance."

"Hey, Roy. Can you come by the Red Onion? I'd like to report a disturbance."

I could hear papers rustling in the background. "Sure, what's going on? Welcome party leave Bernie and Mac three sheets to the wind?"

Yeah, those two were normally the reason. "Not this time. It's Chazz and Dixon Hennington. I think you should come over."

"Sure," he answered hesitantly.

Dixon pulled out his cell phone, but Kane grabbed it. "I don't think so, asshole."

"I'll have my lawyers pull your tapes, and I'll own this piece of shit establishment and everything else you hold dear."

Again, Kane chuckled and held up his finger. "Wouldn't you know it? When I took Alexa back to the office to do the books, I decided to turn off the camera so I could back up what we had. Funny how that worked out."

In the next instant, Dixon swung, and Kane froze, allowing Dixon's fist to connect with his face. Mariah was barking, but Kane held his hand out. *Good thinking, Kane.* I grabbed my glass. "Looks like we'll have the shiner to prove the disturbance now. Thanks, Dixon. A toast?"

He remained silent.

"No? Well I'll toast to putting your ass behind bars."

The lights from the police car flashed out front, and I headed outside to see if I could get Roy to buy us some time. Technically, we still had nothing. "What happened?"

"Dixon swung at Kane. He wants to press charges."

Roy shook his head. "Shit. Are you sure you want to go down this road? I pulled Chazz over for drunk driving last year, and his lawyers had him sprung in no time."

Here goes nothing. "Yeah, I need another favor."

"What?" Roy leaned around me, looked inside, and let out a sigh.

Well, he probably wasn't going to like this next request either. "I need you to postpone letting them make any calls and keep them separated."

"What?"

"Dixon is behind the drugs with Teagan. And I think they're connected to Lloyd's death. I think he's behind a company trying to buy up our land named Milano Incorporated, as well."

"Son, listen—"

"I'll have the proof in two hours. I just need you to stall. Get Travis over here and take them to the police station separately."

"Drake," he warned.

This was our only hope. If they went free now, we'd never catch them. They would completely cover any and all tracks. And I'd have to look over my shoulder for the rest of my life. If they went free, Dixon would get his revenge, and it would be aimed at Lex.

That. Could. Not. Happen.

"Roy, I've never asked you for a favor, but I'm asking for one now. Dixon and Chazz were at my place, trying to break in, a week ago. Mariah got the scent and identified them tonight, but I know a dog's ID won't hold up. So I need to get you the proof. And there's probably more that I don't know about."

He shifted his weight. "You have two hours. After that, I have to give them their call."

"Deal."

Roy called Travis in. After a couple of minutes, he pulled up, and Roy explained what was going on. Travis looked me in the eye. "All bullshit aside, you really think he was involved with Teagan?"

Thank goodness he wasn't going to give me grief. The last thing I needed was some stupid age-old misunderstanding to get in the way. I looked him straight in the eye. "Yeah, I do. And if we don't do this right, he'll get away with who knows what."

Travis and I hadn't gotten along in years. Lex had reminded me that Travis had dated Teagan in junior high. I knew he'd been trying to track her down. Maybe he wouldn't be a prick. I pressed on. "I think he's our only chance at finding Teagan. Two hours. We have to keep the lawyers from springing them or letting them communicate with anyone."

"Done," Travis said. "You have two hours. Make them count."

"I will."

CHAPTER
Forty-One

Drake

We pulled up to Chazz and Raquel's home. It looked like Irene wasn't there, which was good. If she wasn't, it gave us more of a chance to catch Raquel off guard. Lex hadn't said much after I filled her in. She seemed almost numb. Normally, I'd have given her a little more time to process, but we didn't have that much time left. We'd already spent too much time going over what we knew.

But I was worried. This was how she'd been when her dad died—withdrawn and uncommunicative.

Hayden and Kane had come as well. No one moved to get out of the truck until Lex did. She stared at the front door. I felt the pressure of the clock ticking. We only had an hour and a half left. Finally, after about five minutes, Lex said, "I want to be the one who confronts her."

"I'll go in with you."

She nodded and got out of the truck. Kane and Hayden

got out, as well. Before Lex hit the doorbell, a cop car pulled up and Travis got out of the car. *Hell, what is he doing here?* I had a sinking feeling that somehow, they'd been set free.

"I figured you might need me to take a statement on the spot. Chazz and Dixon have been confined into separate places at the station. Roy is stalling."

Thank fuck. I released a breath and extended my hand. "Thanks."

"I want to be the one to confront Raquel," Lex said to Travis. "Then you can do whatever is necessary."

I asked, "All right. How do you want to do it?"

"Kane and Hayden stay out here. You and Travis come with me."

No one argued, and Lex pressed the doorbell. The same woman in the black-and-white uniform answered. "Please tell my *sister* I'm here. And she's going to want to see me. It's about Chazz."

The woman's eyes grew wide, and she nodded. "Yes, ma'am."

It was only a few minutes before Raquel opened the door. "What's going on?"

"Can we come inside to talk?" Lex asked in a cold, distant tone.

Travis stayed behind and said something in his mic.

Raquel screeched, "What's going on? Is Chazz okay?"

Before Lex could answer, Travis walked in, saying, "May I?"

Nodding, Lex gave the floor to Travis. "He's in police custody," Travis said as he stepped further into the foyer. "I just got word that he's willing to testify against Dixon. If you don't want to join your brother-in-law, you need to tell us what's going on."

Her face contorted. "What are you talking about?"

Her denial fueled Lex's anger, and I saw my girl coming back. She was ready to fight. "Dad's death. The letter. The land. His *will*. Milano Incorporated. Teagan. Montgomery."

The blood drained from her face. "I—I don't know what you're talking about."

"I'm going to press charges. And you'll be in jail for the rest of your life as an accomplice. Travis, do we have enough to book her?"

"Yes."

Well, that was a lie, but hopefully Raquel was buying it.

She took a few steps back. "I don't want to go to jail."

"Then tell me what happened, Raquel."

She pursed her lips. "I need you to swear you won't press charges."

Everything was getting convoluted. I wasn't sure if Chazz was actually testifying. But this might be our only hope to get anything on the brothers. Lex knew this, and she glanced at Travis. He gave a slight shake of his head. So Chazz hadn't said anything yet. Lex closed her eyes, and I knew it killed her to say, "I won't press charges."

Raquel's face was ashen. "You can't send me to jail. I had the letter written."

"What?" we asked in unison.

Raquel started getting more hysterical, pointing at Lex. "When your dad died, I figured why not make you more miserable. Why not take away the man you loved, too? Turns out you had it all. My father is a drunken fisherman from Ketchikan. You had it all. And I hated you for it."

"You tried to ruin my life."

There was no sign of remorse when she responded, "Yes."

Irene walked in through the front door. "What is going on? Why are the police here?"

Oh no. If Raquel kept talking, Mom might make her stop. We needed to separate them.

Travis walked over to Raquel. "I need you to come with me. There are questions about Dixon and Chazz Hennington's involvement and how much you knew about it that I need answered. You'll need to make an official statement."

"Yes, okay. No charges, right?" Raquel looked at Lex.

For Lex, it must have been a bitter pill to swallow. "I'll keep my word as long as you keep yours. Tell Travis everything you know."

She nodded.

Travis and Raquel walked silently to the car, but Irene followed them, yelling questions. Travis didn't pause to answer her; instead, he helped Raquel into the back of his cruiser.

The car pulled out, and I laid my arm on Lex's shoulder. "You ready to go home?"

"Yes."

As we made it to the doorway, Irene stormed back in with a wild look in her eyes, and I stiffened. "What did you do? Why are the police here to take Raquel?"

She took a few steps toward us, and I stepped in front of Lex. "I suggest you keep your distance. If Lex wants to talk to you, she will. If she doesn't, we'll be leaving."

Now it was up to Lex how this played out.

CHAPTER
Forty-Two

Alexa

Emotions were welling up inside me, and I was on the edge of completely losing it. Raquel had forged the letter, but I wasn't sure what else she had done. *Was she involved in Dad's death?* There were so many unanswered questions and no concrete proof. Everything hinged on her statement. The guys said that Chazz might turn on his brother, but I wasn't sure.

And now my own mother was looking at me with pure hatred.

"What have you done?"

"Did you know about the letter Raquel had forged?"

Suddenly, she was silent.

I was fuming at Raquel's admission. *My own mother.* "Why do you hate me so much? I don't get it. I'm your child, too."

"Because your father was going to leave me. I had to get

pregnant to keep him. And once you came into the world, nothing else mattered. You were just the means to keep a roof over Raquel's head."

Her words were like a slap in the face, and I visibly recoiled. *No more.* This woman would not hold any power over me anymore. Yes, I was crushed, but I wouldn't be her pawn. Never again. "You tricked Dad into marrying you?"

"It was him or the broke fisherman who drank himself into oblivion. The choice was simple." There wasn't an ounce of remorse in her. None. If she had to do it again, I knew she would.

It was time to set things straight. "You have two choices."

"Who are you to speak to me? I'm your *mother*."

"No. No, you aren't. You never have been. I'm sure the prosecutors can figure out a way to tie you into this mess. You knew about the forgery, so I'm sure I can press charges against you. To save her own skin, I'm sure Raquel will let us know what part you played in all this."

She gasped.

"I will keep my word to Raquel, but you weren't part of that deal. It would be terrible for Raquel's mother to be in jail. I bet she'd have a hard time finding anyone suitable if Chazz leaves her."

If the woman could have killed me with the fire in her eyes, she would have.

"What do you want?"

"The B&B."

"This is extortion. It is rightfully mine." She slammed her fist on the table.

"No, it's not. You tricked Dad into marrying you. He never added your name to the deed. He revised his will and left it all to me." I shrugged. "It's your choice. Let me know what you decide." Turning to Drake, I said, "Take me home."

"Of course. Let's go, Lex."

We made our way to the door. Maybe what I was doing was wrong, but I wanted them out of my life. And I wanted things to be as Dad had intended.

"Alexa, stop."

I kept walking.

"Fine! You can have it."

I turned around and looked at her, but I felt no emotion toward her. For years, she'd done nothing but hurt me. Going forward, she would no longer have the satisfaction. "Get it settled tonight. I don't care what you have to do."

"I'm your mother. You can't treat me like this."

Mother. The word tasted sour in my mouth. "No, you were the woman who gave birth to me. I don't have a mother."

And with that, I walked out the door without a glance back.

Back at the cabin, I sat in front of the fire, leaning against Drake's side for warmth. Since we'd gotten home, a bone-deep chill had set in. The reality of everything hadn't fully hit me yet.

The entire Foster clan had been out here to check on me. Amie and Ike brought food and simply sat with me. I hadn't said much, but even Hayden and Kane hugged me before they left. I loved them with everything I had. If it weren't for the Fosters, I would be lost.

While everyone had been here, my mother brought the

paperwork to have the B&B transferred to me. Hollis had his lawyer look it over and validate it. I stared at the papers where they sat on the ottoman. The Fosters were following Mom back to make sure the locks got changed tonight. Tomorrow Hayden, Ike, and Amie were going to oversee Mom moving out of the house to make sure no damage was done. Mom... the word now felt unfamiliar to me.

It was done. "I can't believe I have it back."

Drake squeezed me. "It's where it should be. I'm glad you got it back. What are you going to do with it?"

"I don't know. I love our home. Maybe I'll find someone who wants to run a B&B. I'll need to find someone to help keep it up during the winter. We'll figure it out."

"Yes, we will. Whatever you need, baby. I'm here."

"And I love you for it."

Earlier, Hollis's lawyer had said if anyone admitted to knowing the will had been changed, I might have a shot at getting the land back. It was a long shot, but I kept hoping.

"How are you holding up?"

That was the question of the hour. "I don't know. I'm hurt, but not surprised. I'm relieved, but sad. It's like there's an opposite emotion for everything I'm feeling. But I'll sort through it. And I want to know what's going on. I mean, if they figure out we really don't have any hard evidence, they'll go free."

I wanted justice for what had been done.

Knock.

Knock.

Knock.

Drake got up. "Let me see who this is."

I looked at the clock; it was late. Way too late to have visitors. Drake greeted whoever it was warmly, which meant it was a good visitor.

Travis walked in and I shot up. "Is now a good time? I wanted to give you guys an update in person."

"Come on in. Have a seat." I motioned to the empty chair.

A knot formed in my stomach, and my heart beat double time. Travis took a seat in the big overstuffed chair. "Alexa, how are you doing?"

"I'm processing."

"Understood. Well, I wanted to update you—off the record, of course. It's been a shitstorm at the station."

Is that good or bad? It was hard to read the situation. Drake took a seat beside me. The warmth of his body comforted me. "What happened?"

He took a deep breath. "Chazz turned on Dixon, confessing to everything in exchange for immunity. Raquel corroborated his story—at least the part she was aware of—in exchange for immunity, as well." Pausing, he raked his hands through his hair. "We had to make the deal. At this point, there's no physical evidence, and we needed the witnesses to make sure Dixon went to jail."

I had dealt with the fact Raquel would be free for the forgery. Before I could process that, I needed to understand the part each person played in this. "So, what did they say?"

Travis scrubbed a hand down his face, clearly tired. It had been a long night for everyone. "Dixon has been piecing together land for oil drilling. He owns Milano Incorporated. It's a shell company. The Hennington brothers are almost broke. They needed this deal to go through. They were going to build oil fields. Apparently, they had people sneak on the land to confirm there was oil. On the piece Raquel had, he'd planned to build a shipping dock."

"How were they getting the money?"

"Investors. They were running out of time to get it finalized. Your dad actually met with Dixon. And refused to sell his land. Dixon was behind your loan getting called in and the way it was written up. The plan had been for you to lose the land as collateral. It's a shitstorm, but charges will be brought against the parent bank in Juneau where the decisions came from. I honestly don't understand that piece of it yet."

"Was his death an accident?" I could hear the waver in my voice.

"No, Dixon arranged it, according to Chazz. The oil was drained from the machine, which then seized. Based on Chazz's testimony alone, we have Dixon on murder charges for everyone who died that day. He had records of the deals that he gave, as well."

But there was no concrete evidence. Yet. My throat grew tighter. *Dad was murdered.* He had been taken from us before his time was up. I closed my eyes in anguish. "So many lives were lost."

"Yes, I'm so sorry, Alexa. Dixon also killed the lawyer, Montgomery, who handled the will. He was poisoned with ricin. The medical examiner was paid off to lie about the heart attack. We've contacted Juneau PD to arrest the coroner there. Chazz had copies of the last version where your father left everything to you. I would suggest you get your lawyers involved. I imagine you can get it back."

"I will. What about Teagan?" Hopefully, there was still a chance for Teagan to be saved. But I wasn't sure what her part was in this. After her words in the hospital, I was sure she knew *something*.

Travis's face turned hard, angry. "Raquel blackmailed her with compromising pictures of her and Donnie to force her to deliver the letter to Montgomery. According to Chazz, Dixon used Donnie to get her hooked on heroin after that. From there, he was able to control her. If she listened, she got more drugs. Apparently, she was becoming more of a loose cannon and wasn't following through. The day you came into town, she was supposed to lure you into a back alley for Dixon to chat with you about the land."

"Fuck," Drake muttered.

"Yes, the night Alexa got into the car with her, Teagan was supposed to bring her into the apartment, too."

So, Teagan had betrayed me first and then tried to protect me in her own way. I wasn't sure what to think about that. But maybe she still had good within her—enough good to want to be saved. "Do you know where she is?"

"No, Chazz didn't know, but he assumes she's dead. Dixon told him she had been silenced." Travis's knuckles turned white.

I expelled an anguished breath.

So much loss.

So much pain.

So much suffering.

And all for some puzzle Dixon was piecing together for money. "Has Dixon said anything?"

"No, nothing. He's not talking. His lawyers are on the way. Chazz did confirm that it was them at your home that night. We're taking DNA samples from Teagan's apartment. If we can match anything to Dixon and the drugs it'll further help the case. Dixon appears to be the mastermind behind it all. Chazz was along for the ride."

What a mess. "So where does this leave me?"

"Just waiting. We'll use the will for evidence. With Raquel and Chazz's testimony and the corroborating evidence, there's a good chance of a conviction. The prosecutors think they have a pretty good case at this point. Any further evidence they find only makes it stronger."

Well, that was a relief. "Does anything happen to Chazz or Raquel?"

"Their assets have been seized. That wasn't part of their deal. So, we'll see where that leaves us."

It wasn't much, but if they ended up with nothing, it was justice in a different form. "Thank you, Travis."

"I hate that we had to cut deals, but Dixon is definitely the worst out of the three."

"Better to have the devil himself behind bars than free," I said.

Travis stood. "True. I'll keep you posted. We may need to talk to you, so stay in town. If you're leaving, just let me know so we can reach out."

"Will do."

He left, and I sat down, unsure what to think. Life was a funny thing. Not everything was black and white, right and wrong. Sometimes things were gray, and sacrifices had to be made for the greater good. It was a bitter pill to swallow. And I hated how jagged it felt, but I was grateful there was some justice.

"How are you doing?" Drake sat in front of me on the ottoman and watched me closely.

"I hate that Raquel and Chazz are getting off. But without the deals, they all might go free. It's hard and complicated. And I walked away from my mother tonight. I was ready, but it still hurts—knowing how she feels about me. It's just... I don't know... it's a lot to sort through. And it's going to take time, I think." It was honestly like being in a boat, drifting at sea, without a sail or motor.

Drake waited for me to continue. "I'm glad it's done with. I'm glad I have closure. And I'm glad I'm free to live my life."

"Me, too, baby. Me, too. And we'll get through this together."

"Together."

CHAPTER
Forty-Three

Drake

Chaos ensued for the rest of the week. Raquel, Chazz, and Irene weren't allowed to leave the area for the time being. The transfer of the B&B had finalized. Dixon was behind bars in Anchorage. In the midst of it all, Hollis had flown his lawyer up to look at the will. With Chazz's testimony, we could prove there had been knowledge of the revised will, and the lawyers were certain Lex would get the missing piece of her dad's land back.

Raquel and Irene had been involved with pieces of Dixon's plan, but from what we could surmise, they weren't apprised of the entire thing. Chazz did whatever his brother told him to do as long as the money kept rolling in. The bank president in Juneau also happened to be one of Dixon's investors who had been behind Lex's loan. Charges were being filed against him.

Things were righting themselves. Well, righting themselves as much as possible. A loss of life could never be right-ed. Innocent people had paid the ultimate price because of greed. Crete had taken it hard because his dad had been a by-stander in the logging incident Lex's dad died in. Among many others. The town was bleeding, but we would heal our-selves and keep moving forward.

Lex had tried to go to work, but everyone—including the news crew—had shown up at the clinic. She and Hollis had decided to shut it down for the time being to everyone but emergencies. I was worried about her. More than worried. To-ward the end of the week, the news people left for Anchorage for the beginnings of a trial there.

Maybe things would get back to normal. On Monday, the clinic would reopen. Right now, Lex needed her work to focus on.

I squeezed Lex's hand as we drove, and she squeezed it back. As the days progressed, I got more of my girl back. She was working through all the shit and, in the end, would be stronger.

I pulled into the driveway and shut off the truck. "Dad's cabin? What a great idea. I think this was just what I needed." She leaned over and gave me a kiss. "I love you."

"Love you, too."

Phew. That could have gone one of two ways. I hopped out of the truck and took her hand as the nerves starting to take over. "Let's go for a walk."

"Okay."

Damn it. She knew something was off with me. *Slow deep breaths.* I led the way to the back of the cabin toward the woods.

Lex was completely relaxed beside me. "I remember taking walks here with Dad. We would spend hours exploring, and he would tell me stories."

Slowing my pace, I allowed myself to get lost in the moment. "I remember you telling me. He told me the same thing the last time we were up here together."

"Really?" She nudged my shoulder and teased. "I remember you saying you discussed something else then, too."

Hell yeah, that's a good sign. I feigned ignorance. "What are you talking about?"

She rolled her eyes and giggled. We kept walking and let the sounds of nature comfort us. Inside I was a nervous wreck, but I was trying to hide it. Earlier, I'd called Mom and Dad to see if they could help me out. Mom was only too eager to get things set up for me.

We came upon the clearing, and Alexa stopped. "What is this?"

In the clearing, a stone fire pit had a low fire burning. To the right, a red and white picnic blanket was spread on the ground with warmer blankets stacked neatly on the end. A wicker basket filled with food sat in the middle. Mom and Dad hadn't left until I let them know we were minutes away. On the blanket were treats Mom had whipped up for us.

When I didn't answer, Lex turned toward me. "Thank you. I needed this more than you know."

She cocked her head, waiting for me to continue. I took a deep breath, took the ring out of my pocket, and knelt on one knee. "This was the place I asked your Dad for his blessing to marry you. And this is where I hope you'll say yes to spending your life with me."

She started to speak, but I squeezed her hand. I needed to get this all out. "Alexa Marie Owens, I have loved you since the moment I helped you change your tire on the side of the road. You changed my life forever. There's no one else who could ever compare to you. You own my heart, my entire being. I'm intoxicated by you. There would be no greater honor than if you were to become my wife."

"Yes! Yes! Yes!" She threw her arms around me. "Yes, I want this more than anything."

"Thank goodness."

I slipped the ring on her finger and spun her around.

This was love.

This was life.

This was everything.

I pulled Lex tighter to me as we lay together in the large sleeping bag near the fire. It would be getting dark soon, and we would need to leave.

Turning over to face me, Lex looked satiated from our lovemaking. "What are you thinking?"

"That finally all of our dreams are coming true."

It had taken what felt like a lifetime to get to this moment. But in the end, I would do it all again if it meant we'd be right in this spot.

Lex looked at her ring. "It's so sparkly. I love it. Thank you. I love you."

She gave me a gentle kiss.

"I love you, too."

She sighed contentedly. "When do you want to tell your family?"

"As soon as possible."

She giggled. I was serious.

"Tomorrow, your mom is having everyone over for dinner. Why don't we make the announcement then?"

"I like that idea."

Her fingers delicately traced some design on my chest. "I can't wait to spend the rest of my life with you."

"Neither can I."

I wasn't sure how fast we could have a wedding, but I wanted this to be whatever Lex wanted. She gave me another kiss and smiled. "I can see your wheels spinning."

"About?"

"How fast we're going to get married."

Man, she knew me well. I waited for her to say something more, and from her teasing smile, it was clear she was going to make me work for it. "And?"

"I want to get married as soon as possible. I want to start our life together as husband and wife."

I rolled on top of her. "I like the way you think."

"Good, Mr. Foster, because you're stuck with me."

"There's no one I'd rather be stuck with, future Mrs. Foster."

Epilogue

WRECKED for YOU

Hayden

I sat in my car and stared at the house in front of me. Lightning flashed, making the white house stand out in the dark night. *Should I be here? Yes, I should.* After Drake and Alexa announced their engagement to the family the previous night, I saw my brother in a whole new light. He was in pure fucking bliss, and I envied him with every ounce of my being.

I want what he has.

The blonde-haired beauty I'd met that summer was on my mind nearly every second of every day. Kory Reynolds. I shook my head, trying to clear it. The last time we made love, something had happened... we connected in a way I hadn't understood.

Then she left.

Her explanation—a three-word text.

Heading home. Goodbye.

Then her number had been disconnected. It was a miracle I was able to find her address. And here I was, outside her place. In my gut, I knew I had to see her tonight. It was unexplainable. But I'd left on the first available flight to get here as soon as possible. I needed to figure out what happened. Something as perfect as what we had couldn't be ignored.

There had been a connection between us unlike anything I'd ever experienced. It was life-changing. And I was ready to see where this took us.

Dive in head first.

I opened the car door and walked up to the door in the heavy rain. It took only one second for me to be soaked through to my skin. I knocked three times and waited. The door opened, and there she stood. My word, she was beautiful. It was hard not to pull her to me and kiss the life out of her.

"Hayden, what are you doing here?" Kory's expression went from shocked to blank.

That wasn't the reaction I'd been looking for.

I blurted out the first thing that came to mind. "Why did you leave?"

She looked around outside and then pulled me in the house. Throwing her arms around me, she held onto me like her life depended on it. This was more the reaction I'd hoped for, and I wound my arms around her, bringing her closer to me. This felt right. So fucking right.

With a sniffle, Kory said, "You came for me. You actually came."

"I'm sorry it took so long. The way you left did a number on my head."

She pulled back, tears in her eyes. "You have to go back and forget you ever met me. You can't be here."

What the hell? That didn't sit right with me. *What's going on?* There was only one thing I could think of that would keep us apart. "Are you married?"

Shock passed over her face. "No. No. Of course not. I would never cheat. It's not that at all. It's… complicated." Taking a step back, she wrapped her arms around herself. "Forget you ever met me. Forget what we were. Please."

What the fuck is going on? There was one thing for certain… forgetting Kory wasn't going to happen.

Wrecked for You will be Coming Fall of 2018

Check out www.authorkristinmayer.com for updates.

Other Books by Kristin Mayer

Available Now

The Trust Series
Trust Me
Love Me
Promise Me
Full-length novels in the TRUST series are also available in audio from Tantor Media.

The Effect Series
Ripple Effect
Domino Effect

The Twisted Fate Series
White Lies
Black Truth

Timeless Love Series
Untouched Perfection
Flawless Perfection
Tempting Perfection

An Exposed Heart Novel
Intoxicated by You

Stand Alone Novels

Innocence

Bane

Whispered Promises

Finding Forever (co-written with Kelly Elliott)

Coming Soon

Wrecked for You – An Exposed Heart Novel

Changed by You – An Exposed Heart Novel

Made in the USA
Lexington, KY
14 August 2018